PRAISE FOR NORA CARROLL

"Nora Carroll's story of hidden family secrets is a tale beautifully woven through time. This elegant novel about a life-changing discovery by a woman returning to the lakeside cottage of her youth will transport you into a warm Michigan summer and keep you there until the very last secret is revealed. Carroll's talent shines brightly in this mysterious, romantic, and mesmerizing debut."
—Darcie Chan, *New York Times* bestselling author of *The Mill River Recluse* and *The Mill River Redemption*

"The love that burned between characters in the book was very deep and emotional. So much so that it left me longing, hoping and wishing for the loves to be united."
—Melissa, *1000+ Books to Read*

"You will be amazed at the ability of Nora Carroll's writing."
—Albert Robbins III, *Free Book Reviews*

The
COLOR
of
WATER
in
JULY

The
COLOR
of
WATER
in
JULY

nora carroll

LAKE UNION
PUBLISHING

Text copyright © 2012 Nora Carroll. Previously published as *Hemingway Point*.

Published by Lake Union Publishing, Seattle

www.apub.com

Amazon, the Amazon logo, and Lake Union Publishing are trademarks of Amazon.com, Inc., or its affiliates.

ISBN-13: 9781503945630
ISBN-10: 1503945634

Cover design by Mumtaz Mustafa

Printed in the United States of America

In memory of ZWL, who appointed me family historian, and CWC, who haunted my imagination.

CHAPTER ONE

JESS, AGE THIRTY-THREE

There must be a precise moment when wet cement turns dry, when it no longer accepts footprints or scratched-in declarations of love; an ordinary moment, unnoticed, just like any. But in that moment, the facts of a life can change.

At the age of thirty-three, Jess thought she knew everything there was to know about leaving places: getting on a plane or stepping into a car, and moving forward, on to the next thing.

She had not yet learned the art of going back.

———

July.

Normally, she didn't go away in July. She usually stayed in the city—a form of atonement. No, that was silly. What did she have to atone for? It was just that she got more work done when the university was mostly empty—found it easier to concentrate on the eighteenth century in France when the marble library was an appealing respite from the New York heat.

She looked through the window grating. If you stood at just the right angle, you could see a sliver of the Hudson—today it was blue. Not a brilliant blue, but still a summer blue, the color of water in July.

"I'm going away for a few days," Jess said.

From where she stood in the living room, she could see through the door into the kitchen where Russ stood at the stove, stirring hot oil with a wooden spoon, his wiry body taut and athletic, his gestures precise. It was warm in the kitchen. From time to time, he reached up to brush his longish brown hair out of his face, to push his wire-rimmed glasses farther up the bridge of his nose.

"Where to?" Russ asked.

"Oh, nowhere. Michigan."

"Conference? Ann Arbor?"

"Well, no." She paused, weighing whether she could end her sentence there. "Actually, my grandmother left me some property that I need to take care of."

She couldn't even say it without feeling an odd squeeze in her chest, a faint flush in her cheeks. Even the expression—*that I need to take care of*—rang oddly in her ears, echoing like a kind of accusation.

Jess remembered the brief conversation with the real-estate agent.

"I see no need to actually be there," she had told the agent.

"Of course you want to be there. I'm sure there are items in the cottage that have sentimental value."

Since then, she had stayed in a keyed-up state of expectation. At night, lying in bed, she could feel her heart thumping in her rib cage, louder, more insistent than usual. The night before, she had pushed away her damp, sweaty sheets, got up to splash water on her face, and stared at herself, wan and surprised-looking in the bathroom mirror.

This could not properly be called returning. There was no call to feel like this. She was imputing qualities—breath, flesh, blood—to a structure made of pine board, shingle, and stone.

Jess truly believed that you could put the past behind you. She had not been back to the cottage in sixteen years.

"Your grandmother left you some property? I thought your grandmother was still alive." Russ was chopping mushrooms now, using a cleaver so that the halves fell neatly apart.

"No, she died . . . last month." Jess paused, momentarily flustered that she had never mentioned it to Russ.

"I'm sorry," Russ said. "Had she been sick?"

"She was old . . ." Jess realized she didn't know exactly how old her grandmother had been. She was born in 1902. Jess did the math her in head. If she were still alive, she would have just turned ninety-four.

"She lived in a nursing home," Jess said. "They told me she died in her sleep."

"So tell me about the house," Russ said.

"It's just a summer cottage. It's been in the family for a long time. I guess she thought my mother didn't want it, so she left it to me."

"What are you going to do with it?"

"Sell it."

Russ turned back to the cutting board, starting to chop the green and red peppers, seeming to let the subject drop.

Had she really gotten off so easily? She was feeling guilty that she hadn't invited him, especially since Russ was always on the scout for new locales for the magazine. Jess knew they were getting to that point, where it was almost expected that they would include each other in their plans—that was the point when Jess, in the past, had tended to bolt.

Well, it was barely worth mentioning. Such a short trip. She would be there and back over a long weekend and the place would be sold.

"How's the piece on the Connecticut farmhouse coming?" she asked, hoping to change the subject.

"Country kitsch in Connecticut," he said. "Would you believe they collect hand-painted duckies?"

"That hardly sounds like *Architectural Home* . . . duckies . . ."

"Very expensive, very tasteful duckies. But they have a ten-million-dollar view of the Long Island Sound. Makes for a great photo shoot."

Russ was passionate about his work at *Architectural Home*.

"Okay, so now tell me all about this cottage in Michigan," Russ said. "I didn't know people did cottages in Michigan. Isn't that a Maine kind of thing?"

Jess pictured the big old gabled cottage, perched up on a bluff above a clear blue Michigan lake. It had been her grandmother's summer home for over ninety years. At one time in her life, it had been Jess's favorite place on the face of the earth.

"It looks out over a spot called Hemingway Point. They say Hemingway used to fish there when he was young."

"You've been there before?"

"Every summer," she said. "Until my mother couldn't make me go anymore. Then, you know, I just . . ."

"Just what?"

"Just, you know . . . didn't want to go there anymore." She hoped Russ couldn't hear the catch in her throat, but he was concentrating on stirring the sauce and seemed to let the subject drop.

A few minutes later, they were seated across from one another at Jess's battered kitchen table, the aroma of Russ's fresh marinara sauce filling the room. Russ stabbed a forkful of spaghetti, expertly wrapping it around his fork so that it neatly tucked into his mouth. "It's, like, a little cabin . . . ?"

Jess should have known he wouldn't let it go that easily.

"It's actually kind of big," she said.

"Big?"

"Nine bedrooms?" She could feel the faint heat of embarrassment rising along her cheekbones. Her apartment in Fort Washington was a ratty sixth-floor walk-up in a marginal neighborhood—its only redeeming feature was the tiny sliver of a view.

"You've just inherited a nine-bedroom cottage on a lake across from Hemingway Point . . . and you didn't even tell me?"

Jess nodded miserably, sorry that she had piqued his interest.

"So what's it like anyway?"

Jess could hear a note of professional interest creep into his voice. Russ was a house junkie—always on the lookout for new locales for the magazine.

"It's very old—probably falling apart by now," Jess said. She looked away from Russ, out the window.

"I'd love to see it," Russ said. He was smiling at her, eager, interested. She should be happy—she had been telling herself recently that she might be in love with him.

"Do you want to come with me?" she said, regretting it as soon as she had opened her mouth.

Russ's eyes lit up and he smiled.

"I was waiting for you to ask."

Jess felt a thud of guilt when she realized that she had been trying to avoid asking him.

———

The road into the Wequetona Club was unprepossessing. Over the years, M-66 had been built up a bit, and so, where Jess had remembered only farms, they drove past the Jiffy Mart, Gail's Nails, and the County Farm and Post. Pine Lake was not visible at all from the road. The gently rolling woods and meadows were unremarkable, except perhaps for a particular clarity of the light. At the crest of a hill, there was a turnoff onto a gravel lane.

"Here," Jess said. Russ wheeled the rental car onto the dirt road, the tires crunching on gravel. Dense woods lined both sides of the road. As the car rounded a bend and the entrance came into view, Jess felt her stomach tighten. Two simple stone pillars flanked the road; a line of stately hemlocks lined up behind them. On one pillar hung a small black sign inscribed Wequetona Club.

Just beyond, Jess saw the white wooden clubhouse, crisply painted and with red geraniums in the window boxes, surrounded by green Adirondack chairs. Off to the left were two lawn tennis courts, and, directly ahead, she caught her first glimpse of the lake. On this sunny July day, it was a fierce and glittery blue.

"Think Martha Stewart," Russ crooned into a handheld voice recorder. "Think Ralph Lauren."

Jess wasn't really listening anyway. She was just looking as the car crunched along, barely at a crawl. The lake, the trees, the prim row of cottages. Close her eyes and she could *still* see it, so deeply was this scene engraved in her mind, and so little did it change over time. Almost impossibly little. And yet didn't it change? Because she herself had certainly changed. The last time she'd been here, she'd been full of dreams. Now, she liked to hide herself in libraries and study the forgotten dreams of others.

She reached over to clasp Russ's hand, but she jarred his voice recorder, and he pulled his hand away, so she turned to look at the lake, so bright it almost blinded her.

"Over here," she said to Russ. "We're the last cottage on the south side. Just next to the woods."

CHAPTER TWO

MAMIE

In those long summer seasons before the war, when the chill of spring and fall wrapped around the languid warmth of endless midsummer days, the only way to get to Wequetona was by water. We arrived in mid-May, coming across Pine Lake on the little steamship *Jefferson*; it stopped right at the Wequetona dock on the way to Horton Bay. In the sheltered circle of the harbor, the water was always calm. But as we steamed out farther into the lake, the water deepened to a menacing indigo, and the brisk wind that blew across Five Mile Point carried the knifelike reminder of a Great Lakes desolation. No matter that the weather was fair, Pine Lake always hinted at her wildness, even on the mildest, most even-tempered summer day.

Every summer, Lila got seasick on the crossing and was peevish. I can still see her clear as day, leaning up against the bulwark, its paint gray and blistered from the lashings of a thousand northern storms. Her blond hair whipped around her face, golden strands catching in the corners of her mouth. With one hand she shielded her eyes, and with the other she pressed against her sash, a queasy greenish look on her pale, angular face.

Nowadays, the area around Pine Lake is heavily wooded, but when Lila and I were girls, the lakeshores were mostly bare. There were still loggers around in those days, unsavory characters, Indians mostly, and some sharp-tongued bearded Scotsmen who appeared never to bathe. They lived in wretched camps in the woods: you used to see the squaws with babies tied to their backs, walking barefoot along the railroad tracks. I remember Daddy saying it was mostly logged out by then. Still, sometimes you'd see patches of smoke from the burning stumps pluming up around the lakeshore in the spots where they were still logging.

The steep canted roof of our cottage was the highest point on the north shore. Its roofline, like a church spire, cut a sharp outline against the sky, mirroring the dark-green points of the few remaining giant pines. Lila and I strained our eyes from the moment we came into Loeb Bay, wanting to be the first to catch sight of our beloved summer destination. Lila usually saw it first; I always suspected that the sheer strength of her impatience made her eyes so keen.

The SS *Jefferson* docked at Wequetona on Tuesdays and Saturdays. Old Joe McKawber would ring the clubhouse bell, and all the Wequetonans would gather down at the dock to collect their mail and to see the new arrivals to the Club. A couple of Indians milled about, ready to heft our many steamer trunks onto their backs and carry them up the steep stairs to the cottage walk. Lila and I stood with arms linked, waiting to feel the boat bump up against the dock—our signal that another summer had begun.

During the war, the *Jefferson* stopped its resort runs. It was converted to a Coast Guard patrol boat, and after the war, I guess nobody thought to bring it back. The roads were slowly starting to improve. Eventually, we began to take the train, and then later to drive.

But I still remember the approach by water: the slant of gables against the blue sky, the sound of the clubhouse bells clanging out over the water, the sight of our dear friend May Lewis, the hem of her white organdy drenched in water, waving a gay summer welcome with her upstretched, white-gloved hand.

Up in Michigan, the summer is brief, crowded between two ends of a desolate northern winter. And yet somehow when you are young, it seems to last forever. A whole lifetime can be hastened to fit between the giddy green leaves of May and the chastened red and yellow of September.

During my long life, I've seen the world constantly changing, spinning around, until the next thing you know, it becomes a place you don't even recognize anymore. But Wequetona doesn't change that much. Summer after summer, it has a way, perhaps an illusion, of seeming much the same. As it was in the beginning. *The pine trees.*

Is now and ever shall be. *The lake.* World without end.

But then there's no such place as that now, is there? Not on this earth anyway.

I've just come home from the lawyer's office, where I signed the papers about the cottage. Tomorrow, I move into Coventry Manor. I was born in the year of our Lord 1902, and in two months, I will turn ninety-four, if it is the Lord's will.

CHAPTER THREE

JESS, AGE THIRTY-THREE

Jess got out of the car and walked down the grassy slope. The back of the wooden-framed cottage loomed in front of her, painted white, with green-shingled gables and dormer windows. To her right were dense woods where white trunks of birch trees shone through like slender ghosts. The gravel road ran along the back of the cottages. The cottage, with its wide porches and tall windows, faced the lake.

Remembering that it had once squeaked, she grasped the green-painted screen door tentatively. Sure enough, the door protested with a raspy squawk. The air inside was a stale combination of mildew and mothballs. The back hallway to the kitchen had always smelled like that, as long as she could remember. She paused before stepping all the way through the doorway, sensing the oddness of the quiet inside. There was no brisk clicking of pumps across the wood floor; no waft of Chanel No. 5. The cavernous cottage was dark and still. Russ let the screen door slam shut with a thud.

———

As her eyes skimmed the room, she was surprised that after all this time everything looked exactly the same. A balcony with a Craftsman-style geometric railing encircled the living room like a wide catwalk. The second floor had no ceilings; you could look all the way up into the exposed pine rafters in the house's vaulted gables. All across the front of the cottage were windows looking out on the lake. The rooms were furnished with Navajo rugs and Indian baskets, wicker furniture and hand-bent hickory rockers. There was a stillness common to rooms that have stood empty, the old house silent but for the creaking of the worn floorboards under their feet.

Russ broke the silence with a loud, appreciative groan.

"This is unbelievable!" Russ exclaimed. "American cottage style, eclectic Arts and Crafts, and look at this Indian stuff. This house could be a cover story."

"Journey's End." Jess whispered the cottage's name so softly she wasn't sure if she had spoken aloud.

"I've got to get on the phone," Russ said.

Jess looked at the view through the warped glass, out toward Hemingway Point. With the lights on in the living room, she could see her own reflection faintly in the windows, her same narrow face, with fair hair in a ponytail. She was wearing button-fly Levi's and a white cotton T-shirt. Exactly what she might have worn the last time she was here, when she was seventeen.

Russ started fingering the Navajo rugs and inspecting the Ojibwa sweetgrass baskets. Jess stood there with their suitcases—there were so many rooms here, most of which had always stood empty. At first, she wasn't sure which room they should use.

"Come on, Jess. Let's put our bags in here." Russ pointed to one of the ground-floor bedrooms with wide windows looking out on the lake.

Mamie's room. Jess hesitated, then decided her hesitation was silly. She grabbed the handle of her suitcase and wheeled it into the room.

———

"I can't find an outlet, Jess!" Russ hollered from his position under Mamie's Victorian writing table. Jess was standing upstairs on the balcony. From where she stood, she could see into the room that used to be Mamie's. It was a feminine room with frilly white curtains and pictures of Gibson girls hanging framed on the walls. Jess's grandfather had run off when her mother was a baby. Her grandmother's room bore no trace of him. All she could see of Russ was his jeans-clad legs and the pointy toes of his expensive leather cowboy boots. His computer paraphernalia crowded the top of Mamie's writing desk; his bomber jacket and camera case were strewn across the bed, lenses, camera paper, and other junk littering the spotless pink-and-white chenille spread. "We're going to need to get set up for Internet access."

Russ had already been on and off the phone with the magazine half a dozen times.

"Classic Gaines," she kept hearing him say. "His signature work."

When Russ wasn't on the phone, he walked around with Jess like a tour guide, showing her things about the cottage that she had never consciously noted.

"See the foundation." Russ pointed to the uneven heaping of gray stones that ran along the base of the shingled structure. "That's local flint. Arts and Crafts style. Characteristic." Inside, he pointed at the walls and ceilings. "Look at the pine board—unvarnished, so Gaines—that golden-honey color." Jess had never really noticed the walls, had taken for granted their warm amber hue.

But she knew that they were pine boards—*number one white pine planks*. Jess almost felt like she could hear a voice, long forgotten, whispering in her ear. She shook her head. *No*, she was not going to think about him. All that was so long ago. Jess ran her hand along the smooth, knotty surface of the wall, feeling the carefully grooved edges, the slightly shirred ends.

"The amazing thing about this place," Russ said, "is that it hasn't had a thing done to it. You just don't find cottages like that. They've all been screwed around with, mucked up."

In the bedroom, Russ was drawn to a collection of small Indian artifacts on the shelf in the corner. They were little tourist trinkets, painstakingly made by hand: a miniature birch-bark canoe, a finely beaded sandal, and two small woven baskets, one with a tiny doll in deerskin cradled inside. Russ handed one of the baskets to her. "Do you see how fine the weaving is?"

She examined the intricate beadwork, the careful stitches. Each basket had a name stenciled on it: *Mamie*, written on the basket that still held the doll; *Lila*, on the basket that was empty, the doll no doubt lost long ago during play.

"How am I ever going to figure out what to do with this stuff?" Jess said.

"Are you kidding? These old handmade tourist trinkets from the twenties are worth a small fortune." Russ picked up a hand-painted toy tomahawk and brandished it toward his reflection in the mirror.

Russ didn't understand, but maybe that was just as well. These were just things to him—to catalog, describe, photograph, and eventually sell. For herself, they were dusty relics of a past that seemed frozen in time—it was hard to know what value to assign to things like that.

———

Russ lost no time getting acquainted with the layout of the rambling cottage. He was upstairs in the alcove now, muttering into his voice recorder. Behind him, the high alcove windows were thrown open, and a fresh breeze from the lake was making the faded curtains flutter.

"Wow, Jess, this picture of your grandmother," Russ called over the balcony. "I never knew you looked so much like her. It's the spitting image of you."

"Is that the picture that was up there in the alcove?"

"Yeah."

"That's not Miss Mamie. That's my great-aunt Lila—Mamie's sister."

"What was she like?"

"I don't know. I never knew her. She drowned in the lake years ago. Before I was born."

"That's sad."

"Actually, it was kind of creepy. Miss Mamie almost never talked about her. Just left her picture there, staring out over the lake. Kids used to say that late at night you could hear footsteps on the balcony and the sound of water dripping—the ghost of old Aunt Lila."

Russ came down the stairs holding the picture.

"It is an amazing likeness though, isn't it?"

Jess looked at the faded image, the face of a pretty young girl, in the old sepia-toned photograph. She looked to be about seventeen, with fair hair and wide-set eyes in a narrow face. There was a faint likeness, she supposed.

Jess had never liked the way she looked that much, blond and ordinary, not at all like her mother, Margaret, who was a black-eyed beauty, with dark hair, prominent cheekbones, and almond-shaped eyes. Margaret used to stand in front of the mirror, combing her thick, dark hair, making Jess feel like a pale wraith beside her. Jess imagined that she looked more like her father—even though she had no idea what her father actually looked like. She didn't even know his name. All her mother had told her was that she was the result of a one-night stand with an Irishman when Margaret was in Belfast reporting on the Troubles. At cocktail parties, Margaret loved to retell the story of Jess's conception, always with the utmost hilarity, including lines about seeing bombs exploding in the sky. Try as she might, Jess could learn nothing about him. Margaret steadfastly stuck to the story that she never even knew his name. Jess's own name, *Carpenter*, was Margaret's invention—she had picked it, she said, because it was easy to pronounce.

For the rest of the afternoon, Russ was on and off the phone. Jess went out onto the wide front porch. She tested each of the porch swings and finally came to rest in the hammock. From there, she could see through the birches and out over the lake toward the beach and sailboat moorings.

The Wequetona Club was set on a sheltered cove where for thousands of years the Woodland Indians had made their summer camps, fashioning arrowheads from the tough, flinty stone and fishing for trout in the clear water surrounded by an unbroken expanse of dense woods. In those woods, there was a grove of the giant white pine that had surrounded the lake. These trees once drove the economy of the region, drawing first lumbermen, then white settlers, and, eventually, summer people to the shores of Pine Lake.

By now, all the giant trees were gone—shipped out to build the great cities of the Midwest. Only one small stand remained, on the plot of land adjoining Journey's End. From the cottage, there was nothing distinctive about them; it was from across the cove, at Hemingway Point, that their majesty could be seen: dark-green towering spires pointing sharply up into the sky.

Lying in the hammock, staring out at the sun-dappled expanse of lake, Jess felt as if she had momentarily stopped time. The hammock was rocking slightly in the gentle breeze. Then, she heard a frail voice calling her name.

"Why, Jess Carpenter, welcome to Wequetona." Jess looked out and saw May Lewis, tiny and hunched over, dwarfed by a woolen suit in a bright shade of robin's-egg blue, coming along the walk.

Jess was startled to see Mamie's friend. It made her grandmother seem closer, the fact of her passing more real.

Jess climbed out of the hammock and walked out to say hello. "Mrs. Lewis. How nice to see you. I'm surprised you recognized me after all this time."

"Why, you look exactly the same, Jess. I'm so sorry about your grandmother. Miss Mamie is missed." Her face was wrinkled, but she had a sharp look in her eye. Jess squirmed under her gaze, wondering if Mrs. Lewis knew that Jess hadn't seen her grandmother for many years before she died.

But Mrs. Lewis was poised, and her friendly smile gave no hints.

"You must stop by The Rafters sometime. You can tell me all about your medical practice."

Jess flushed in spite of herself.

"Oh, I . . . I never did go to medical school . . ." It was half a lie and she stammered through it.

"Well, I'd love to hear what you are doing now," Mrs. Lewis said, smiling. "You were always such a bright girl—you must have accomplished great things."

"Oh, nothing special," Jess said. Nothing that really helped people, as she had once dreamed of doing.

"Well, you be sure to stop by. I'd love to hear all about it."

Mrs. Lewis continued along the walkway until she reached the woods, and then she circled back.

Back up on the porch, Jess turned her face away from the lake and tried not to think about her grandmother.

———

The sun began to set over Pine Lake, turning the water to a silvery sheen. Russ and Jess sat on the front porch drinking white wine.

"They want it to be a kitchen and solarium focus." Russ's sharp voice intruded upon the silence.

"What?" Jess said absently.

"For the magazine."

"That ratty old kitchen?" Jess was surprised. "Why would they want to do a story on that?"

"Well, of course, it's a makeover story, and those usually have the kitchen as an important focus."

"A makeover story?"

"You know, beautiful old cottage brought up to date, with Sub-Zero appliances and stuff."

"I thought you said the best thing about this place is that it's never been tinkered with."

"That's right," said Russ. "It's a designer's dream. You can leave the authentic look and just improve upon it. That gives it a kind of 'old money' look that's hard to fake."

"Russ, this place is going to be sold this week. How on earth are you talking about remodeling?"

"I've got some of the best people in New York who'll work on it. I think I have a real shot at getting it on the cover of the magazine."

"On the cover?" Jess said, honestly surprised.

"An original Gaines? Jess, this will be a real coup. Couldn't we just sit tight while I try to pull this together? The place will be twice as valuable when we're done."

Jess looked at Russ's boyish, eager face. He was a bit thinner than the average guy, wore little intellectual glasses, and had a nervous way of leaning forward and barely resting in his seat. His jeans were jet black—she had seen him turn them inside out before he washed them so they wouldn't fade. And those fancy leather cowboy boots, hand tooled, were clearly designed for walking on cement. Everything about him said city boy. Not the kind of guy who had spent time poking sticks in the mud as a kid. Not the kind of kid who knew the names of birds and trees. Unbidden, the names of birds that someone had once taught her came back: kingfisher, pileated woodpecker, pine warbler, golden loon. *Stop*, Jess thought. *Just stop.*

She looked out at the lake again—there was something about being here that was bringing the past into sharp and uncomfortable focus. As though her life was a continuum of connected parts—not a past life and a present that had been sharply divided in two.

"Please," Russ said. "It would really be a good thing for my career . . ."

"Oh, all right," Jess said as much to herself as to Russ. "You can do whatever you want."

Russ leaned over and gave her a kiss, but she turned her head so that his lips just grazed her cheek.

He looked at her, puzzled. He didn't read her well, didn't often know what she was thinking. Then, he grinned a happy grin and picked up his cell phone, punching a number on his speed dial.

"Milo," Russ crowed into the cell phone, "start booking blocks of flights up to Traverse City. It's all systems go." He gave her a thumbs-up sign, then stood up and walked out toward the porch, the phone pressed hard to his ear.

Russ was talking and examining one of the Indian blankets. He looked so out of place here—but that was good, wasn't it? For years, she had kept looking for the same kind of man that she had once lost—now, finally, maybe she'd given up on old dreams, and changed for good.

Jess carried her empty wineglass into the kitchen and set it down next to the sink, and then she ducked into the pantry off the kitchen, a short, narrow hallway that had always been used as a storage space.

She pulled the string hanging from the single bulb, and a thin light lit up the room. She looked around but soon spotted what she had been looking for, leaning up against the wall in a dusty corner. It was a long switch of pine, carefully stripped of its bark, then whittled smooth. She picked it up slowly and examined it, running her fingers along the sides to feel the knife marks ticked vertically along it like measurements.

Then, she ran her fingertips over the two initials carved into it: *J* and *D*.

Up until that moment, she had been able to keep her emotions at bay—but now, they flooded over her and she felt startled awake, like being splashed by cold, clear water from the lake.

CHAPTER FOUR

JESS, AGE SEVENTEEN

That year, the water level in the lake was unusually low. Most years, the water lapped up against the wooded shoreline, except right at the swimming beach. Along the rest of the shoreline, you could only get to the lakefront by cutting through the sedge marsh, thick brambles and saplings, and sharp razor grass.

But that year, you could walk all the way out to Loeb Point along the beach. Flocks of birds congregated in the sand, and minnows swam in the shallow, stagnant pools near shore.

Jess liked to walk down the solitary beach alone. As she rounded the bend of the cove, she slipped out of sight of the beach where the sunbathers congregated, and she could not be seen from the cottages up on the bluff. None of the other summer people ever seemed to walk that way, as though there were nothing in the empty beach or woods that could interest them. But Jess loved the quiet along the beach; she watched as the seagulls that had flocked there took flight in white swirls, rising above the mallard ducks that swam along placidly at the water's edge.

Down at the far end of the beach, Jess had found a fresh cold spring bubbling up out of the sand. In years past, the spring must have fed directly into the lake, but this year, it was visible, just a bubbling in the sand. When she stuck her foot into it, she felt icy-cold water, and her leg slipped down as far as her knee. Jess took to sitting there by the little spring. In the afternoon, she could slip away from the bathing beach with a book and stay there by the spring, reading and watching the birdlife on the water. Not once had any of the other bathers ventured in her direction.

On one of those days, Jess was seated on a flat rock next to the bubbling spring, reading a book. There were clouds in the sky and the weather was changeable. When the sun was out, the water was calm and blue, but then a dark cloud would pass with a gust of wind, and the water would turn slate colored, with tiny whitecaps. Because of the threat of storm, few boats were out, and so Jess was surprised when she saw a canoe slip around the corner of the cove. A young man with his shirt off was paddling, his clean strokes slicing through the water.

The canoer seemed to take no notice of her. Perhaps he couldn't see her because of the sun that had just flashed out from behind a cloud, and which must have been shining in his eyes. Jess, on the other hand, had the sun behind her, and she immediately noticed his stillness and unusual ease in the canoe. His fluid motions as he paddled made him appear to scarcely move, but she could see the muscles in his deeply tanned bare torso, slipping across his ribs as his oar plunged into the water.

To her surprise, as he drew nearer to shore, with one graceful motion he jumped out of the canoe, pulling it up on the sand not fifteen feet from where she sat, although he still didn't appear to have noticed her. Closer, she could see that he was a boy of about her age, wearing faded red swim trunks, with an unruly tangle of brown wavy hair streaked through with gold.

His motions were slow and deliberate. He pulled the canoe out of the water and then laid his wooden oar across the seats. The canoe was also a faded red, like his swim trunks. Jess sat perfectly still, perched on the rock, almost directly in front of him.

Finally, he put his hand up to shade his eyes from the sun and looked straight at her.

"Have you seen the great blues?"

In spite of his quiet movements, he had a quick smile. Jess could see that the sun had burned the end of his nose, which was peeling, leaving pink skin and freckles showing through. The rest of his body was brown and glistened faintly with perspiration.

"I don't know," Jess said. She did not want to let on that she had no idea what he was talking about. "I've been reading."

"Well, I've seen you sitting here before. You scare the birds away."

Jess felt the pit of her stomach tense up.

"I do not! I've always seen a lot of birds while I'm sitting here."

"Not as many as there would be if you weren't sitting here. The blue herons have been coming—were coming—until you started bothering them."

"I did not come here to bother the birds," Jess said. "Look at them." She pointed to several ducks pecking in a shallow pool.

"Oh, the mallards . . . they don't scare easy. It's the great blue herons I'm interested in. They never used to come around here, but now with this mudflat . . ." He stopped speaking for a moment, scanning the sky. "I've been trying to shoot them."

"You have no business shooting them. They're wild birds."

He laughed, tipping his head back and showing his even white teeth. "No, I mean taking pictures," he said.

He reached down into his canoe and pulled out a camera, with a variety of lenses hanging in their cases from the strap. Again, Jess noticed his unusual grace.

"I like to take pictures of birds. Usually, around here it's the woodland birds, you know, black-throated green warblers, American redstarts. But now, with the mudflat, we're getting some of the shoreline birds."

Jess didn't say anything else and she looked back down at her book, but she could feel that the boy was still looking at her. She did not know the names of any birds—except pigeons, of course. If the blue herons had been there, she did not believe she would have noticed.

When Jess's cheeks stopped burning, she hazarded a glance toward the boy. Now, he was squatting ankle deep in the water, his telephoto lens pointed out toward Hemingway Point. Jess examined him carefully, though all she could see was the side of his face and his back.

This summer, she had noticed that most of the American boys had their hair cut short and were wearing these expensive Ray-Ban sunglasses. This guy's hair was kind of long, and his body was lean. He was kneeling in the sand holding his camera with the telephoto, but Jess couldn't see what he was looking at.

"There they are," he said softly, almost to himself.

Jess looked up at the sky but still saw nothing, looked back at the boy who still crouched motionless on the sand.

"I don't see them," Jess said.

"Sh . . . ," he whispered. "They won't land here while we're sitting here. You can tell them when they're flying. They have a wide wingspan and they stutter."

"Stutter?"

"Yeah, I mean that's what it looks like. It looks like they stutter."

Jess scanned the sky again, wondering what stuttering looked like.

"Do you think I could get you to hold the light meter for me, for just a sec? I don't want to lose my focus."

Jess stood up from the flat rock, hesitating awkwardly for a second.

"It's in the canoe, the little flat thing, looks kind of like a flash."

Jess walked over to the canoe and rummaged in the camera bag. She picked up what she thought he was talking about.

"This it?"

"Just hold it up," he said. "About a foot in front of me, a little to the left."

He took his eye off the camera and glanced up at the light meter.

"Perfect," he said, and squeezed the shutter several times in rapid succession. "You can just throw that back in the bag."

Jess stared at the empty sky again, wondering what it was that he could see. She saw a couple of birds, black blobs at this distance, an airplane, and a number of scattered cumulus clouds, white on top, their undersides purple. All of a sudden, he jumped up, threw his camera into his bag, and swiftly dragged his canoe back into the water, leaping into it the second it began to fully float.

Jess was left standing there stupidly watching him push. Her ears burned. She hadn't even learned his name. She wanted to ask him, *Were those the blue herons? Did you see them? What did they look like?* But before she had prepared herself to open her mouth, he was gone.

He was paddling away, toward the point and the South Arm. Just when he was almost out of earshot, he called over his shoulder, "See you around." Then, slicing clearly through the water, his canoe rounded the point and disappeared from sight.

———

Jess was up at the cottage counting sheets with Mamie. Every year,

Mamie opened the cottage, putting fresh sheets on every bed in all the bedrooms. They rarely, if ever, expected visitors. Sometimes, a few of Cousin Edith's daughters would come up from Texas for a week. But most of the time, it was just Mamie and Jess—Mamie downstairs in the master bedroom, and Jess upstairs. She always slept in the same room, the front bedroom with a dormer overlooking the lake on the side adjacent to the woods.

Jess knew that kids said the cottage was haunted; there was an old story about her great-aunt Lila, who had drowned in the lake, ages ago, way before Jess's time. But Jess found the old cottage homey and familiar. She appreciated its rambling space since she lived in a city apartment for most of the year.

Mamie was holding a yellow legal pad on which she had written at the top, in her distinctive hand, *Journey's End Sheet Count*. This, like everything else, was a yearly ritual. Every year they counted sheets, and any that were frayed were either mended or cut into rags. Mamie had always ordered the heavy cotton sheets from a special supplier in Savannah, until one year, the mill closed down. Mamie bought ten sheets and carefully laid them away, folded in crisp white tissue paper on the back of the top linen-closet shelf. Now, she would dole them out one by one as though parting with jewels. Mamie didn't like change, in sheets or in life, as Jess saw it.

"Jess," Mamie began, clearing her throat a bit, as if she had something important to say.

Jess looked up at her grandmother warily. They rarely talked to each other about personal matters.

"When a young woman gets to be your age . . . I know that sometimes she starts to think about young men."

Mamie spoke with an old-fashioned soft Texas drawl. "Living all around as you do, with your mother . . ."

"All around," Jess thought, was not entirely fair. Her mother was a journalist. They lived in Paris now, before that London, and sometimes Milan. Other people, Jess had noticed, found their itinerant lifestyle interesting, even admirable. People seemed amazed that she could speak French and that she had visited so many far-off places. Not Mamie though, who seemed to see those cities, all of them, as indistinguishable, foreign parts.

"Well, I just want to remind you, Jess. At Wequetona, there are nice boys from families we know, families we've known since your great-grandmother Ada's time."

Mamie was folding pillowcases into crisp squares, matching up the hand-stitched embroidered hems just so.

"Look around while you're here, Jess. I don't want you meeting someone . . . uh . . . in a foreign country . . . Someone who might not . . . quite fit in . . . at the Club, you know."

Jess smiled at Mamie in a way that she hoped was pleasant. Jess was used to her grandmother. She knew what Mamie thought, what she cared about. She was old, Jess thought, and as rigid as the stays in her corsets.

Jess's mother, Margaret, could never take this kind of thing from her mother. "Mamie!" she would holler. "Just stay out of what you don't understand, which is most things!"

But Jess took a more diplomatic approach with her grandmother. "Well, Miss Mamie," she said evenly, "I'll try to bear that in mind." Margaret could never accept how set in her ways Mamie was, but Jess admired Mamie in a certain way. Life with her mother had always been exciting and rootless, in equal parts grimy and glamorous. Mamie represented another way. She knew how she did things, the same way as her mother before her.

Jess picked up another of the oblong pillowcases, worn to a silky softness from years of use. All the sheets and pillowcases were identical, but some were more than seventy years old. A few had stamped black initials inside, *LT* and *MT*, ones that her grandmother and her great-aunt had used when they were girls. Jess loved the way these old ones felt between her fingers, so soft and worn, and yet the warp and weft of the fabric still maintaining its basic strength.

"I still remember, Jess, my dear daddy standing in the center of the living room downstairs. He pointed up around the balcony. 'Look how many bedrooms,' he said. 'My grandchildren will come here. And their children too.'" She picked up another pillowcase, matched the corners smartly, and laid it on the bed, smoothing it with quick, sure strokes as she spoke. "You will marry well, my dear, and the cottage, someday, will go to you." She considered her words.

"Not to your mother, Jess," she said. "The way she lives . . ."

Jess's cheeks burned. She hated it when Mamie criticized her mother—could never think of the right way to respond. Most often, she said nothing. But this time, she was thinking about Mamie's words. Why was Mamie so sure that Jess would "marry well"? It wasn't exactly something that ran in the family, and what did it even mean?

Losing husbands and fathers seemed to be something that the women in her family specialized in. Her own father was a one-night stand, and Mamie's husband hadn't stuck around for long. Perhaps it was understandable, Jess thought, that she had little conception of the married state, nor any reason to think she'd be especially good at it.

"Well, who knows what will happen," Jess said. "I may never get married. I'll just have a career."

Mamie peered straight at Jess, over the top of her glasses. "Young women have a lot more choices nowadays. This is a good thing. I just have one piece of advice for you, Jess. Figure out what matters, then hold on to it. That's how you keep things together. By not letting go."

Jess stared out the window of the upstairs bedroom toward the trees, a dense wall of green that blocked out the light. For a while, they continued their task in silence. Jess and Mamie each sat perched on either side of the bed, ankles crossed neatly, folding pillowcases in the same precise way, and then stacking them between them on the chenille bedspread. "Miss Mamie," she said finally, "you know the other cottage down around the other side of the Tretheway woods out toward Loeb Point . . . Any idea who lives there?"

Mamie laid down the pillowcase she was folding and smoothed it several times before she answered. She prided herself on knowing all the goings-on around Pine Lake. Of course, nowadays, there were lots more condos and time-shares—people up from downstate—weekenders. Those people just didn't count, didn't mean anything, were basically invisible to the "real" summer people, ones like Mamie, who had spent a lifetime of summers along the piney shores.

"The Painter family," Mamie said firmly with a hint of distaste. "Not our kind of people."

Jess, in her mind's eye, could see the boy in the red swim trunks paddling off toward the point in the red canoe.

CHAPTER FIVE

Mamie

When I first visited Coventry Manor, three years ago, I was wearing my little mink jacket. It was a cool, bright Texas day. I had planned my first visit for January, when the weather is chilly, because I tend to think that there is no occasion that can't be improved by dressing in mink.

At the time, I was in quite good condition, except for my palpitations, and had dressed with care for the visit. I wanted everyone to know that I, Mrs. Mamie Tretheway Cleves, had choices about how I would square things away.

The thick plate-glass front doors of Coventry Manor swoosh open as you walk through them. Inside, there are marble floors and various sitting rooms, furnished with Queen Anne–style mahogany chairs and stiff little velvet settees. I was going to move there before I needed to, before I became a burden to Margaret, when I could still install myself with pleasure into my new little home. Then, I knew how it went after that. At Coventry Manor, they would move you upward, closer and closer to the uniformed nurses and the motorized hospital beds. Up and up, closer and closer to heaven.

Margaret, bless her heart, came all the way from London to help me move in, but I was the one who arranged the furniture and placed the cutlery neatly into the sideboard drawers. I had only lived in an apartment once before in my life, and oh, the pleasure of it. Not more than five steps to anywhere. I reveled in all the clean, gleaming surfaces, and in the order; no more than needed and no less, yet still pretty and pleasing to the eye.

One of Margaret's greatest failings, if I may say so, is in her housekeeping. That girl was positively piggish, right from the start, shoelaces untied, ribbons falling out of her hair, leaving her things in a tossed-off trail behind her, here a school paper, there a sock, and a few steps later, a shoe. It was just like that when she came to help me move into Coventry Manor. She sat on a sofa in the middle of the room, feet up leaving marks on the coffee table, saying to me in that ridiculous drawl of hers, "Now, Mother, you shouldn't be straining yourself."

I was grateful, though, to have an opportunity to talk to Margaret about the cottage.

"About Journey's End," I said to Margaret the second afternoon she was there. Margaret was sitting on my good green-brocade sofa, holding her cigarette so as to balance the long ash that was sticking out the end. I was anxiously eyeing the sofa, wondering if it would be ruined and whether my upholstery man was still in business or had already retired.

Margaret looked at me blankly, a look that I knew well, a look that she had perfected as a child. Margaret looked right at me, and she said, sweet as can be: "Journey's End . . . What in the hell is that?"

It wasn't her incessant cursing. I had long grown used to that. It was that implacable face, that innocent tone of voice . . .

The long ash on Margaret's cigarette tumbled off, missing the green brocade, leaving a little soiled pile on the tufts of the cream-colored carpet. I picked up the sheaf of papers I had before me, my notes about Journey's End written out in blue ink on a yellow legal pad.

"I own a piece of property in Michigan, as you know." I read to her from my handwritten notes. "There are two separate matters. One is the cottage with its contents, and the other is the adjacent woods."

Margaret continued to look at me without curiosity, as though I were describing a completely unfamiliar place, though she had spent every summer of her childhood there.

"Last month, I donated the woods to the Little Traverse Conservancy—a charitable organization that will preserve the woods in their natural state and protect some bird habitats. For now, I have retained the cottage and its contents."

Margaret leaned over and stubbed out her cigarette.

"Upon my death, I have appointed the trustees of the Wequetona Club to act as executors." I stopped for a moment, watching Margaret, wondering how she would react.

"I have chosen to let the cottage pass out of the family, Margaret. There are many worthy Wequetona families . . ." Margaret didn't look up. "The proceeds from the sale, of course, will go to you and Jess."

"That's fine, Mother. Just fine. Whatever you want to do . . ." Margaret wasn't even looking at me; she was picking some dirt out from underneath one of her fingernails. I never could understand that girl. I paid for her to go to the very best schools, and she always affected this lower-class drawl, and the most repulsive kind of personal hygiene you could imagine.

"I'm afraid that's all there is," I said.

It was the last kernel of my daddy's once-impressive fortune. I think I have lived in a way that was appropriate to a woman of my station. I can't say I have ever had to scrimp on anything, and I was careful to set aside whatever might be needed for the future.

About Journey's End, though, I confess a muddleheaded sentimentality. In the cottage above Pine Lake, I could always close my eyes, and there they would all be: Mama before her nerves set in, Lila smiling and skipping down the walk, even Daddy, tall and clear-eyed, cheeks flushed with success.

For the longest time, I thought I could hang on to that thread, imagined passing the cottage on to Jess, taking her through it step-by-step, teaching her the rhythm of the year. Open it in May: throw wide the windows and let in the light. Close it in late September: shut it up tight as the fall chill creeps into the air. At Wequetona, I see that other families have managed to do it, passing their cottages along from generation to generation, just as they pass their characteristic blue eyes or stooped posture or thin hair.

I've arranged it so that Jess and Margaret won't have to return to Journey's End in order to pack it up and sell it. The Club will handle the sale, and I know that they will see to it that the cottage goes to the right kind of people—another family that will doubt-less go in and brighten up the inside with fresh paint and colored summer chintz. New people, new dreams, another try.

That first night, after Margaret left, I slept in my own bed in Coventry Manor, in my little white room, with only three pieces of my mahogany furniture: a bed, a dresser, and a vanity table. Two sketches of Pine Lake, one in rain, one in sun, hung on the pastel wall. Even with the TV on low, sitting in my bed, I could hear the hum of the elevator as it sped along its tracks, the electric ding that it made when it stopped at my floor to let passengers out.

I thought, *Mamie, you're a free woman again.* I didn't sleep much at all that first night, awakened less by the few buzzy and metallic sounds in the building than by the absence of the familiar creaks and groans of the old houses where I had spent my life. And when I needed to use the bathroom in the middle of the night, I was shocked by the cool angularity of it: smooth, pale linoleum and sleek, unstained porcelain that had seen nothing of having lived a real life.

CHAPTER SIX

Jess, age thirty-three

"Of course, we can't do anything ethnic . . ." Russ was saying. He was hunched up in a wicker settee in the living room, knees jutting out, poring over the Fine Dining section of the *Northwest Michigan Guide*. "You can't do anything ethnic between Yonkers and Oakland."

"Oakland, Michigan?"

"Oakland, California. You know. Gertrude Stein. 'There isn't any *there* there'?" Russ flipped the pages of the newsprint throwaway impatiently. "But at least *there* they have decent ethnic food."

Russ was something of a food snob—something that Jess knew she should appreciate more. He took her to excellent restaurants, and made gourmet meals for her. But her own taste had always run to simple stuff, something that Russ didn't really understand.

"I know a place that makes good burgers," Jess said. "Of course, who knows if it's even there anymore."

"Let's do it," Russ said. He slipped his arm around her as they made their way toward the car. She shrugged it off, and then stole a glance at him, but Russ wasn't the sensitive sort, and he didn't seem to notice that she was pushing him away. Maybe that was one of the reasons that she'd stuck with him, and that everyone assumed they were getting serious—because when she pushed, he stayed around anyway.

———

They circled downtown three times, looking at all the restaurants lining Main Street: whitefish houses, soup restaurants, and ice cream and popcorn shops.

"I'm so disoriented," she said. "I would have thought I could find this place blindfolded . . ."

They were about to give up, when Russ turned one more corner and she spotted the old neon sign with half the tubes burned out.

Th D cksi er

The Docksider

Inside, same scarred-up tables, same jukeboxes on the tables with old seventies tunes you could flip through while waiting to order. The Wequetona kids used to come here a lot, probably still did as far as Jess knew. They would ride their motorboats into town late in the evening and dock at the city marina.

People were smoking at the bar. The waitress showed them to a darkened booth in the corner and Russ ordered two beers. Jess looked down at the battered table and remembered nights from the old days, coming in bone chilled and windblown from the boat ride across the lake, when the scent of beer and cigarettes, boy-sweat on crew-neck Shetland sweaters, and the jukebox playing

"Midnight at the Oasis" made her feel all buzzy inside. At age seventeen, she used to light up a cigarette and blow smoke rings at the ceiling. Now, she sat fingering the initials of the unknown lovers carved into the battered tabletop.

Russ was talking—telling Jess everything he'd read in a local guidebook: about the lumbering business at the turn of the century, about Ernest Hemingway's descriptions of Indians in the Indian camps. She could tell he didn't know she wasn't really listening. She rubbed the beads of condensation that had gathered on the outside of her beer glass, looking, without really meaning to, over Russ's shoulder, past the shiny bar top, to the door.

Jess had watched someone walk out that door once, his back to her, leaving her behind. Now, it seemed as if only minutes had passed since that night, and that soon the door would swing open again. Jess reached down and fished around in the bottom of her purse. There, in the zippered lining, she felt a forgotten cigarette, bent and shabby like an old tampon, and the familiar bulge of her lighter. She pulled them out and lit up, inhaling deeply on the first breath.

"I thought you quit!" Russ said.

"I did," Jess said, forming her mouth into an O.

Just then, the bar door swung open, revealing a pretty woman whose shiny chestnut hair was pulled away from her face, and behind her a taller man with dark, wavy hair, worn longish. He was wearing a plaid polar-fleece shirt jacket, and, strapped to his chest in a baby carrier, there was a baby about six months old. Startled, Jess stared past Russ toward the doorway, which now framed the couple, the man with his arms looped loosely around the baby. His knees were slightly bent and his hair framed his face. His stance was one of particular grace—at once athletic and nurturing of his baby child.

"Oh, not here," Jess heard the woman say. "Look, people are smoking."

Jess felt herself straining, almost rising from her seat. Was it . . . ? Could it be *him*?

"Yeah, let's try the Villager," the man replied in an unfamiliar voice. As he turned to follow his wife out the door, the streetlight illuminated his face, and Jess saw the face of a stranger. She sank back down in her seat.

"Are you okay?" Russ asked. "You look kind of pale . . ."

"It's the nicotine," Jess said. "I'm not used to it anymore."

Jess picked up her glass and took a long swig of beer, letting the cold liquid sear her throat. Heat was rising along her cheekbones.

Russ reached out and put his hand over hers—even Russ, obtuse Russ, had picked up on her agitated state, on the awkward bulkiness of her shapeless desire.

He smoothed a lock of hair from her cheek and sat silently, looking at her face. She felt like telling him everything—just getting it off her chest.

"Russ . . ." She studied his face, wondering if he would actually listen if she opened up and told him what was really on her mind.

But Russ liked to fill silences with the sound of his own voice. "Hey, we've got to make sure we get some blueberry jam. It's a regional specialty . . . made with berries gathered by hand . . ." Russ wasn't a good listener—but wasn't that one of the things she liked about him? Unlike other men she had dated, Russ wasn't that interested in her past—not interested enough to want to pry.

By the time they got back into the rental car, Jess had whittled her desire down into a more manageable lump; it started somewhere underneath her collarbone and sat in the pit of her stomach, leaden but contained. She was not like her mother. She knew how to keep her passions simmering well below the surface.

———

Ardor unleashed was something she knew all about from

Margaret. "Look what the cat drug home," Margaret liked to say to Jess over breakfast. Jess would look up from her breakfast and see a bland and rather ordinary-looking fellow. Jess imagined her mother literally snatching these men unsuspecting off the streets, where they would find themselves not much later tangled and moaning in the sheets of Margaret's bed. Margaret always paraded around the apartment stark naked, her poofy breasts bobbling, sometimes the fishy smell of sex still upon her. Early on, Jess thought she understood sex pretty well: it was actually quite common, but people pretended not to notice; it had a tendency to be noisy and to stink. The part Jess never got was where all the painful leave-taking came from—every love to Margaret, no matter how unpromising at the start, ended inevitably in fountains of tears and frantic phone calls from train stations. That was how Jess gained her early impressions of love.

During the ride back to the cottage, Jess had the window rolled all the way down so that the sound of the rushing wind made conversation nearly impossible. Russ tried shouting to her a little bit, but she kept saying, "What, I can't hear you?" and finally he fell silent.

———

Toni Miller Barnes came highly recommended. She was a Miller, of the Miller cottage, a Wequetona girl who had married badly and gone local. Still, she had a small trust and enough affectation to make it in the business of catering to cottagers, a little interior decorating, a little real estate, and a sure eye for teaching new money how to look like old.

"Chippewa sweetgrass baskets," Ms. Barnes was saying. Jess and Russ had spent the morning combing the cottage for anything that looked Indian, taking everything down and lining it up on any available tabletop in the living room. Actually, Jess did most of the work. Russ had brought an astonishing variety of books in his overnight bag. *The Navajo Rug, The Ojibwa of Northwest Michigan, The Appraisers Guide to Native American Handicrafts and Antiques.* He spent most of the morning lying on the wicker settee in the living room, reading aloud to Jess from the books while she moved systematically from room to room, picking up objects that seemed to have possible value.

Jess had been washing dishes at the kitchen sink, looking out the back window, when Toni Barnes pulled up behind the cottage in her navy Volvo station wagon and marched toward the back door of Journey's End. Jess dried her hands on the clean waffle-weave dish towel and stepped forward to open the back door.

"Jess!" Toni cried out. "After all this time! You look exactly the same. Exactly!"

Jess poured lemonade into tall blue-glass tumblers and led Toni through the cottage. Toni was chattering brightly as they walked through the shadowy interior and out onto the sunny front porch.

"I'm so delighted that you called me, Jess. Of course you know that Miss Mamie was something of a landmark here at Wequetona. Everyone in the Club has been wringing their hands worrying about the cottage's sale. Everyone wants Journey's End to stay with one of *our* families."

Russ got up from the hammock and walked over to where Jess and Toni were standing. Slipping his arm around Jess, he said, "Ms. Carpenter wants to get the best possible price, and it should be worth quite a bit more as soon as we finish the renovations and do the photo shoot for a national magazine. Nothing else interests us at all."

Jess was surprised, but not ungrateful for Russ's action. She was perfectly capable of dealing with her own transactions, but she really couldn't stand Toni Barnes, had never liked her. It was only bad luck that they were dealing with her at all. When she had called the RE/MAX office, the receptionist had said, "Wequetona Club—oh, that would be Toni Barnes." Jess didn't at first realize it was Toni *Miller* Barnes. After they had spoken by phone and the connection had been made, it felt like too much trouble to look for anyone else.

"I thought the Club had dropped all the ridiculous membership regulations," Jess said.

"Well, there was some awkward legal story, someone threatening a lawsuit or some such. The board went through an emergency process, and the regulations were dropped." Toni leaned forward and lowered her voice slightly. "Everybody seemed to think that doing things informally, within the Club, would be a better way to go. Inside sales, word of mouth, that kind of thing."

Jess mainly wanted to sell the place soon and get back to New York. With Mamie gone, she found it unbearably sepulchral: a tomb for summer memories, a repository for long-forgotten souvenirs. But she didn't want to be hoodwinked into selling the cottage for a song either. As a research librarian in the French manuscript collection, in New York, her small salary didn't go very far—she was still paying off student loans, and her mother was so profligate that she called occasionally, rasping into the phone, "I'm broke and in Bangkok, can you wire me some money, please?" as though Jess were the Bank of New York, and not a poor librarian who spent her time arranging and stacking old manuscripts.

"I wonder if Jeb and Allison Cartwright are looking to buy," Toni went on, acting as though she hadn't heard anything Russ had just said. "Lovely couple. Jeb's in securities."

"If there is someone who is willing to come in with a good offer and accept the renovations sight unseen . . . we'd be willing to talk to them. We need to settle this as soon as possible and get back to New York."

Jess was intrigued to see Russ, obviously so much in his element, dealing with the real-estate agent. He had taken on a vaguely proprietary air that she had never noticed before. She was exhausted and felt the beginnings of a migraine coming on. Russ had his arm around her and he kept saying "we." It was such a relief not to have to deal with Toni Barnes. After a while, Jess picked up one of Russ's magazines and went out on the porch. She let Russ do all the talking.

CHAPTER SEVEN

"The Millers are here," Mamie said, not looking up from her mending. Her pale-blue glasses were perched on her nose. She was sitting on the porch swing, rocking slightly as she sat. "The *David* Millers."

"Are they?" Jess said without much interest. This was a summer ritual, Mamie telling her the comings and goings of the cottagers. Few stayed all summer as they did. Most came for two or three weeks at a time and then left, replaced by another batch of cottagers, each group barely distinguishable from the last. "I thought the *Sam* Millers were still here," Jess said, knowing as she said it that she had no idea who was in the Miller cottage.

"Left on Friday," Mamie said.

Jess pulled the faded floral bolster under her head and flopped over in the hammock. She was starting to hate summer, even to miss her crazy mother with her oddball journalist friends. Before this, she had always loved Wequetona—the easy summer alliances, fast friendships that formed and faded just like summer tans, soon forgotten but leaving behind a reminder of the season's warmth. But this summer was different. She kept running into people's mothers who peppered her with news. *Oh, Kristen misses seeing you. She stayed home to work this summer. David's not coming up this year. Summer school.* Jess was picking at the strings of the hammock where it was starting to fray. Staring out at the lake, feeling drowsy from boredom.

"The Miller girl. Isn't she a friend of yours?" Mamie asked.

Jess rolled onto her back and closed her eyes. *The Miller girl?* There were five sons in the Miller family, all of whom shared the cottage. They had some complicated time-share system. Besides, they all kind of looked alike—angular, bucktoothed, and blond. Nobody could ever keep the Miller family straight.

"Do you think it's *Toni* Miller?" Jess felt a little wave of dismay. They were around the same age, and people always expected them to be friends. They often ended up hanging around together, but they had never been close.

"Is that David Miller's daughter? The pretty blond one?" Mamie said. "Yes, I think that's the one."

———

It was 5:30. Jess knew because her grandmother had gone into her dressing room to change for dinner. Mamie still dressed for dinner every night, even though now it was just the two of them sitting down to simple meals at the kitchen table in the add-on kitchen in the back. She never said anything to Jess, didn't suggest that she change out of her jeans. The clubhouse had been closed for—oh, it must have been almost ten years, but Jess knew that Mamie still imagined that she heard the clubhouse bell, precisely at six, and could stroll down the walk like they used to. They gathered around the Tretheway table, in the drafty old wooden clubhouse with the linen-covered tables and worn wooden floors. The Club still held Vespers there on Sunday evenings; some of the older folk still went, including Mamie, of course. But for years it had been Mamie and Jess alone at the dinner table, Mamie dressed, with fresh makeup. Every night, they unfolded a fresh linen tablecloth and spread it out over the table, even though neither of them cooked much: they ate frozen dinners or canned chicken noodle soup.

"We didn't even have a kitchen until after the war," Mamie said to Jess more than once. "Most of the Indians were gone by then, and we couldn't find staff for breakfast. I had it added on just for breakfast, you know. Never did I imagine . . ." She spread her linen napkin in her lap, folding her hands on the table to say grace. "That we would dine here, Jess. Lord knows I never intended that."

———

"Don't you think you should stop by to see the Miller girl? Maybe you girls could spend some time together. Have a little fun." Mamie was spooning cream of mushroom soup into her mouth, pausing between each mouthful to carefully dab at her lipsticked mouth with her napkin.

"Um, yeah, I guess so."

"Don't say yeah, Jess. Say yes, ma'am."

"Yes, ma'am. I guess so."

———

At a quarter to six the next evening, there was a knock on the cottage door. Toni Miller was standing on the porch, wearing Levi's and a red stretch tube top, smelling strongly of Hawaiian Tropic tanning oil. Toni threw her arms around Jess, who could feel the slick sheen of tanning oil on Toni's bare skin. It was a relief to see someone her own age, even if it was Toni Miller.

"A bunch of us are going to picnic on Hemingway Point tonight. We're going in Phelps's boat. You wanna come?"

"Phelps is here?"

"Got in last night."

Jess hadn't seen Phelps around for several summers. He was a couple of years older, already a student at Yale. She remembered him well though. He had always been a leader at Wequetona, team captain for the relays, winner of the sailing cup, a little too arrogant for her taste. Besides, his mother, Mrs. Whitmire, had always struck her as kind of judgmental. *How's that mother of yours?* she used to say. Even as a small child, Jess had understood that Mrs. Whitmire was not asking because she wanted to know the answer.

"So are you coming?" Toni asked.

"Of course."

"We're meeting at the dock at eight."

After Toni had left, Mamie emerged from her bedroom, dressed for dinner in a blue ultrasuede suit. Her feet were shod in slingbacks of precisely the same shade of blue, and there was a small sapphire nestled at her neckline.

"Who was that, dear?"

"Toni Miller. She invited me to go to a picnic on Hemingway Point."

Her grandmother paled slightly.

"At night? Hemingway Point?"

"Toni said that Phelps is going to take us, in his boat."

"Is that Phelps Whitmire? That good-looking Whitmire boy?" Jess could hear that plummy tone in her grandmother's voice, the one she saved for *certain* Wequetona people.

"Yeah, I guess that's the one."

"Well, all right then. If the Whitmire boy is going."

———

Toni was leaning out over the bow of the Whitmires' red Chris-Craft wearing a pink bikini that had a thick white-plastic ring holding the two triangular pieces of the bra top together. She was still fragrant with the coconut scent of tanning oil. Jess was sitting in a vinyl-cushioned seat alongside the inboard's housing, holding on tight to a grip handle, wishing Phelps Whitmire would slow down. Phelps was standing at the rudder, one hand clapped to his head to keep his Yale lacrosse cap on. Even though it was approaching dusk, he was still wearing his Ray-Bans. There was a bottle of Wild Turkey in a brown paper bag braced between his feet. He was pushing down hard on the throttle, cutting the turns sharply to make the boat crash over its own wake.

Jess gripped the side rail tightly. She hated the way the boat skidded across the water, skid, bang, bang, skid, bang, bang, bang. The sound of the motor was deafening, and the stench was unbearable, old canvas, dead fish, and diesel fumes. Despite a lifetime of lakeside summers, Jess had never really learned to like boats. Hemingway Point was close, so close some people could swim to it. It couldn't possibly be taking this long. Phelps reached down to pick up the Wild Turkey, wrenching the boat hard to the left as he did.

He turned around to look at her.

"Wild Turkey?"

Jess stood up a little to grab the bottle from him, falling back onto the cushioned seat as the boat whacked the water.

"Why not," she said, tipping up the bottle and downing some of the fiery liquid. She sloshed a little as the boat hit another wake. She felt the cold liquid dribble down her chin.

About two hundred yards offshore, Phelps cut the motor and idled.

"I'm gonna swim in," Toni said, already shimmying her jeans over her hips. She stepped out of them, leaving them in the bottom of the boat, the legs crinkled up like two empty sausage casings. She had long, slender feet with frosted pink polish on the toenails, covered with a faint dusting of sand. Without waiting for a response, Toni stepped up onto the boat's gunwale and dove cleanly into the lake, making the boat sway in the quiet water. Jess froze for a second. The shore still appeared far away to her. She was ashamed to admit it, but she was afraid to swim. Mamie's sister had drowned in the lake, years ago, and Mamie had never really let Jess learn. While the other children were swimming and boating, Mamie had always flooded her with streams of cautions: be careful, watch out for the drop-off, stay near shore—not an approach that led Jess to feel confident in the water.

"Come on," Phelps said. "I can pull up at Lauder's dock. No need to get wet." Standing with his hand on the throttle, brown-bagged whiskey bottle now braced between his feet, he put the boat into forward and they chugged slowly down to the little dock.

The narrow strip of beach that ran along the edge of the woods was studded with sharp rocks. As they rounded the curve of the shoreline, the beach widened slightly into a ribbon of white sand. From there, Jess had a clear view across the cove. First, she noticed the woods that were adjacent to Wequetona, with their uncommonly tall trees. She could make out Journey's End, though it was too far away to see clearly. Then, along the crest of the hill, like pearls on a knotted strand, the other Wequetona cottages lined up. They looked like dressed-up ladies, their paint making bright splashes against the dark green of the surrounding woods. She could see the Wequetona dock, the brightly colored cabanas on the beach, the moored sailboats and motorboats. The kind of place you might look across at, from somewhere on the lake, and think:

Aren't they the lucky ones? Dusk was falling, and the water had taken on a purplish hue.

Turning back toward the beach, she made her way over to the bonfire where some of the kids had gathered. Toni was already there. On the other side of the fire, Jess saw a solitary figure, only his silhouette visible through the flames. Mostly what Jess saw was the graceful curve of a solid shoulder, and the hair, longish, framing his invisible face. Jess recognized the boy from the canoe.

Though by now it was very cold except right next to the fire, Jess could see that Toni had not put a shirt on over her bikini top, and her lean brown arms were glowing a bit—the tanning oil had lent them a perpetual shine. Toni was talking to the boy from the canoe, leaning so that her long feathered hair kept falling forward, each time just brushing the boy's forehead before she flipped it back behind her shoulder again. Their words were not audible, but Jess could hear the low rumble of the boy's voice as he spoke. He seemed pleased by whatever Toni was telling him—Jess couldn't help but notice his easy smile.

The time spent around the campfire passed in a warm blur. Jess couldn't remember how many people were there. Or what they ate. Or how many bottles Phelps Whitmire produced. For a while, everyone had been talking, and then the talking had died down. A group of kids left in somebody's motorboat, so just the four of them were left: Jess, Toni, Phelps, and the boy, whose name was Daniel. Now, they sat around the fire, hearing the pop and spit of the burning wood.

Jess felt soft and relaxed from the fire. The skin of her face was warm from the heat of the flames. She was staring through the orange licks of the fire at the face of the boy on the other side. She thought he was staring at her too, but maybe that was just a trick of the light. She felt like she knew him from somewhere. But that was impossible. She had never seen him before, except that one day at the sinking sand—still, there was something about him that she recognized.

Slowly, they edged toward each other. Finally, his shoulder touched a small patch of her bare arm, and she felt her skin light up like a runway at night, tracks of light in the darkness. She leaned into him, felt the bulk of his shoulder, smelled for the first time the scent of his body, a mix of clean laundry and something like fertile soil. They hadn't spoken directly to each other yet, were barely touching. Jess felt a heat at the base of her neck flushing outward. Her toes curled into the cold, damp sand.

"Hey, it's getting late, guys," Toni said, breaking the silence. "Jess, want to swim back with me?"

Jess looked out across the water. Wequetona, she knew, was just across the cove. Not more than half a mile. You'd think you'd be able to see porch lights but none were visible. She could see some points of yellow light in the darkness, but they looked farther away than they should have.

Toni threw her clothes off and started walking toward the water.

"Count me out," Phelps said. "I've got the boat."

"You're too drunk to drive your boat," Toni said.

———

Daniel pulled off his white T-shirt. Jess could follow the shirt's faint white arc through the air when he tossed it. Shirtless, he was almost invisible until he came into the light of the fire.

"Wait here, Jess. I'll be back soon," he said to Jess. "I'll go with Toni and get the canoe." The sound of his voice speaking her name made her flash hot, quick as a leaping flame.

"Unless you wanna swim with us?" he said.

Jess looked past Daniel out toward the water, feeling her heart beat faster and her throat get tight.

"I'd rather stay," she said.

"Only the crazy ones gonna swim," Phelps said, flopping his heavy arm on her shoulder. His speech was slightly slurred.

"Wait for me," Daniel said, looking at Jess. "I have to get the canoe."

She understood. It wouldn't be smart to get into the boat with Phelps in this state.

With yelps as they hit the cold water, Toni and Daniel took off swimming. Within seconds, they had disappeared entirely from sight.

The moment they were gone, Jess became aware that Phelps was now holding her uncomfortably tight. When she tried to back away, he threw his other arm around her and drew her in close.

"No, I . . ." she said, confused, trying to pull away from his unexpected embrace. His breath was hot, sour with booze; she could feel it coming fast on her cheeks and neck. He pressed the full length of his body against her, the bulge of his belt buckle biting into the soft skin of her belly where her T-shirt was pushed up.

"Lay off," she said, a little loud, now aware that there was no one around to hear.

Jess could feel her heart beating rapidly; she could feel bile rising up the back of her throat. She could smell him, the sharp stench of perspiration cutting through the soapy smell of Coppertone.

"Let go," she said, breaking free. He stumbled a little, fell down on one knee. She ran down to the water's edge, pulling off her T-shirt and dropping it onto the sand. "I'm going to swim."

"Come on, baby. I'm sorry." He didn't sound sorry.

Jess backed away from him, until she could feel the icy water lapping at her ankles.

"Come on . . . ," Phelps said, his voice suddenly crooning. She crept backward, wincing as the sharp rocks cut into the soles of her feet. The water was lapping up around her calves now—the slope was not gradual off Hemingway Point. She edged back another step, tapping her foot behind her along the silty ground to feel for the drop-off.

Turning, she strained her eyes trying to see across the dark lake: the water was blacker than black. The far shore looked distant and indistinct . . . She could just barely make out the gables of Journey's End, the yellow light that shone through in a square in the third-floor window. Or was it? Was she even facing in the right direction? Straight across to Wequetona wasn't far, but a miscalculation and she'd be heading out into open water . . .

Cutting into the silence, a motorboat ripped across the lake, its headlight making a jagged, bobbing path across the water.

Phelps was just standing there, not moving, harmless probably. Jess hesitated, fixing her eyes on the pinprick of light that seemed to be telescoping farther and farther away. Her toes were going numb; the water was frigid. Feeling her resolve wilt, she stepped back toward the shore.

Phelps shoved her onto the ground so fast she didn't even see it coming. The fall knocked the wind out of her, sickened her. She gulped for breath. His hands grabbed at the button fly of her jeans. Scratching at him, she pushed, flailed. He was stronger than she was; the bulk of his body pinned her down.

This is happening, she thought stupidly.

———

Everything ached, especially her head. Knowing she was awake, she lay with her eyes closed, afraid to open them, and listened. No wind, just silence and lapping water. She realized that her cheek rested not on the ground but on something smooth, something that felt like polished wood. She opened her eyes slowly, completely disoriented, and saw that her cheek was on some kind of step. All was quiet and dark. She was half sitting, half lying on a rough, mildew-smelling blanket.

She saw a round yellow light that she suddenly realized was a flashlight and, behind the light, a dark male outline.

Abruptly, scared, Jess sat bolt upright and could feel herself rocking back and forth, the ground underneath her not ground at all but something vertiginously choppy. She reached out to steady herself and felt the fiberglass gunwale. She was in a canoe.

"Jess," came the voice, low, urgent, tender as a caress. "Jess, are you okay?" Now, the flashlight moved so that the speaker's face was illuminated, and Jess could see tears streaking down his cheeks.

Jess sat stock-still and perfectly silent, until a shudder, both cold and fear, racked her thin shoulders.

With memory returning, she looked down, embarrassed, at her pants, to see if they were still down around her knees. But they weren't, they were pulled up into place, although Jess could feel that they were unbuttoned. Her feet were sandy and bare.

"I'm sorry," Daniel said softly. "I didn't know what you wanted me to do . . . You were out for a couple of minutes. I thought I should get you to the hospital . . . Are you okay?"

He picked up another rough blanket from behind him, wrapped it around Jess's shoulders. Without realizing she was crying, Jess felt her cheeks turn cold from the wetness of tears.

"I really think you should let me look at your head," Daniel said.

"I think I'm okay."

"Let me just look." Jess did not protest and Daniel shone the flashlight around her head, touching her hair, here and there, ever so tentatively with his hand.

"Ow." Jess winced when he touched the back of her head, reaching up with her own hand to feel the lump on her head.

"I thought I could stop him by cracking him on the head with the paddle, but I think I ended up whacking you too. I'm so unbelievably sorry . . . I feel terrible . . ."

"No, really . . . I'm okay . . ." Jess wasn't sure what to say. "Where's Toni?" She suddenly remembered. It would have taken them a while to swim across. It seemed like a lot of time had gone by.

"She didn't really swim across, just swam over to Lauder's and took Whitmire's boat. She was trying to do him a favor. She knew he was too drunk to drive it. I came back right away. I didn't think . . ."

"How long was I out? Long enough for . . . ?"

Oh God. Jess crossed her hands over her chest tightly and closed her eyes. She didn't remember exactly what had happened.

"Don't worry. He didn't . . ." Daniel paused, his voice hesitant. "I got to you before . . ."

Jess wanted to think of something grateful to say, but she didn't quite have the energy to put the words together. The canoe was rocking, her head ached, and she was trembling in little violent bursts.

"Can't you just take me home?" she said. "Row me, or whatever you were going to do?"

"I'll paddle over to where my truck is parked," he said.

———

Jess stayed quiet during the short ride home in the truck. She could feel her heartbeat slowing to normal. Daniel was looking straight ahead, out at the dirt road. She was struck by the way his hands rested on the steering wheel, relaxed yet firm.

But as soon as the back of the cottage came into view, she felt the equanimity slip away from her. She slumped against the pickup's door and started sobbing, completely silent, but her body racked by shudders and her face awash with a flood of tears.

Daniel didn't move. Through her tears, Jess could see the way his hands were gripped tight around the steering wheel now. Then, he reached over and put his hand on her chin, gently cupping it, turning her face toward his.

"Jess, I'm going in to talk to your grandmother." She was surprised, both that Daniel knew she lived with her grandmother, and that he seemed to realize, without being told, that she couldn't possibly see Mamie until she changed her clothes and washed the sand out of her hair.

Jess nodded in assent. Daniel slid off the truck's red-vinyl seat and headed down toward the cottage, cutting around to the front.

———

In the morning, when Jess came downstairs, every muscle in her body was stiff and sore. She found Mamie sitting at the kitchen table, ankles crossed, with her cup of Ovaltine in front of her, doing the crossword puzzle in the *Chicago Tribune*.

"Good morning, Jess," Mamie said. "I had a word with Judge Whitmire last evening."

Jess couldn't think how to answer, so she said nothing. Just walked over to the bread box to pull out some bread for toast.

Mamie stood up and took a step toward Jess; there was an awkward hesitation in her step, just a slight hitch of indecision. Briskly, she patted Jess twice on the arm, just two brief taps. "Young Phelps won't be bothering you anymore."

Jess turned her head and looked away, wishing that Mamie would drop the subject, acknowledging the gesture by just the barest nod of her head.

Mamie walked back to the table and resumed her crossword puzzle, taking a small sip of her Ovaltine from time to time.

Jess sat down at the table next to her, forcing herself to nibble on the toast, which felt like sawdust in her mouth.

After a long period of silence, Mamie looked up at Jess.

"And stay away from that Painter boy! He's nothing but trouble."

Jess felt her sore and tired muscles clench. The image of Daniel Painter pulling up her jeans and dragging her off the beach was so burningly painful to contemplate.

She hoped passionately that she would never see him again.

CHAPTER EIGHT

Jess, age thirty-three

"Jess, what say we do a little Hemingway today?" Russ said as he and Jess sat across from each other at the breakfast table, sipping black coffee and reading a three-day-old *New York Times*.

"Read Hemingway?"

"No, *do* Hemingway. You know, take a little walk in the woods. Commune with nature a little bit? What do people do up here anyway?"

"Sail," Jess said. "And play golf."

"Well, we don't sail . . ." Russ said. "Do we?"

"No, we don't sail, Russ."

"What we need to do is traipse through the woods carrying a musket and looking for Indian signs, you know, like Ernie would have done."

"Indian signs?" Jess said. "Honestly, Russ, aren't you going a little too far with the Hemingway thing?"

Russ was unfazed. "Well, I don't think it would be right to come to Hemingway country and not walk in the woods. Come on, let's get it over with."

Reluctantly, Jess agreed. Why shouldn't she go into the woods? She had come to the cottage. No point in treating the woods like some kind of sacred space. As a child, Jess had thought of the woods as being trackless and indefinably vast. She now understood the geography of the place much better. There was a little pie-shaped area of undeveloped land, cutting between the road and the lakeshore. People said that in the winter, when the trees were bare, you could see right out to the road. It was in those woods that the last of the giant white pine stood. She hadn't known that as a child, didn't remember anyone mentioning it. It wasn't the kind of thing—golf scores, sailing races—that Wequetona people usually talked about.

So she would take a little walk in the woods with Russ. She was sure he would soon tire of looking at trees. Russ went into the bedroom to get ready, and when he came out, Jess bit back a laugh. Out of his usual city garb, he was wearing a neon-yellow Columbia Sportswear jacket and hiking boots that looked like they had been designed to withstand a trek into the Himalayas. In one hand, he held *The Field Guide to the Deciduous Trees of North America*, and in the other, a little combo gizmo that looked like some kind of a compass/flashlight/hunting knife.

Instead of turning left at the front walk that led back toward the other cottages and the beach, they turned right where the walkway shortly turned into the woods and led over a rustic footbridge. It soon became a narrow path, so thickly covered with pine needles that their footsteps made a hollow, thumping sound when they walked.

Just beyond the footbridge, not more than twenty yards into the woods, Jess noticed a sign that she did not recall having seen there before: LITTLE TRAVERSE CONSERVANCY. CONSERVATION LAND. NO HUNTING, FIRES, OR DISTURBING PLANT LIFE. STAY ON CLEARLY MARKED PATHS.

"That's funny," Jess said, reading the sign. "Mamie always told me that these woods were part of our property. Her father made his fortune in lumber, but Mamie told me that when the loggers were set to clear-cut through these woods, he bought the land right out from under them and then left it untouched. Supposedly, almost all the hardwoods were gone by then, but this little patch was left because it was farthest away from the mill."

"An early visionary of conservation?"

"No, not exactly that. What I heard was that the loggers would have set up camp in the woods—Miss Ada, my great-grandmother, didn't want the camp there, on account of the smell."

"What smell?"

"The Indian smell."

"Well, maybe your grandmother donated the land—it's not a bad write-off, you know."

"Oh, that's impossible," Jess said. "Margaret would have told me. Besides, Mamie wasn't exactly the nature-preserve type. She hated the woods. Never set foot in them, as far as I know."

"The whole story about your great-grandfather was probably just made up. Most stories like that are, you know."

Russ was hitting his stride. He had his Peterson field guide open and was reading from the introduction—reading, with a tone of authority, about single leaves and leaf clusters, leaf scars, and leaf buds. It had seemed a bright day when they had set out, but now Jess suspected that the sky had clouded over. Though she couldn't really see the sky through the canopy of leaves, it was dark in the woods, and little sunlight seemed to be filtering through. The woods did appear to go on forever, but if she listened carefully, she could hear the low rumble of cars out on the highway. Jess looked over her shoulder and saw that the cottage had already disappeared from sight, even though she knew it couldn't have been more than a couple of hundred yards away.

"The paper birch tree . . ." Russ was reading to her all about the unusual tree with the white scored bark that gave the North Woods their distinctive look. "The bark was used for canoe making and as a treatment for rheumatism . . ."

Jess felt relieved that nothing around them looked familiar. She saw trees everywhere, some birch, some beech with the smooth gray-green trunks, a few of last winter's pale, dry leaves still clinging to the lower branches under the canopy of green. She felt no special resonance here, their quiet footsteps on the forest floor, Russ's loud voice. *These woods,* she thought, *evoke nothing.*

Then, without warning, she realized that they had entered the stand of giant white pine. Around her on all sides, there were tall tree trunks, ruddy brown and covered with rectangular markings. The trunks rose up straight as the masts of schooners and then disappeared above the beech, poplar, and maple leaves. Jess knew that the branches of the giant white pine spread out above them, forming a supercanopy over the other trees.

"Russ," Jess whispered, her voice hushed. "Look!" she said.

Russ glanced up from the field guide for a moment, and looked around him.

"What is it?" he said in a voice that seemed to Jess to be much too loud. "I don't see anything."

"It's the giant white pine—see the dark trunks of the taller trees?"

Russ looked around, and then back down at his book.

"Giant white pine, giant white pine . . . Ah, here it is . . . Nope! There aren't any around here. Logging. They've all been gone since the turn of the century."

Jess looked at the spot where she remembered once feeling deep reverence. She could hear the echo of a modest, worshipful voice. Jess felt tired then, and she sat down on a sawed-off tree stump, a stump that still bore the traces of hacking and burning left by loggers—poachers, no doubt—almost a hundred years before. She could hear birdsong now. A lone pine warbler, wasn't it? At first, she felt sure it was a pine warbler . . . but then she felt less sure, and finally decided she did not know. She watched Russ's yellow jacket bobbing down the path ahead of her, and then she stood up and followed the path out of the wood—to where the sidewalk started up again, flanked on either side by the green of neatly clipped lawns.

Just as they stepped out of the woods, it started to pour. Russ pulled the rip cord tight on his Gore-Tex jacket, smiling the smile of a little boy with a new toy. Jess felt the cold raindrops penetrate her thin T-shirt, and with a shiver started to jog back to the cottage.

———

The rain did not let up. They returned to the cottage—Jess damp, Russ dry—where Jess lit a fire in the fireplace. The old cottage was shadowy inside. Russ got absorbed again in doing research on cottage architecture, and Jess roamed around the cottage aimlessly, feeling as if she was looking for something but couldn't quite remember what.

A stack of leather-bound photo albums caught her attention. Mamie had been a meticulous album maker, carefully labeling her photos and aligning them with little black paper corners. Jess looked through the albums, starting with the ones that showed herself as a child, always prim and proper with a white ribbon in her hair. She remembered posing for pictures, always doing Mamie's bidding: Here is Jess with her dress on, on the way up the walk to dinner. Here is Jess in her first two-piece bathing suit, with the little strawberries that dangled from the bows on the side. When Jess stopped to think about it, Mamie must have bought most of her clothes. Jess had always worn American clothes; she remembered that her clothes used to arrive in boxes from time to time: Florence Eiseman dresses, and patent-leather Mary Janes that had to be buttoned with a little metal hook.

Jess put aside the pictures of herself and looked at the pictures of her mother. There were few pictures of Margaret, and in most she seemed a little out of focus: Here she was on her tricycle. Here she was swinging on the hammock. In this one, she was twirling on the lawn; in another, she was running away and laughing, looking over her shoulder. Jess could just imagine that Mamie would have had little patience for that, could imagine her saying: *Margaret, I won't take your picture at all if you won't stand still.* Jess knew Margaret had never minded Mamie very well. She had always wondered how her mother had dared to defy her grandmother.

Most of the pictures showed Mamie's family in their prime. There were stiff formal portraits of Mamie's parents. Mrs. Ada Tretheway dressed in heavy brocades that only exaggerated her ample bosom. Mr. Harris Tretheway had a long, thin face and bright, clear eyes—looked more like Lila than Mamie. Even though Mamie's father died when she was in her teens, Mr. Tretheway had left enough money to keep Mamie throughout her life, even paying Margaret's way through expensive private schools and colleges. But his death had taken an emotional toll on the family. After he died, his wife took ill, then, a few years later, Mamie's sister drowned. The family that had once joyously filled the rooms of the large cottage had shrunk down. During all the summers that Jess had spent with Mamie, the cottage had always seemed cavernous and lonely, and Jess imagined that her mother's childhood must have been much the same.

Jess studied the images of Lila. In a picture with her husband, they appeared the image of 1920s sophistication, both in light-colored golfing clothes; both fair, they looked like pictures she had seen of F. Scott and Zelda Fitzgerald. Jess studied the picture of the young fair-haired man, his foot resting on the running board of a two-seater roadster. In brown, spidery script on the white border was written the name *Chapin Flagg*. Though Mamie never talked about Lila, Jess had heard her mention Chapin Flagg from time to time when talking to her old friend May Lewis. Jess had always thought it an odd name. She had understood, without really being told, that Chapin Flagg was somehow a bad fellow. *If it hadn't been for that Chapin Flagg,* Jess had heard her grandmother say more than once. She had no idea what he might have done, or what had ever become of him, but she had understood that it was somehow his fault that Lila had drowned.

There was one picture in particular that really grabbed Jess. It showed the two sisters, Mamie and Lila, wearing woolen bathing suits that came down to their knees, with towels wrapped around their heads and bulky wool fisherman's sweaters pulled around their shoulders. The caption read: *Mamie and Lila, setting out to swim across Pine Lake.* Mamie looked radiant, her smile wide and full of life, some of her wild curly hair escaping from under the turban, somehow making the photo look more modern, more life-like. Lila, standing next to her, eerily pale, even in the photo, had a smile on her face too, but a look in her eye, so vacant, so haunted, that she seemed to see herself drowning already, sliding under the blue water.

After that, there were no more pictures of Lila or Mamie. In fact, it was the last photo in that album.

Jess realized that Russ was looking over her shoulder.

"We can use those."

Jess looked up at him, confused.

"They'll look good in the pictures. I like that old-album look in this kind of setting. It helps evoke the twenties thing we're going for. You can unload them after that if you want."

For a second, Jess felt stunned. This was her family, her life history. Russ wanted to sell them? Then, she tried to imagine the albums, dusty, taking up space in her tiny apartment. Life with Margaret had taught her to be disciplined about what she saved and what she discarded. "You're right," she said, reluctantly closing the album and placing it back on the pile. "I don't think I'll keep them. I just don't have the space."

"They've got some sale value," Russ said. "You'd be surprised how many people are poking around antique stores shopping for likely-looking ancestors."

———

Later that afternoon, the sun came out, and Jess and Russ went into town. Russ wanted to see if he could find more books about local architecture, so they headed for the bookstore. When they got there, the shadowy interior didn't look as appealing to Jess as the bright day outside, so she decided to take a walk down along the marina while Russ was looking for books, and to meet him at the coffee place in a few minutes.

The day was balmy and the air was dry, so pleasant in contrast to the humidity of the New York summer. She looked at the boats in the little city marina—big, hulking cabin cruisers with folding lawn chairs on the decks, enormous sailboats with their names painted in gold leaf: *The Harriet Ruth, Tipsy Topsy.* There was an art fair going on in the park in front of the marina, artists with their wares spread out under white tents. The paintings were mostly bright watercolors with summery themes: sailing boats and lighthouses, children in striped bathing suits with sand buckets on the beach.

Jess saw families walking around, dressed in crisp vacation clothes, bright white tennis shoes and polo shirts in pastel colors. Jess saw two brothers, certainly twins, maybe about six years old, throwing pieces of bread to the ducks that swam along in the sullied water just at the marina's edge. Both children had tousled brown ringlets. She saw one boy bending forward on chubby legs, fingers wrapped around a bit of bread he was getting ready to throw, the other hand pressed down on the blue baseball cap he was wearing. His brother, his brow furrowed in concentration, was holding the bag carefully.

Some of Jess's colleagues at the library had children. She would sometimes see them on their way to private schools, the boys wearing blazers, the girls bare legged with knobby knees above their woolen kneesocks. That was probably how she had looked as a child—crossing city streets with her hand gripped roughly in a nanny's hand, or climbing awkwardly into a taxi with her satchel, her violin case whacking her uncomfortably in the knee.

The boys ran out of bread and sprinted back to their mother, who was wearing black bike shorts and a white sweatshirt with pictures of sailboats on it.

"Come on, guys," the woman said. "Let's go meet Daddy for a Happy Meal." And off they walked.

Jess imagined that if she and Russ ever had a child, it would be more likely to slurp sesame noodles out of a paper takeout carton than to ever eat a Happy Meal. A Happy Meal . . . Well, she and Russ hadn't discussed having children much, except for the obvious fact that in New York City, they would never be able to afford to have more than one.

Jess walked back to the coffee place, where she saw Russ sitting at an outside table with a black coffee and a stack of books in front of him.

"What did you find?" she asked him.

"There is some pretty good small-press stuff here. Look, here's one about the history of lumbering in this area. This one's about the Earl Young houses, these cottages on the north shore made out of stone. This one's even up your alley—it's got some poetry in it."

Russ handed Jess the slim paperback volume, bound in shiny blue paper. She turned it so that she could see the title: *Cathedral of the Pines: Musings of a Sometime Woodsman*. She didn't even need to read the author's name, because there was his face, on the back cover.

She opened the book slowly. The dedication caught her eye.

For J.

CHAPTER NINE

JESS, AGE SEVENTEEN

As it does in the north part of Michigan, the weather had suddenly turned colder and stormy, and there was an almost autumnal feeling in the air. Outside the warped glass windows, the lake had gone silver, studded with scallops of whitecaps. The tree branches that hung down over the window were shaking, and the sky over the lake was gray streaked with purple: dark, menacing, and cold.

It was Thursday, the day each week when Mamie went to Petoskey with May Lewis, and this Thursday was no exception. Mamie had put on her raincoat, snapped plastic galoshes over her pumps, and tied a pink kerchief around her head; then she had left as usual, gliding her town car down the back road toward The Rafters, where she would stop and pick up May.

When Jess heard the screen door closing behind Mamie, she felt herself relax, just a little. It wasn't until she felt her shoulders drop an inch that she realized how tightly she was holding herself. She was still stunned by what had happened at the beach picnic the night before.

Jess was wondering whether she should have called her mother. Of course, it wasn't easy to reach Margaret in Namibia. She was following rebel camps in the South, but the AP could always get in touch with her, and, as Jess knew, she frequently flew out to Johannesburg for R&R. She might be at the Sofitel right now, and Jess could just pick up the phone and dial.

Then again, they weren't much in the habit of speaking to each other during the summer. Jess rarely tried to get in touch with her on assignment. Just the idea of trying to reach Margaret in Namibia gave her a headache. Jess thought about Margaret and Mamie. No use to her, either one of them. She would, as she usually did, forge on alone.

Just a few minutes after Mamie left, she saw Daniel's white pickup pull into the spot next to the garage where Mamie's Lincoln Town Car usually sat.

Her first thought was to run upstairs in the cottage, to hide and pretend she wasn't there. But it was too late. He had caught sight of her through the window, and his face, so serious-looking, had eased into a smile. She stood up from where she sat at the kitchen table folding clothes and walked to the back door, pushing it open.

There was an awkward moment of silence, Jess staring down at the scuffed green-and-white linoleum, unable to meet his eyes. She thought he was going to offer sympathy, and felt that the slightest kind word would send her dissolving back into sobs. She stared resolutely at her feet.

But Daniel did not offer sympathy. Instead, he grasped her arm gently and guided her out the door into the soft rain.

"If it's okay with you, I want to show you something." Holding his green windbreaker over their heads as they walked, he headed them toward the path into the woods.

"Where? Where are we going?" Jess was walking along beside him, close enough to bump elbows, ducking to stay under the impromptu canopy.

"Just a minute, I'll show you." He slowed to a walk as the path into the woods got so narrow that they had to walk in single file. He still held the windbreaker over both of them. The air underneath it was close, with a vinyl odor. Fat raindrops were falling on it occasionally, making loud splats.

Daniel stepped off the path and led Jess through the thick, wet, knee-high brambles that slapped against her pant legs as she stepped, trying to avoid the thorny vines. After a moment, he stopped, pushing the edge of the windbreaker off his head, and he knelt down on the wet forest floor, assuming a posture that looked almost like prayer. It wasn't raining hard now, just the occasional splatter falling through the trees.

"Look, Jess. Look here."

Gently, he held back the branches so that she could see, but she didn't see anything special, just green leafy underbrush hugging the ground.

"What, what is it?"

"Come down and take a look."

Jess knelt down beside him, feeling the damp soak through the knees of her jeans. Tenderly, Daniel held up the low heart-shaped leaves. Underneath, she saw clusters of wild raspberries, each one beaded with a gossamer of moisture: perfect rose-colored globes.

"They're dwarf raspberries," Daniel said. "It's an endangered plant. You almost never find them." Carefully, he disengaged his hand and left the berries to rest hidden under their leaf canopy. "The whitetails will certainly eat them soon, if the squirrels don't get to them first." He reached over and plucked a single berry from the plant, then, gently pressing on her chin, he dropped one sweet starburst into her mouth.

Daniel led her farther down the path. "Here," he said. "Tell me, what do you see?"

Jess looked around and saw nothing but trees and more trees.

"Lie flat on your back," he said.

They lay on their backs staring up at the canopy of leaves above them, dampness seeping through the back of her jeans. Jess noticed that there were a number of trees with long, straight trunks that appeared to leave the forest entirely and rise up into the sky.

"This is it," Daniel said. "The last stand of giant white pine hereabouts. The lake used to be ringed by them, but these are the only ones to survive."

"Survive?"

"Lumbering. They chopped them all down to make planks from them. You know all that wood in our cottages? Number one white pine planks. Just lie here for a minute and get the feel for it."

Jess and Daniel lay side by side on the wet, mossy ground in silence. Jess felt uncomfortable and vaguely foolish. The ground was wet, and there were sticks poking into the small of her back. She really did not know what she was supposed to be looking for. She just kept staring upward at the ever-shifting patterns of branches and leaves. She stared until the long, straight shafts of the trees seemed to converge overhead.

"Do you see it?" Daniel asked.

"See what?"

"If you look long enough, it looks like a vaulted ceiling."

Jess shivered as she murmured assent.

"I call it the Cathedral of the Pines."

———

Cutting through the woods, they got to Daniel's cottage in just a matter of moments. It was surprisingly close, straight through the forest, just on the other side.

Daniel and Jess walked up the worn wooden steps of the small cottage; its weathered green shingles were just slightly paler than the surrounding woods. A cottage sign, TREETOPS, hung over the porch.

"Is anybody home?" Jess asked, suddenly shy.

"Nobody's here but me," Daniel said. "I'm staying here alone for the summer. I'm doing an independent project, photographing birds."

When Daniel pushed the warped cottage door open, the interior looked warm and inviting. Treetops, the Painter cottage, was cozy, decorated in dark reds and greens, with soft woolen Hudson's Bay point blankets draped over corduroy sofas.

Even inside, Jess was still shivering.

"I'll make a fire," Daniel said. He took some logs from the hearth and stacked them on the grate in the large fieldstone fireplace that took up most of one wall. Jess curled up in the corner of one of the overstuffed sofas. She pulled a multicolored woolen blanket around her shoulders.

"He should be arrested," Daniel said. "You should press charges."

This was Daniel's first reference to the events of the previous night. Lying in the woods, looking at the trees had calmed her. Now, her stomach started to churn. Jess did not disagree with him, but it had not occurred to her to do something like that. Already, Jess sensed that she would not know what to say the next time she saw Judge Whitmire, a tall, slightly stooped man with white hair, always elegant and courtly in a navy-blue blazer and white pants. Things came up at Wequetona from time to time. To call the police would be to turn it into a "townie" matter. Mamie would never want to handle it like that.

"I just, I just don't think I could . . ." Jess pulled the soft blanket around her shoulders and moved a little closer to the fireplace as the flames began to shoot up. "You think I'm chicken, don't you?"

"I think you're brave," he said. And he said it in a voice so grave and so serious that Jess could feel tears pricking her eyes.

Daniel went into the kitchen and came out with a steaming bowl of chicken noodle soup and some saltines. Jess took the plate and balanced it on her knees, letting her salty tears stream freely down in the bowl as she took sips of the steamy broth. Daniel didn't say anything about her tears, just came over and brushed them off her cheeks ever so lightly with his callused yet gentle fingers.

The Painter cottage was not part of the Wequetona Club. It was a little farther down the lakeshore, on the far side of the south woods. Though the cottage was not more than a quarter mile from Journey's End, if that, it looked out at the lake at a different angle, out toward Five Mile Point. At the end of the lawn, there was the lake, light green-blue close to shore and then a vivid midnight blue out farther, where Jess knew the water was deep. Though the wind had died down on shore, Jess could see that in the middle of the lake, the surface of the water was still troubled.

She looked around the interior of the cottage. Someone in the family must have been a fly fisherman; there were several trophies of rainbow trout on the wall, mouths gaping in perpetual surprise. There were also old black-and-white photographs of Ironton, back when it had been a poor lumbering town; one showed some Indians in logger clothes standing next to a sawed-off stump, and another showed giant logs loaded onto a tiny flatbed railroad car.

"Can I have some tea?" Jess asked.

Daniel stood up and walked toward the kitchen, smooth on the balls of his feet. From where she sat, she could see him filling the kettle with water, his hair falling over his eyes. He was barefoot and wearing a pair of frayed khaki shorts, with a soft dungaree shirt hanging out, rolled up at the sleeves. His skin was quite brown, and she noticed that his calves were exceptionally well muscled, like a runner's. The sight of him making tea in the kitchen unnerved her, made her go soft around the middle.

———

Jess and Daniel spent days like that, inside the cottage, sitting apart, sipping tea, and talking or listening to music. As long as she was home by dinnertime, Mamie never asked where Jess had been. She was probably relieved that her granddaughter was gone somewhere so that she could avoid awkward opportunities to discuss what had happened with Phelps.

With Daniel, Jess sat, mostly, arms buckled around her drawn-up knees. Her brain felt cottony, her muscles stiff, every painful shift of her limbs a reminder of what she had been through. Daniel alternately lounged and padded around in bare feet, now fixing some food for them, now changing the record album. On occasion, he took out his camera and stood on the front lawn, almost motionless, for what seemed to Jess to be an eternity. He spent a lot of time in his darkroom, down in the basement, with the red lightbulb on, making black-and-white prints of birds. To Jess they looked indistinguishable, but patiently he showed her: See the two black wingtip feathers? See the white around the eyes? Daniel seemed to take it as a matter of course that Jess rarely moved, that he would disappear for an hour or two and she would still be sitting there, curled up like a walnut, staring at the water.

Sometimes, he sat next to her and named the birds flying near shore.

"How'd you learn so much about birds?"

"Before my mom remarried, she used to bring me up here on weekends, with her boyfriends."

Daniel was lounging on one of the sofas, his arm flung over the end and his brown hair cascading over the side. Joni Mitchell was playing softly on the stereo. "Always by sometime Saturday after-noon, the boyfriend would start giving me *the look*."

"The look that said 'I'd be screwing your mother if it weren't for your presence'?"

Daniel rolled on his side and looked at her. "Yeah, exactly, that's the one. Anyway, my mom would always say, 'Daniel, why don't you go outside for a while and take a walk in the woods.' I used to think, is she crazy or what? There's nothing to do alone in the woods."

"My grandmother never let me set foot in the woods . . ."

"Well, my mother thought the woods was just the place for me. Anyway, I spent so much time out there . . . I used to play this game I called The Last Man on Earth, and after a while, in spite of myself, I did like the woods, and I started watching the birds."

"Are you in college?" Jess asked.

"Yeah, Ann Arbor. I'm majoring in environmental sciences and art."

"What are you going to do with it?" Jess asked, hating the question, the one that grown-ups always asked.

He looked hesitant before he answered, raising his eyebrows a little, as though wondering if she really wanted to know. "I take pictures and then . . . write poems about them, and essays too . . . about the outdoors. At least that's what I really like to do. What about you?"

"Well, my mom is a reporter. She goes to places where all this awful stuff is happening, and then writes about it, without actually . . . doing anything, you know what I mean? I would like to be able to actually do something practical, and . . . you know . . . helpful." Jess felt her cheeks flush slightly even saying it. That wasn't the kind of thing you could say around Margaret and her crowd—that you wanted to "help." The expat crowd her mother hung around with would chuck her under the chin and snicker if they ever heard her say a thing like that. It was okay to want to do things "just for the hell of it." Seeming sincere though, now that was a cardinal sin.

"So I'm planning to go to medical school."

They both sat silently for a moment, listening to Joni Mitchell's voice glide and plunge as she sang "Little Green."

"Just be careful. Don't sell out."

"I won't." She looked at Daniel. "I mean, I don't think I will. Do you think you can really know . . . if you're gonna sell out, I mean?" She paused again, listening to a saxophone riff through a plangent solo; she was studying the planes and contours of his face.

"I know I won't," Daniel said. "Where are you going anyway?"

"University of Texas."

"Oh," Daniel said. "Not anywhere near here."

"No, not anywhere near anywhere, really."

"Why there then?"

"That's where Mamie wants me to go."

"Is that a good reason?"

"She's paying for it."

———

It was the end of an unusual week of unremitting cold weather. Daniel was stoking the fire, trying to warm up the living room in Treetops, which had settled into a bone-rattling chill except right by the hearth. Jess was looking at Daniel as he tended the fire. The stiffness had eased out of her muscles, and she felt a little less raw, less bruised, every day. She watched the careful way he handled the fire tools, the orange flames casting light upon his face.

He turned his head away from the fire, looked at her, and smiled—a crooked smile over even white teeth. Jess had to smile back at him. And she smiled him a smile that was an invitation, and the distance between them melted away.

He was warm sand. He was the smoke from a campfire. He was the soft wool of a Shetland sweater, scented gently of wind and sweat. She was lying back on the sofa, and he knelt beside her on the floor, his rough hand gently stroking the hair off her forehead. Jess looked up at his face, the brown cheeks, the pink at the end of his nose where the skin had peeled off, with pale hints of freckles. She looked at his brown eyes, dark pools in the low light. She slipped her arms along his warm, bare chest, shimmying his flannel shirt off, feeling the buttons popping off as she pulled it over his head. For a moment, she lay her cheek against the warm, firm expanse of his chest, then as she raised her chin to meet his soft lips, her own parted to taste his salty pad of tongue.

Jess did not know how long they lay like that, entangled on the sofa. They were so close to the fire that they were almost scorched on the side nearest the flames, and Jess first took off her shirt, and then unclasped her bra by its front hook, letting it slip off to the sides. She felt her breasts flatten out under the weight of his chest, their chests glued together with slick, hot sweat.

Daniel slipped down on the floor beside the couch and gently, gently reached for the button at the fly of her jeans. But feeling the hands on her jeans, she flashed on Phelps's face in front of her. Jess felt herself go rigid, and she curled up, knees to her chest, and said, "No. No, I can't."

Daniel laid his head, soft with fine brown hair, gently on her sternum between her breasts, then he stood and turned away, banging his forehead rhythmically against the wall, muttering, "Sorry, sorry, sorry . . ." so softly that Jess could barely hear.

She stood, scooping up her bra and pulling her shirt closed to cover herself, and walked into the bathroom, feeling at the same time weak-kneed with desire, cold with fear, and burning with shame.

When Jess came out of the bathroom, with her hair combed, shirt buttoned, and face damp with cold water, Daniel was in the kitchen making Kraft Macaroni & Cheese out of the box. Jess had never seen cheese made out of powder, and she giggled as he poured in the bright-orange powder and mixed it with butter and milk. "I've never seen mac and cheese come out of a box," she said.

Daniel looked at her. "Seriously? That's impossible."

"We mostly eat out," Jess said. "I'm sure my mom would love mac and cheese in a box," Jess said. "She hates to cook."

Outside, the sky was darker than ever, almost purple, and the rain was coming down in sheets, not the usual brief downpour with thunder and lightning, more like a winter storm, cold, steady, and relentless. In no way did it seem like early July.

They sat close together, knees and thighs pressed against each other's, at the chipped Formica table, forking the small cylindrical noodles into their mouth. They tasted, Jess thought, disgusting— but she was starving and so she shoveled the little orange noodles into her mouth, and then they would lean over the plates and kiss each other, the powdery, salty orangeness mixing up in their mouths. Joni Mitchell's *Blue* was playing in the background while Jess filled Daniel in on some of the crazy details of her life.

"What's it like over there anyway? In France. Do you like it?" Daniel asked.

Jess shrugged. "It's okay," she said. She thought of their small, messy apartment, her walk to school under gray skies. She and her mother moved around a lot. Michigan always felt more like home.

"We'll go there sometime," Daniel said. "You can introduce me to your mom who doesn't like to cook. I'll bring her a box of Kraft Mac and Cheese as a present."

"I would like that," Jess said.

Daniel kept hopping up every couple of minutes, saying, "I like this part," thumbing the needle up off the vinyl and letting another Joni Mitchell riff repeat.

"Listen to this!" and he would close his eyes, chin tipped up, legs lightly flexed, and rock back and forth in time with the music.

And then Jess would have to stand up and go over to him, embracing him tightly, and kiss him again, pressing up against him, cheek to cheek, and they would both let the bright risings and fallings of the music pour through them.

Finally, Jess reached down to unbutton her own pants, letting them drop to her ankles, and then she stepped out of them. Without a word, Daniel led her by the hand up the staircase and down a narrow hall. Compared to downstairs near the fire, it was freezing up there, and she felt gooseflesh rise on her naked legs. Then, flannel sheets, dark green, warm, and smelling like the warm earthy woods themselves. She brought him to her, unfolding to him, and they rocked and rocked, deeper and deeper, and then down, down, into a heavy, dark-green sleep.

When they woke up, Jess imagined for a moment that she heard the clubhouse bells, clanging out the first bell, the fifteen minutes to dinner warning. But fully awake, she heard only silence and the sound of Daniel's even breath. The rain seemed to have stopped. Glancing at the bedside clock, she saw that it was a quarter to six. She sprang out of bed and pulled her jeans on, calling over her shoulder that she had to be home for dinner with Mamie. She ran the quick way, down the path through the woods, and managed to skid into her seat right at six.

"I thought I heard the clubhouse bells," Jess said, slightly breathless, as she sat down across from Mamie in the kitchen, "the warning bell for dinner. Isn't that funny?"

"I still hear them too, Jess. After all these years, I still swear I hear them on occasion."

———

The next morning, the rain cleared and the sun came out. It was summer again, only now it seemed like a brand-new summer, no problems with Phelps Whitmire, no lonely vigils at the beach. *This* summer, she was with Daniel, and she was in love. He took her out in the canoe across to Hemingway Point so that she could see the tops of the giant white pines. He taught her the names of birds, what their markings looked like, and how to recognize their calls. They spent hours down in the basement, elbow deep in chemicals while he showed her how to process photos, and they kissed under the red darkroom light. They ate ramen noodles and Cup-a-Soup, and listened to Joni Mitchell's *Blue* over and over and over again, each time the record ending with a *scratch-scritch* and then the automatic arm lifting up, moving over, and setting itself back down with a *scritch* again.

CHAPTER TEN

JESS, AGE THIRTY-THREE

Poison, Jess thought. *This is pure poison. I quit smoking ages ago.*

She sat out on the porch, feet tucked underneath her in one of the wicker rockers, smoking a Marlboro Light; a pile of dusty old novels she'd pulled down from the shelf was sitting on the table in front of her. One was open on her lap, except that she realized she had been reading the same phrase over and over again. Every time Jess let her eyes lift from the page to look out over the lake, she would drift back into her memories of the summer she had spent in love with Daniel Painter. The summer she had learned the names of trees that she had never even distinguished before: tulip poplar, black walnut, blue spruce, paper birch. And she had looked at birds for the first time, looked at birds doing anything besides strutting around dirty in city streets, pecking at bits of garbage.

Enough, Jess thought. It was like writing and rewriting a paragraph until she couldn't understand her own words anymore. A long time ago, she had put that summer with Daniel between brackets—big, bold, black brackets; it was one subject that she had thought about enough. She should be honest—thought about way too much.

Jess could hear Russ's voice inside the cottage, talking with the architect, Paul Banyer, who had arrived late the evening before. They were talking about weight-bearing walls, islands, and peninsulas—it seemed to have something to do with kitchen counters—and Corian and granite. This was Russ's stuff, and it had always pleased Jess, so concrete and tangible, so unlike the intangibles around which she tried to make her life's work.

No, she rarely indulged herself in thinking about Daniel Painter. Now, she could recognize the cauldron of emotions that as a young girl she had mistaken for love. She had left her mother, not just for the summer but, in every real sense, forever. She was going to college, and though she had always called herself an American, she was planning to live in America, really, for the first time.

Then, there had been that awful thing with Phelps Whitmire. Oh, she'd been pawed on a time or two since then, and gotten much better at seeing trouble coming and fending it off.

Even now, it pained her to think of what had happened to her after that summer—struggling as a premed at the University of Texas. She had been so distracted, so lost in her thoughts, so chewed up and burned by the flash of experience she had mistaken for love. Still, she had maintained straight As in the premed program, until . . .

Jess reached down and picked out another cigarette from the new pack of Marlboro Lights she had bought last night when they'd picked up Paul at the Traverse City airport. She shrugged slightly and lit up, the unread novel lying open on her lap. The acrid taste in her mouth made her grimace. It was one thing in a bar, with her mouth awash in beer, but here on the front porch with the clean lake smell in the air it made her feel dirty. But—she thought, taking another puff—now that she was started, she might as well keep going. There was a sailboat race going on out on the lake, the boats heading west past Loeb Point. They had their bright-hued spinnakers out, making brilliant dots on the water.

Jess was thinking about how she had decided to be a premed in the first place. There was a famous picture of her mother, Margaret, the kind of picture that kept showing up in photomontages, like the greatest one hundred journalistic photos of this century. Her mother was a young woman then, one of the few women reporters in Vietnam. She looked just like Joan Baez in those days—long, jet-black straight hair, and piercing eyes under dark eyebrows that formed a straight line across her forehead. Margaret was shoving a microphone into the face of a young American soldier who was lying in the dirt, gazing up at Margaret as though she were the Madonna herself. The photograph took in the face of the boy, the microphone, all of Margaret's intense hippieish beauty, and the pool of blood, dark against the ground, that was forming around the boy's leg, shot off below the knee.

Jess saw that photo—saw it a million times—but she still remembered the first time she had seen it, the overwhelming *wrongness* that she felt, like she had caught Mommy in the act of doing something private and embarrassing.

"Why didn't you help him with his leg, Mommy?"

"Because I'm not a doctor, darlin'," she said. "My job is askin'. Askin' how does it feel to get your leg blown off, young man? Then the doctor'll come around later and fix him up. That is, if the poor bastard isn't dead by then," Margaret laughed.

So Jess made up her mind that she wanted to be a doctor. She would go with her mother to all the places that she was always leaving for, and follow behind, and after Margaret was done with her asking, Jess would sew them all up and send them on their way in much better shape than she had found them.

And then there was Gary. For a while—Jess must have been about twelve—Margaret had dated a doctor, from Doctors Without Borders. Gary was nothing like most of Margaret's boyfriends. He had a thick wave of golden hair that flopped into his eyes from time to time, and sapphire-blue eyes that were both penetrating and gentle. Jess had been fascinated by his stories of working in refugee camps on the Thai border, and of going into Biafra during the famine. He didn't seem like a real grown-up to her; he had a bushy beard and always wore worn-out corduroys with hiking boots. Once, Gary had taken them along to a presentation about Beirut at the American Church in Paris. They sat in one of the cold wooden pews near the front; the stone Gothic building was half-empty, only a smattering of wives here and there, American women with overbright makeup, purses clutched two-fisted in their laps.

Jess remembered that she hadn't wanted to go; she had brought her homework with her and had planned to do it with her books balancing on her knees. At first, she had squirmed uncomfortably in the wooden pew, not listening, peeking sidewise at Gary, who was both leaning forward listening intently and at the same time fondling her mother's knee. But then, the words of one speaker had started to captivate her, to draw her in. The speaker was a midwife, British, who described attending to refugee women in labor, in primitive conditions, while the bombs were raining down around them. The woman was stout and rather plain, with gray hair pulled back in a stern knot, but her words were full of compassion as she described her credo: to make the world better "one healthy baby at a time." Walking out of the building with Margaret and Gary, Jess had shyly spoken of her admiration for the woman.

"Oh, she's incredible, isn't she? She's single-handedly kept the maternity program going in the refugee camps . . . Dropped the infant mortality rate by more than fifty percent," Gary said.

Jess had felt her blood rise along her hairline and under her ears, a small flush of pride because of his approbation.

"Gawd," Margaret hooted. "I couldn't stand her. What was all that 'one healthy baby at a time' crap? The world is far too big a place to help people one at a time—let the babies die and storm the barricades. That's what they ought to do."

That was a moment when Jess passionately hated her mother. She felt the burn at the pit of her stomach, stared down at her scuffed shoes on the pavement, looked out at the gray water of the Seine as they walked toward the Pont de l'Alma, wishing that she could think of a rejoinder, hoping desperately that Gary would.

But Gary only laughed and yanked on Margaret's arm, pulling her closer so that he could nuzzle her neck there at the nape where a fine fringe of black hair grew.

"Bravo, darling. Go ahead and storm them," he said, laughing.

"I'll help the babies," Jess whispered, but neither of the grown-ups gave any sign that they had heard.

Gary was gone not long after that. "Off somewhere," Margaret had said offhandedly. "Saving people," she had snorted. But Jess had harbored the image of the plain woman in the church, her voice ringing with the clear tones of conviction, and Jess had bided her time, and studied her science and hunkered down to wait, believing that she could do it; believing that it could be done.

Staring at the lake, taking a long searing pull on her cigarette, Jess remembered that it hadn't exactly turned out that way . . .

She had ended up studying French, a language she had learned growing up in France. After graduation, she had gotten a job in a university library, a job whose quiet, orderly concentration was as far from her life with her mother the foreign correspondent as anyone could possibly imagine.

Sometimes, she regretted that she had never gone on to medical school—it was hard to imagine she was helping anyone now, except the few college professors and graduate students who needed her resources.

But youthful dreams are just that—dreams. Jess scratched at a mosquito bite she had gotten when she and Russ were in the woods. She closed the novel, suppressed a yawn, and turned to face the cottage, telling herself she would dwell on the past no longer.

Russ's voice, self-assured, businesslike, was audible through the screen door, mingling with the lower, softer voice of the architect. She had always loved to hear Russ talk about business. She listened to his voice, sharp, clipped, and to the point. "I'll talk to Karla over at Viking—they're always looking for product placement."

I love Russ, Jess thought. Managing affairs, doing business, tidying up the past, and moving on. *That's what love feels like.* Not like a hash, a swamp, and a stew. She stubbed out her half-smoked cigarette in the enamel ashtray and stood up to join the men in the cottage. She was eager to see what plans they would have to bring the cottage up to date, to bring some light in, to make it look more like a beach cottage and less like a mournful dirge, an old never-sung tune.

She gathered up the books to carry them inside. She was keeping Daniel's book wedged between the others, holding it so that she couldn't see it, so that not even her fingers would touch the shiny edges. Jess could not even bear to look at the cover of the book, much less open it. But this was something that she would not admit, even to herself, and so she carried it in, disarmed, among the other books, which she laid down on Mamie's table, a tidy, academic-looking pile.

———

Tonight, Jess, Russ, and Paul were sitting around the Formica table in the breakfast nook, the table littered with empty and half-full takeout containers of Chinese food: moo shu pork, scallion pancakes, and steamed pot stickers, now cold and congealed to the side of the white cardboard box. All the lights were on, and Paul had even dragged in several standing lamps from the other room, saying that he couldn't bear dark spaces. There was lots of fast, loud talking, and Paul's beeper kept going off every twenty minutes or so. Sections of the *New York Times* were strewn across the tables, some with grease spots from the Chinese food. Jess was feeling altogether much more like herself, her *real* self, as she thought of it.

"You know, that whole dressing-room area, between the living room and the kitchen, can come down. It's not a weight-bearing wall. The cost will be minimal. I can get my guy to do it, as a favor. We'll throw a skylight up here over the work-triangle area, then you won't believe the place." Paul's speech was staccato. He was wearing a denim shirt and thick black horn-rimmed glasses.

Jess was leaning close to Russ, pressing her shoulder into his side. In front of her on the table was a half-empty glass of red wine, a plate with a pot sticker with one bite taken out of it, and some wilting shreds of cabbage. Russ was sitting on a bar stool; she had to tilt her chin up so that she could look at his face as he talked.

"God . . . you know . . . it'll be so much better . . . so much more light, and a kitchen you can actually do something with."

Jess saw the enthusiasm in Russ's eyes. For barely a moment, she let herself slip into thinking that they would keep the cottage, modernizing it. They could spend summers here. Summer in the city was awful, and normally she could barely afford a vacation— much less her own summerhouse.

"You need to go through the stuff in that hallway thing and decide if there's anything you want in there. Empty it out so we can take out the wall."

"Sure," Jess said. "I think I know what's in there. Sheets. A helluva lot of white sheets."

"I found some papers in an old trunk marked *Linens*. I was trying to find a towel and I opened it."

"Papers?" Jess said, surprised. "Mamie wouldn't have left anything important in a linen closet, I don't think."

"Well, you should look through it anyway, just in case . . ."

Papers in an old storage trunk marked *Linens*? That was not Mamie's style. The lawyer had told Jess about the perfect order of Mamie's affairs, the bequests to charity, the trust fund for her cleaning woman, the gift of the cottage to Jess. Curious, she agreed to take a look.

———

Jess sat cross-legged on the smooth old floorboards, looking through tidy stacks of dusty, yellowing papers. Her instincts were right. There was nothing of interest here. It was just a storage place for housekeeping details. There were bundles of summer receipts, each labeled with the year that the items were bought, going back to 1952. A complete set of Mamie's dining-room and telegraph bills from the Wequetona Club, and a packet of business cards from every small-tradesperson she had ever dealt with. Jess looked with bemusement at the neat collections of schedules: the SS *Jefferson*, some kind of a boat, with docking times right at the Wequetona dock. Timetables for the Chicago-to-Charlevoix train on the now-defunct Pere Marquette Railway. She saw a yellowed paper, "Rules of the Wequetona Club," with orange thumbtack marks in the corners.

Dutifully, Jess sorted through the papers, the mundane details of a lifetime of cottage summers. At the very bottom of the trunk, there was an ornate embroidered folder. Jess picked it up and could feel that there were more papers inside.

She opened the folder slowly, afraid that a dusty mess of papers would spill out. Inside, she was surprised to see that there were some photographs. On top, there was an old tintype that Jess had never seen before, of people wearing dungarees standing barefoot on the front porch of a wooden shack, a few scrubby pines and a mule in the background. There was a packet of postcards, black-and-white, of watering holes in Europe, faded-out blood-colored ink with short statements on the back: *It's great here, loving it* . . . Addressed to Mamie, signed *Lila* in a loopy, spidery hand.

Jess was about to put the folder back into the trunk, when she saw another parchment envelope, medium sized and yellowed with age, that was tucked behind the portraits. Jess pulled the envelope open and saw more photos of what must have been Margaret as a baby and very young child. In one, she was holding the hand of a man wearing a doorman's-type uniform, and in another, she was sitting on a young Mamie's knee, one hand reaching up and grasping a lock of Mamie's thick curly hair. Underneath that, there was an official-looking document, a birth certificate that appeared to be her mother's, although the name was misspelled, issued by the county courthouse of Folsome County, Indiana. It read:

Margaret Lila Trathway
Mother: Margaret Adele Trathway
Father: none
Status: illegitimate
Born May 30th, 1922
Place of birth: LaSalle, Indiana (born at home)

Status: illegitimate. Jess stared at the words, the reality of their meaning starting to sink in as she tried to remember what she actually knew about her mother's birth.

She remembered the story she had heard growing up: Mamie was terribly in love with Thomas Cleves. In fact, they were engaged to be married, with a Christmas wedding planned, when her sister, Lila, tragically drowned. Miss Ada, crazy with grief, had insisted that they defer the wedding indefinitely. Thomas and Mamie were so in love that they couldn't stand waiting. They eloped, had Margaret, and shortly thereafter, Thomas was gone. Jess had asked Mamie once what happened to him, and she didn't really answer. She just said, "Thomas Cleves was a good man." One thing was for sure—Mamie didn't need a man. As the last surviving Tretheway, she had inherited her family's fortune and moved into the family's mansion. After that, she was a woman of independent means.

Jess held the yellowed document in her hands, scanning the words again. So Mamie had never been married in the first place. Of course, that would pretty much explain everything. She couldn't believe it had not been obvious to her before.

Jess looked down at the ridged lettering of an old manual type-writer. It was just a simple story, after all, an out-of-wedlock birth, a marriage that never was. Jess noticed that the clerk in the court-house hadn't even bothered to correct the typos. Her mother's last name was misspelled, and the year was typed wrong—1922, not 1923. She could almost picture the clerk, a young woman with cheap, bright lipstick, wearing a red polka-dot dress cinched tight at the waist, a patronizing look in her eyes. Jess could imagine a young Mamie standing at the polished wooden counter, draw-ing her shoulders up square, insisting that the clerk type it again because her name was spelled wrong, the woman in polka dots, drumming her red-painted fingernails on the countertop impa-tiently, saying, "Come on, honey. What difference does it make? *To someone like you.*"

Jess tucked the pictures and the birth certificate back in the envelope. She would show this to Margaret. She put away the rest of the papers, the old faded postcards. She looked again at the tin-type of the dungareed people standing in front of the dusty shack; thinking about keeping it but remembering Russ's comment about "likely-looking ancestors," she returned it to the folder, which she placed in the trunk.

When Jess went to stand up, her legs were stiff and she had pins and needles in her feet. She had been so absorbed in looking through the papers that she had completely lost track of time and forgotten all about Russ and Paul—and even forgotten where she was for a moment. She wiped the dust off the back of her jeans and walked out of the little closet hallway into the kitchen, carrying the envelope that contained the pictures and birth certificate. After sitting in the little hallway illuminated only by a single sixty-watt bulb, Jess blinked back the bright afternoon sunlight that flooded the kitchen.

CHAPTER ELEVEN

MAMIE

They say all babies are born with blue eyes, and Margaret was no exception. She was a bit of a thing, small enough to cup in your two hands, and her eyes were the blue of smoke when it hangs low over water; but when I looked at her tiny naked body, I could see from the start that there was something about her that was different. I knew from Cousin Edith's babies that nipples were supposed to look like tiny rose petals, the palest of pink with filigrees of blue veins showing through. Margaret's tummy looked white enough to me, but her nipples were amber, the color of sun-warmed wet sand. She had a fuzz of hair on her at birth, and long black hairs growing from the tops of her ears. I wasn't quite sure what to make of it, but right from the start, I knew she wasn't quite like the rest of us.

When she was just tiny from being born, I thought I'd call her Meg—I liked the softness of it—but she was looking reproachfully at me, waving with her tiny fists, wailing her most anguished cry, and *Meg* just didn't stick to her. She had a mind of her own, and she needed a name to suit her personality. Even as a tiny baby, *Margaret* fit her better.

I'll admit, I longed for a soft cooing baby, a cuddly little girl to share my lonely days. But even as a tiny one, Margaret had such strong opinions. Sometimes, when I tried to hold her, she tensed her tiny baby body as stiff as a washboard. I made her bottles of warmed-up milk with Karo syrup in it, and when she had a mind to, she would fling it right back at me, her eyes in injured slits. I used to imagine that if she could talk, she would tell me how angry she was at me. I tried to be good to her. Lord knows I did. But only the good Lord could tell me if I was truly doing the right thing.

We lived in a building called the San Remo, and though it was simple, I loved it. There were only two real rooms, connected by a long hall, and a small kitchen, tucked away toward the back, with a pink-and-black tiled floor. The apartment was furnished, and, as if by grace, it seemed that there were just exactly the right number of things in it, neat and compact.

I took good care of that baby, better than any nursemaid, and I did everything myself, even down to the dirty diapers that I soaked in a pail with borax and bleach. It gave me pleasure to stand near the sunny window looking at the tree leaves, ironing her tiny bibs and sleep sacks, breathing in the fresh scent of hot, clean linens as I worked. I would push her wicker basket so that a panel of sunlight fell across her, making her fresh flannel blanket look even whiter, her lips pursed in a soft bow while she slept.

But it seemed like before I knew it she was walking, running, back and forth across the wooden floor: Mommy, can we go to the park, can we go outside, can we go for a walk? That girl never stopped chattering, words spilling upon words in her little birdlike voice.

She kept me company with her chatter, which was good since I knew no one. Were it not for our daily conversation with the elevator man as we were coming and going, I would have had no conversation. I was not alone in being a single woman in the building. There were other girls, clean and respectable-looking, who would come and go dressed for work, but maybe we all had stories we didn't want to tell, as we instinctively kept our distance, limiting our contact to brief nods as we passed.

I confess I lived with a still, small sadness at that time, but I tried to stay busy. Tending to Margaret, who smelled like sweet warm milk, I felt like there was a quiet melody that ran through our days. I listened as I tended to the baby, my eyes on the sun-dappled backs of leaves that fluttered in front of our window. Watching those leaves move in the wind, I thought that was about as close to God as I could get.

There was a school down the street from us, just at the far edge of the park. In the morning, the children used to go into the square brick building in twos and threes and run shouting through the fenced-in play yard. Little Margaret, by the time she could barely sit up in her carriage, loved to pass by the school yard and watch the children. Maybe a baby knows when they're lonely and feels that absence like an ache, I don't know. She was tiny, with thin matchstick legs and enormous black eyes, but words flowed out of her mouth thick as prayers from a preacher on a radio show. By the time that child could walk, she learned to talk, without the slightest trace of babyishness in her voice. We would walk by the school in the morning, she and I, and she would say, "Mommy, I want to go to school." And I would say to her, every morning just the same, "You can't go to school. You're not old enough."

"But, Mommy, how old do I have to be?" And I said to her, "You have to be five to go to school, Margaret, and you're not five yet, you're still a baby."

"I'm not a baby," she stormed.

"Yes, you're a baby," I said, never wise enough to keep my mouth shut.

I wished she didn't sound so grown-up. I used to watch the other mothers at the park with their children, and I did not see any like Margaret who were so tiny and at the same time so accusatory.

One day in the park, she was playing with another child, a chubby girl with blond wisps of hair and chapped pink cheeks. Margaret was half a head shorter and half the width around, but that voice of hers was always crisp and imperious, not a child's voice at all. The other girl's mother, a plain, respectable woman in a green-paisley dress, bent to ask her what grade she was in in school.

"I haven't started school yet," Margaret said, her fluted words each crisply enunciated. "I'm too little."

"She's four," I blurted, a little too quickly.

"Oh my," the woman said, "she sounds so grown-up. I thought she was older."

My face blushed a deep crimson, and I gripped a little too hard as I dragged Margaret down the sidewalk toward home.

That was the fifth year of our exile, and I wanted to go home. Margaret would never understand exactly why she always seemed so grown-up, because to tell her the truth would be the unraveling of my story. Mercifully, not long after that, Miss Ada died. It was time for me to bring little Margaret home. The two of us left the sunny solitude of our life in the San Remo behind and returned to the big family house on Sycamore Street.

———

The house was too big for us, built to proportions that were gran-
diose, not human at all, and haunted by mournful faces of the
dead. My mother was sick for several years, and died alone; when
the maid saw that she was poorly, the minister was called, but
he arrived to find that she had already departed. She never once
reached out to me. I felt no animosity toward her, only sadness that
circumstances had conspired to make me break her heart.

Margaret and I did not take up much space. We were ill
suited to living in the big gloomy rooms whose tall windows were
shrouded by heavy curtains, and whose spaces were stuffed with
heavy furniture too big for a slight woman and a small child. But
the big house had one advantage: it gave us bulk. Never again
would we be the object of pity. A woman with a large house and
enough money to pay her servants well need not think about pity.

I was not ashamed. I held my head high. On Sunday, I walked
straight into the Ironton Congregational Church, my hand gripped
tightly around Margaret's fragile wrist. I wore navy crepe and she
wore velvet, and we both walked right down the center of the pews,
looking neither right nor left, my eyes shrouded by a little net veil
that I had adjusted just so. I paid no attention to the whispers coming from either side. To me, the murmuring was just the sound of
lapping waves, of Pine Lake gently ribbing the woody underbrush.

We took our places in the front right pew; we stood up tall to
sing the Gloria Patri:

Glory be to the Father and to the Son and to the Holy Ghost . . .
And glory be to the mother and to the child.

After that, Margaret and I were home. I took up my church
circles and Red Cross and golf, and come the middle of May, I
headed off to Wequetona, where I stayed through every summer. I
never listened to the whispered gossip that I knew followed us like
shadows on a sunny day, and I kept my chin held high.

Before I knew it, that girl was grown up and gone. Margaret and I shared a little piece of a life; not a lifetime, no, not a lifetime at all.

CHAPTER TWELVE

JESS, AGE SEVENTEEN

The days had been glorious. A string one after another of sun-drenched days, each twice as long as a winter day, and three times as bright. Daniel had been reading Indian lore out loud to Jess as they sat on the beach together. The Painter cottage had a wonderful library, shelves and shelves of faded leather-bound books with crumbling bindings and fading gold-leaf titles. Someone in the cottage had collected nature lore. The books were mostly from the twenties, and many had Indian legends and stories in them. There were also a number of illustrated botanicals with detailed descriptions of the local trees. Each day, Daniel would bind up one or two of the old books in a blue bandanna, and they would carry them down to the secluded part of the beach next to the sinking sand.

Daniel was stretched out on the flat rock, knees bent and head propped on one hand. He was wearing the same faded red shorts that he had on the first day Jess had seen him, the ones that she thought matched his canoe. He was holding the book at an angle that would block the sun, turning the pages occasionally. Jess was lying beside him, eyes closed, facing the sun.

"Listen to this," Daniel said excitedly, rolling into a sitting position so that he could hold the book more comfortably. "Listen, Jess, this is about the sinking sand. They call it spirit waters."

Daniel began to read from the crumbling book:

The local people have legends concerning the souls of lake people, who they say can be seen very rarely at the edge of the lake, only in years when the spirits are strong. They call these years spirit years, when along the water's edge, cold water, like spring water, bubbles up from under the sand. According to the Indian legend, souls of people who have perished in the lake return, bubbling up at the water's edge, spitting out the cold water that filled their lungs when they drowned so that they can join their ancestor spirits. According to the legend, these spirit years are uncommon, and some souls have to wait for many, many years for the spirit waters to appear. When asked to point to the location, our brave pointed to a spot well out into the water and said that his people say that it is there. He says that the tribal elder is the only one of the tribe who remembers seeing the bubbles. Furthermore, they say that if people use a branch of the giant pine to reach as far as they can down into the sand, that this helps free up the drowned spirits.

"Doesn't that sound like our sinking sand?" Daniel asked. "Have you ever seen the water level this low? Usually, the waterline goes right up to the trees; that's at least fifteen feet back. Last summer you couldn't even see the flat rock, much less the spring."

Jess looked at Daniel's face, lit from within with delight. She loved that he could be made so happy by such simple things. Jess felt that her mother had raised her to be world weary and skeptical.

"It's true that I've never seen the water level this low. Mamie says that it hasn't been like this since the teens. When she was a girl, they used to walk the beach all the way around Loeb Point. It's never been passable since then."

Daniel continued reading silently from the book, while Jess stood up, refastening her bathing-suit top, and walked over to the spring in the sand; she tentatively pushed one foot into its center. The sand immediately gave way. When she pulled her lower leg out, it was coated with gray clay all the way to her knee. She stared down into the bubbling sand, and then out across the calm blue water toward Hemingway Point.

"You know," Jess said, "I actually know of a spirit that might need to be released. My grandmother's sister drowned in the lake, a long time ago. She was trying to swim across the lake."

"Right, right, the beautiful girl with the long green hair, the footsteps on the balcony, and the sound of dripping water . . . All the kids on the lake know that story."

"All the more reason to free her. How'd you like to spend eternity dripping water on Miss Mamie's balcony? Don't you think it's high time we let her out?"

"You're right," said Daniel. "Let's emancipate her. I'll get a stick."

Daniel, Jess had noticed, was the kind of guy who always had a pocketknife, even in his bathing-suit pocket. He took it out and cut off a long switch from a slender young pine growing up from the underbrush at the edge of the sand. Jess was surprised to see how easily he was able to strip the bark and twigs off the switch to come up with a long, smooth stick. He made little horizontal cuts along its length, and, down where the branch was a little thicker, carved their initials, *J* and *D*.

"Hey, where'd you learn to do that?" Jess said, admiring his effort.

"There used to be an old Indian guy around here, did odd jobs and stuff—he could make almost anything by carving it. Used to make Noah's arks and wooden blocks and stuff and sell it to tourists in Ironton."

"Yeah, I remember those."

"Anyway, I followed him around one summer. He would teach me how to do stuff with the knife if I did some of his work for him. He was weird about the lake too, said one of his brothers drowned and you could hear him screaming in the winter when the ice cracked. Now, that one kind of freaked me out."

"Maybe we ought to let him out too."

———

So Jess and Daniel danced around the bubbling sand, shoving the stick farther and farther down, giggling and chanting, "O spirit of the dead, we liberate you. Spit out your cold water and go to your ancestors." The sun was high in the sky and the air was still and humid, so finally—hot, damp, and exhausted—they threw themselves into the freezing pool. Because of the underground spring, the sand felt like it collapsed underneath them and they sank as far as their waists. The clay dried on their skin in a layer of sticky gray. Even when they dove into the lake to clean off, the greenish-white powder still stuck in the crevices between their fingers and toes, around the edge of their noses and margins of their faces.

———

Jess was upstairs, lying across the white bedspread in her room, telling herself she was reading, but the book beside her on the bed was closed. She was tired, so tired that even to open her eyes was an effort, much less to reach over and pick up her book, which felt as though it weighed a thousand pounds. Two days earlier, she had picked up a little test kit in the drugstore, a test kit that showed a little cross.

Was it strange, Jess wondered, that she had to force herself to think about it? That during the normal course of the day, she didn't think about it at all? In a few days, she was going to be leaving Wequetona, and instead of returning to France, and to her mother, she was going to start college. The whole thing seemed unreal—all of it. She had never visited Texas, and had trouble even picturing it in her mind. She was going to have a baby? Well, it seemed odd, but she figured she would manage—after all, her own mother had done the same.

By contrast, it was easy to think about Daniel, the curve of his back, sliced by the sharp angle of his shoulder blade, the way his hair fell in front of his eyes, his calf muscles so taut that they snapped like rubber bands each time he took a light-footed step. She thought of him standing in the middle of the room with his eyes closed, stereo cranked up, swaying back and forth on the balls of his feet; of the perfect stillness of his crouch as he prepared to photograph a bird far out over the water. She had been avoiding him, telling him she was busy, going into town on pretense, protesting that she was not feeling well, which of course was true. She missed him desperately, with an ache that felt like a bottomless pit. But she did not want to tell him.

But why? This question was gnawing at her as she lay there on the bed, so still that she appeared to be sleeping, because every time she rolled over she felt like she was going to vomit. Why didn't she want to tell him? She started and restarted in her head: *Daniel, I . . . Daniel, I . . .* But she never got to the end of her sentence, and in her heart of hearts, she knew exactly why. Because she was afraid that as soon as she told him, it would be over—because she would see the look of disappointment on his face, and she would not be able to love him anymore. Jess could not bear the idea of not loving Daniel anymore, and she ached at the pit of her stomach, an ache that got all mixed up with the acidy, throw-uppy feeling she had, an ache that never seemed to let up at all, even for an instant. She had thought, he had thought, that they would keep this love going, long distance, while they got through college, and that when they got older—because obviously, they were too young and that was a problem. They had found each other, Jess thought, at the wrong moment. And now this.

But there was no doubt in Jess's mind that she loved this baby. She loved the baby so much that she didn't want to give Daniel a chance to say that he didn't feel the same way. Maybe she would tell him later. But not now. Not until it was too late for anyone to tell her that they didn't think she should have the baby.

Jess was so lost in her thoughts that she was surprised to hear the tapping of Mamie's pumps coming up the wooden steps toward the second floor. As a rule, Mamie never approached Jess, but rather, waited until their paths crossed naturally in order to speak to her. So when Jess heard the sound of Mamie's pumps, she immediately felt uncomfortable, felt as though Mamie's approach was ominous. A week had now gone by since she'd realized that her period was not going to come. The summer was rapidly drawing to a close. In less than a week, she'd be on her way to college. She was gripped by intense inaction. But, of course, Mamie knew nothing of this. Perhaps, Jess thought, she suspected that Jess was sick. But Jess did not think Mamie would ever guess the truth.

Jess heard three stiff raps on her bedroom door.

"Jess, please open your door. I need to speak to you right now!"

Jess swallowed hard on the acrid bile that she felt rise in her throat as she sat up and opened the door for Mamie, who was dressed in a green-linen suit, pale stockings, and patent-leather pumps. On her lapel was a ruby bumblebee pin. Jess could not read her face—Mamie appeared bent on something, and Jess felt intensely self-conscious, as though she were standing naked at the doorway, although she was fully dressed.

"Jess, I shall not mince words," Mamie said, making no move to cross the threshold into the room.

"As a woman, I am not unaware of certain laws of nature that govern the way that the female body functions. As we have not discussed the subject, I do not know what the state of your ignorance may or may not be. I have made an appointment for you with my gynecologist, Dr. Coggins. Am I making myself perfectly clear?"

Jess stood in front of Mamie, who was half a head shorter than she, and listened with increasing incredulity as Mamie gave her little speech. Her grandmother was standing square on both feet, looking straight at Jess, without the least embarrassed air about her. Jess's knees felt weak. She steadied herself.

"But how could you . . . ?"

"Everything that goes on at Journey's End is my business, even, how to put it delicately, the content of the wastepaper bins. I've been very worried about your recent conduct, running around with that Painter boy, and I've made it my business to know."

Bile forced its way up into her throat, and she shoved past her grandmother and ran down the hall to the bathroom, where she slammed the door shut, locked it, upchucked into the toilet, and then lay down on the floor, pressing her cheek against the cool linoleum, which was slightly grainy, always, with traces of beach sand.

Mamie did not, as her mother would have, follow her down the hall and bang on the door, hollering, wheedling, eager to continue the discussion no matter what. No, apparently Mamie thought that she had made her point, and since it was clear that Jess had understood, then enough had been said.

Jess lay there quietly on the floor, and her swirling cauldron of emotions sifted down to just one specific feeling. Anger. She was furious at Mamie. What possible business was it of hers? Jess could certainly not imagine Margaret stooping so low. Her mother would never, ever have dreamed of prying into her affairs in that way. The more that she lay there, in the bathroom, staring up at the white porcelain curve of the toilet, the bright-pink paint that was flaking off the old cast-iron bathtub in places, the more that Jess felt she had been treated unjustly—and the more she bathed in that feeling of having been wronged, the more she wanted to tell her friend about it, her best friend. Surely, he would understand; surely, he would take her side.

When Jess finally came downstairs, there was no sign of Mamie. There was only one phone in the cottage, and it sat on Mamie's ornately scrolled writing table. Jess used the phone rather rarely. But today, she felt that she needed to call, right then and there, and decided to grab the moment when Mamie was out. She thought that Daniel was probably spending the morning in the darkroom, and she wasn't even sure he would answer the phone. She dialed the number and then stood letting it ring, six, seven, eight times. Jess was gripping the phone hard, willing him to pick up.

Finally, on the tenth ring, she heard his voice. "Hello?" He sounded rushed. Clearly, she had interrupted him.

"Daniel," she said. "Remember in *The Way We Were*, that part where Barbra Streisand breaks up with Robert Redford and then she's crying and crying, and finally she calls him up and says something about how she needs a friend and he's the only one she has?"

"I'm coming to get you, Jess," Daniel said. "Just hang on."

In the end, Jess just blurted everything out, right there in the truck, before they even got back to Daniel's cottage. Jess could watch Daniel's profile through her tears, but, careful driver that he was, he didn't look over at all, just let her talk, about the late period and the little chemical cross, about Mamie spying on her, and about the appointment with Dr. Coggins, and about how her own mother would probably expect her to have an abortion but that she was having some kind of a chemical reaction and didn't really think she could do something like that.

Then, they sat there in silence for a while, until Daniel pulled off the road and down the short white-gravel lane, two tracks with grass growing between, and pulled up behind the Painter cottage. Daniel, still silent and grave-looking, turned the key to switch off the ignition. When he saw that Jess wasn't moving, but just sitting lumplike in her seat, he came around and swung the car door open, stretching his hand out to her. Quiet now, she got out, unable to believe the torrent of words she had just dumped on him, and terrified, absolutely terrified, to find out what would come next.

Once inside the cottage, Daniel didn't speak right away, just went into the kitchen, filled the kettle with water, and set two mugs out on the counter. Jess stood back, searching his expression for clues to his feelings, but she saw none. His motions were steady and deliberate. Daniel said nothing until he had poured the hot steam of water over the two Lipton bags, releasing their fragrant scent. Then, grasping one mug in each hand, he turned to Jess. He looked straight at her with calm, smiling eyes, his face open and containing no reproach. She reached out her hand and took the steaming mug from him, and followed him out to the screened porch where the view of the lake was obscured by a canopy of green.

There they sat, until the sky was dark and the stars were peeping through the trees, talking to each other in urgent, heated voices, in the voices of youth and love and infinite possibility. Daniel was going to graduate soon. He would be able to work and support them; he would move to Austin and work while she went to school. Eventually, Jess would become a doctor; she would make enough money that he could pursue his photography and his poetry. They would not stay in Texas but would move back here—well, not quite here, a little farther north, maybe on the Upper Peninsula, where it was a little wilder. Maybe Jess would be a doctor in a rural clinic, or on an Indian reservation. The sky got darker. It was a hot night, and very still, and the hours passed. They ate nothing, feeding on the strength of their hopes, their dreams—solid imaginings, so real that the dreams themselves seemed ample sustenance. And each feasted on the face of the other, knowing that now, they would never be torn apart.

———

Later that night, Jess lay tossing, unable to sleep. She was wearing only a thin T-shirt and underwear, and had all her blankets thrown off at the foot of the bed, her shirt bunched up under her breasts. It had been a hot day, and the night had not cooled off at all. Upstairs in the cottage, the air was hot and close. Jess lay in bed cupping her tender, rounded breasts, letting herself feel the promise they signaled. Ever since she'd missed her period, she had felt, as a sub-text, this aliveness. Now, she was letting herself, little by little, try on that feeling. She imagined in her mind's eye the picture, like a tadpole in a water balloon, that she had seen in a book about pregnancy. And feeling herself full, full of life-giving life, pregnant with possibilities, Jess drifted off into a dreamless sleep.

It was before dawn when she awakened, just the palest pink and yellow light slivering through the trees. Already, this early, the sun's rays had a scorching intensity. She awoke with a start, drenched in sweat. At first, Jess felt an ominous sense of foreboding, but then she realized it wasn't fear—it was pain. A horrible cramp shuddered through her, unlike anything she had ever experienced before, as though her entire midsection were caught in a vise. Then, the pain ebbed away, gone as soon as it had come, and Jess lay there wringing wet and sticking to the sheets. She looked at her clock and saw that it was not even 5:00 a.m. yet. She was so hot that she couldn't stay in bed, and so she unstuck herself from the sheets and slid on some shorts, hooked her bra, and pulled on a fresh shirt. She would have loved to take a shower but did not want to bother Mamie this early in the morning. The old pipes in the cottage made a terrible racket whenever anyone bathed.

Figuring it had to be cooler down by the lake, Jess slipped out the front door, taking great pains to make sure that the screen door didn't squeak, and headed barefoot down the path toward the sinking sand. Halfway, she was gripped again by a pain so intense that she had to stop in her tracks, doubled over with the intensity. Jess was breathing hard, and sweat beaded up on her forehead and trickled into her eyes. She looked toward the lake, which appeared flat and gray at this time of day. This heat, so early in the morning, was odd. The pain gone, Jess stood up and walked on until she reached the small beach. She waded directly into the bracingly cool water, up as far as midthigh. Jess looked up and scanned the horizon; usually heat like this would quickly be broken by a thunderstorm, but the pale predawn sky was free of clouds.

Again, Jess was gripped by a severe cramp, this one barely letting up before another one started. She waded out of the water and sat down on the beach, hugging her knees to her chest, bracing herself for the pain to start again, but it did not. Jess sat perfectly still, hoping that the pain was gone and would not come back. She hoped it wasn't anything serious. She could feel a dull ache in her back now. Probably, it was nothing. The pain was going away on its own—she hoped.

The air felt like a blanket. The lake was as flat as glass, and the trees were perfectly still. Several mosquitoes were buzzing around her face and one landed on her arm, leaving a few drops of blood when she swatted it. If only she could get cool. She dragged herself over to the gray chalky spot where the spring bubbled up and stood there, letting her feet sink down, until she was submerged in the glacial water up to her waist. The water was so cold that her legs felt completely numb. Her face though was still sweaty, with her bangs stuck to her forehead in sticky streaks. The morning sky changed steadily from gray to pale blue as she sat, immersed in the water.

Finally, Jess's toes were so numb they started to hurt. The pain had subsided. She was just starting to pull herself out of the water when she felt a cramp so strong that she moaned out loud. Suddenly, a tremendous heat spread between her legs, like a fire from below, and Jess saw the white sand start to bubble up around her in crimson streaks. She felt herself go light-headed. Just as she realized that she was going to faint, she felt strong arms grasp her under the armpits and lift her up.

Daniel cradled her in his arms and sprinted up the path toward Journey's End. All the while, bright-red blood was pouring down her wet thighs in rivulets, red streams against the chalky white silt that clung to her.

CHAPTER THIRTEEN

MAMIE

It was not even June yet, but unseasonably warm. We were planning a picnic on Hemingway Point. At first, we thought to have Thomas row us across, but instead we had decided to swim.

It was odd that year. The waterline of the lake was much lower than usual. You could even see little bubbling springs in the sand along the shoreline. In most years, it would have been out of the question to swim so early in the season, but that summer, the ice floes had melted early and Pine Lake, though always bracing, was bearable to swim in, especially when the sun was out and the air was hot.

Later, people used to say that Hemingway Point was named after Ernest Hemingway, who used to like to sit there and fish, but it was in fact named after a Mr. Charles Hemingway, who ran a tree farm out on the point. Pine Lake was first settled by lumber-men, but most of the giant white pine was already gone by the time that Lila and I first visited Journey's End. My father, Harris, had made his fortune in lumber, and so he took quite an interest in what Mr. Hemingway was doing, going over to the point a few times to converse with him about logging, which by then was just about finished. My daddy always said that to make money in lumber you had to find virgin forests to log out; there was no money in cultivating trees. Looking across the cove at the odd scrubby trees that were growing there, I thought my daddy was right. I used to spend a lot of time correcting people about why the point was called Hemingway Point, but after a while, I noticed that people were more attracted by the legend than interested in the facts. If people wanted to believe that Ernest Hemingway used to fish out there, who was I to tell them no.

This particular day, the day of our planned picnic, I remember as if it were yesterday: warm and clear, with the lake settling into its friendliest shade of blue. The sun shone down gently, warming the skin on our bare forearms and the backs of our necks.

"Can't we swim?" Lila said, first thing in the morning, sitting in the clubhouse dining room sipping her morning tea.

This came as a surprise to me. Lila had seemed ill to me ever since she had come back from Europe. She never looked herself, and she was so quiet all the time. Before her trip, she had been lively and athletic, the first to play tennis or go for a swim. But since returning, she wasn't like that at all.

I set my cup back on its saucer gently. I had developed the habit of treating her like she was a small child who might easily startle. Behind her, I could see the blue water out the big clubhouse windows. We were almost alone in the wood-floored dining room. Here and there, a family sat at a white linen–covered table, but mostly the big old room was empty. The doors were flung open, and through the screen doors floated a summery breeze.

The day was warm, but Lila had covered up in a bulky wool wrap. I thought she might have gotten poor blood over in Europe from eating all the wrong kinds of foods, and I begged her to agree to take a treatment from Dr. Lewis. Each time, she just averted her eyes and said that she was feeling well enough. She was cold all the time, always wrapped in heavy coats and sweaters, and though it was true that the cottage could be drafty this early in the season, her chill seemed to be inside her, of the sort that even a warm sun could not penetrate.

I studied my sister while she wasn't watching me. Less than one year of marriage, and she seemed to have lost most of her prettiness. Her complexion was not so much fair as sallow, and her hair had a lifeless cast.

Lila had always had a faraway look, but of late it had been positively distant—sometimes she seemed not to even notice that I was in the room with her, and I would say "Lila" just to see if she would turn her head. It seemed as if she had gone away somewhere, so I kept by her side. I was expecting her to come back at any moment.

"You want to swim?" I said.

It was not unusual for us to swim to the point. We Tretheway girls were strong swimmers, having spent so many summers near the lake. Miss Ada always believed that lots of fresh air and exercise improved our complexions, so we were avid on the golf course and at lawn tennis and could swim without fatigue well out into the lake.

"I see the sun out, and it makes me want to swim."

Lila's pale face glowed white except for a bit of a blush at her lips and up along her cheekbones. Her face and arms were so painfully thin, and her figure, for she had always had a lovely figure, now seemed stiff and bulky, as though she moved with difficulty or pain. She pulled her wrap tighter around her and shivered.

"It's not yet June, and the water must be frightfully cold," I said.

"I'm so hot," Lila whispered. "I want to swim . . ."

It did seem odd that she would want to swim, but I thought that the exercise might breathe some blood into her bones.

When we finished our tea and toast, Lila and I returned down the front walk. Back at Journey's End, I had the pleasure of provisioning us for our little picnic lunch. Miss Ada was feeling unwell that day and had decided to stay in bed. That was not unusual for her. She simply said that she was "going to the country" and refused to leave her room. My mother suffered from nerves, and I feared that Lila was following in her footsteps.

My delight was that our party included Thomas Cleves, who was planning to row us across to the point in a small wooden rowboat. The cook at the clubhouse had provided us with fried chicken and corn muffins and several kinds of pickles, as well as a pot of cherry preserves. I can still remember my joy as I put that little basket together, each bundle of food wrapped in a clean redchecked napkin, the cutlery nesting just so, and a bottle of fresh milk, still cool from the icehouse. The party was to leave from the wooden dock in early afternoon. Through the window, I could see that the sun was high and the sky cloudless. It did, in fact, seem a marvelous day for a swim, and I was looking forward to the tired ache I would feel in my muscles when finally we sat down on the warm spit of sand at Hemingway Point to eat the little meal tucked so pleasantly in the basket.

I confess that my mind was also on my beloved Thomas Cleves. Since the Cleves Cottage was not properly part of the Wequetona Club, there was no chance for meeting by happenstance, and though he came to visit every single evening, oftentimes motoring into town with some friends to a picture show, or over to the Loeb estate for some of their Sunday-afternoon baseball games, still the moments and hours that we passed apart from each other seemed like agony—the moments together so brief and so sweet. Our wedding was planned for Christmas, and so aside from my worries about Lila, I had plenty of pleasant images in my head with which to pass the time.

I wish I could say that it occurred to me even once that morning and early afternoon to ask myself *Where's Lila?* I could not even say where we had parted after breakfast. Did she stop at another cottage, or did we part on the steps of Journey's End? All that comes back to me is myself in the cottage, puttering around with the picnic things, the warm woolen blankets to take with us, my wool-flannel bathing suit.

We planned to meet at about one o'clock, and at that time of day, the weather promised by the morning sunshine had come true—it was a day as warm as midsummer. There was a very slight breeze. The lake water was a pale green close to shore where it was shallow, then a deep sapphire farther out where the water was deep and always several degrees colder. I was wearing my woolen bathing dress, navy blue with white piping. Over it, I wore a heavy fisherman's sweater. At just a minute or two past one, I saw Thomas come around the bend of Loeb Point in the white rowboat. I never once laid eyes on that man that I didn't feel my heart tug right away, and it was no different that time; though he was much too far away for me to make out his face, there was something in the steadiness of his motions that could have been no other man but he.

It was only then that I realized that I hadn't seen Lila; up until that moment, I had assumed that she must be up in the cottage getting dressed. Lila was known to be punctual, and she could have been in Miss Ada's room, tending to one of our mother's whims. I was completely ready, dressed for a swim with the picnic basket on my knees. Thomas would reach the dock in a few minutes, and I did not want to miss even a moment of his presence. I set the basket carefully on the gray-painted steps and went inside the cottage, whose interior seemed gloomy after the bright sunlight.

"Lila!" I called up the stairs, loud enough, I hoped, to get her attention, but hoping at the same time not to awaken Miss Ada if she slept.

Hearing no answer, I climbed the stairs and circled over to Lila's bedroom, which was on the north side of the cottage, the opposite side from mine. I saw that she had laid out her bathing suit and a thick wool sweater on her bed, but she was not there.

Downstairs, I rapped lightly on Miss Ada's door, and when there was no answer, I cracked the door open slightly and saw Miss Ada's sleeping form.

Back outside, I scanned the cove. I could no longer see the rowboat, so I knew that Thomas had pulled across and was now out of sight. I felt unsure what to do. If I ran down to the beach to tell Thomas that we were running late, I might miss Lila as she came out from wherever she was. I decided to sit and wait there on the steps a few minutes longer, thinking that if Thomas did not find us, he would moor the boat and come up to the cottage.

I think I first heard a crackling in the underbrush. It wasn't unknown for a deer to crash out of the woods and find itself blinking in the bright sun of the cottage lawn. When I looked up though, I saw Lila, still clad in the same dress and wrap that she had been wearing at breakfast. She was just emerging from the path in the woods. Though I was right in front of her, she gave no sign of seeing me and she had a very odd look on her face, almost as though she did not even know where she was. I was shocked yet again by her pallor. My sister was clearly not well.

I truly wish that I could say that I gave more thought to my sister's frail health, but in fact, I could think only of Thomas, who was certainly now looking toward the path up the bluff, wondering when we would emerge.

"Lila," I said sharply. "Lila, if we're to swim, you must change immediately. Thomas is already waiting down at the dock."

"Thomas?" Lila said, as though she scarcely remembered who he was.

"I'll meet you at the dock," I said, and, picking up the picnic basket, I hurried down the walk in front of the cottages toward that path that led down to the dock, thinking that if Lila saw me leaving, she would be more inclined to hurry along.

I still remember clearly that combination of joys, the sun warming my hair and heating the wool sweater I was wearing, making me break out in a gentle sweat. The lake so lovely in its blueness and the prospect of Thomas waiting for me, who though I had seen him just the evening before, still seemed like a whole world of newness each time I saw him again.

As I rounded the bend, I caught sight of Thomas—sun shining in a crest on his dark head, one foot balancing on the rowboat's gunwale—peering up the path at me, shading his eyes from the sun. Then, how long were we there together, passing the time in the warm sun next to the blue lake, waiting for Lila to come?

In truth, I do not know how much time passed, but before I had thought to worry, she came, dressed as I was in a woolen bathing suit with a thick wool sweater covering her almost down to her knees. I was surprised at the thinness of her bare legs, but do not remember noticing anything other than that.

"Hello, Lila," Thomas called out. "I see you come ready to swim."

"Are you sure you want to swim?" I said. "I was thinking how lovely it would be to let Thomas row us in the warm sun."

Lila looked out over the lake toward Hemingway Point and appeared to take measure with her eyes.

"I want to swim, Mamie," she said listlessly.

What was I thinking that day? How many times have I asked myself that question? So many times, I've tried to remember exactly what happened, but my memories come back like a series of images—still photos in an album—that I study to look for hidden shadows. A sunny day, a young girl in love, and a ghost story, getting ready to be told for the first time. What I keep from those moments next to the lake, just before we set out, is not a memory of Lila. It is the image of Thomas, his brown hair catching the sun, his broad knuckles grasping the wooden oars, the soft thick pad of his pink lower lip. Try as I might try and try for all these many years, and I can't bring to mind an image of Lila. How cruel it seems that in memory she was already gone.

But I do have a photograph, taken by Thomas just before we set out to swim. I do not remember the moment it was taken at all. Lila appears pale, spectral, almost vanishing. In front of her, on the ground, is a dark shadow. Many times, I have studied that shadow in the photograph, wondering how it was that on that day, none of us could see it.

We set off swimming, Lila and I, Thomas rowing beside us. The water was almost unbearably cold, so that my teeth started chattering. The surface of the lake was glassy; there was almost no wind. Every tingle of water made me feel so alive. Each time my arms windmilled through the air, they were stroked by the warmth of the sun, so that quickly I began to warm up. About a hundred yards out, the water was suddenly much colder, a second shock to my system, and also murkier below us. I pulled more rapidly through the water, trying to warm myself.

Lila fell a bit behind. She was the graceful one of us Tretheway girls, and though several years my junior, she had always been able to beat me in tennis and golf and at swimming races. I had always known her to be able to run and swim without tiring, and so when I realized that it was I who had a slight advantage this time, I pulled even faster through the water, finding a rhythm to my breathing, and noticing that the water no longer felt like icy slashes across my legs.

"Come on, Lila!" I called to her, teasing, treading water. But she did not perceptibly change her pace, her slender arms pulling skillfully through the water at a steady, even rhythm.

It is about a quarter mile from the Wequetona dock to Hemingway Point, but you only swim a short way through wide-open water, for the point is a spit of land that reaches out in front of the Wequetona cove. It is always difficult to measure distance when you are in water, and I remember that day that almost from the start, I kept looking out toward the point and thinking that we were almost there.

It is an odd thing about swimming—or I should say it *was* odd, for I have never been able to stand swimming since that day—but there is something about the rhythm that turns you inside yourself; the noise of breathing, bubble, bubble, bubble, out, out, out, three times, then turn your head and gasp. I would look up periodically to search for the rowboat, the flash of white paint with red trim helping me to stay my course, or sometimes I would look at the white necklace of sand on the point; the land always looked close, but at the same time, it never seemed to get any closer.

I know that we were well past the midpoint when Thomas rowed ahead a bit. I had not until that moment sensed any fatigue, nor thought much about the depth of the water below me, but when I looked up and saw that the rowboat was about a hundred yards ahead, I had a sudden sensation that the lake had become infinitely larger; I looked below me at the dark blue of the water, and noticed again the icelike current that ran just below the surface. Suddenly, my arms began to ache and I feared that it was too far to the point and that I might not be able to make it. Treading water, I measured the distance to the boat with my eyes, wondering whether if I called out, Thomas would hear me. Though the water had been still as glass when we set out, now there was quite a bit of chop. I could not tell if the wind was picking up or if it was just the normal roughness that far into the lake.

"Thomas!" I called, unsure if he could hear me. "Thomas," I said, "you're getting too far ahead."

I turned away then to look for Lila.

Disoriented, I did not see her. Scanning the open expanse of lake, I saw nothing. I felt panic squeezing my chest. Again, the lake seemed monstrous, enormous, infinitely wide and deep. I began looking about frantically, spinning this way and that, until I had completely lost my bearings and could not figure out even where I should be looking.

Feeling dizzy, I scanned the bluffs on the shoreline, searching for a recognizable landmark. There, I caught sight of the bulk of Journey's End. Right in my line of sight, about twenty-five yards behind me, came Lila, swimming steadily. Turning back toward the point, I saw that Thomas was closer now—evidently he had heard me and started to circle back. I took off swimming again, pulling myself strongly through the water, wanting to be done with this frigid swim, back on the shore, warming myself in the sun. Thomas turned the boat around again and was rowing steadily in front of me.

For the rest of the swim, I did not speak or look up. I took glimpses every few strokes or so: there was the boat's red gunwale; the scrubby pine of the point; the flash of Lila's white arm, keeping pace with me, a few yards behind.

About ten yards out from shore, the water grew warmer again; the silty, rocky bottom grew visible, and the water's tone turned from deep blue to a pale, murky green. I felt that warm water like a prayer of welcome, and I sprinted the last few yards, tearing my lungs full of air, until it was so shallow I could swim no more, and I stood stumbling on the sharp rocks that cut into my feet— and then running, at once freezing and tired and cold and sun-warmed, propelling myself forward with the sheer joy of the air filling my lungs, the sun shining down, and my beloved there on the beach, holding out my sweater in welcome.

CHAPTER FOURTEEN

JESS, AGE SEVENTEEN

After it was over, Jess lay in her bed alone. It was still hot and stuffy upstairs in the cottage, although finally that afternoon the weather had broken with a thunderstorm, and the air had cooled. She was running over the events of that day in her mind. Daniel had been coming down to take pictures, thinking that the still air would attract birds to the spring, when he had seen her. Mamie, with a quick look, seemed to know what to do. She folded three snowy-white towels between Jess's legs, towels that rapidly changed color to crimson. Mamie let Daniel sit with Jess for an instant; she disappeared into her room wearing only a dressing gown and her blue-velvet mules, and somehow reemerged a moment later wearing stockings, pumps, and a spotless pink linen suit. With Jess in the backseat, towels clenched between her legs, Mamie drove quickly to the hospital.

Dr. Coggins was an older man, tall and sinewy, with a crew cut and military posture that reflected his years as a navy doc. Jess recognized him from the Ironton church, where he was a vestry member and often read the Collect, his voice rumbling. His blue eyes, which peered at her over bifocals, were harsh and she could see he judged her unkindly.

"Well," he said, as he probed deep inside her with his long fingers while pressing down hard on her belly. "You're a lucky girl," he said, though his voice was not kind.

"You could have easily bled to death." He jabbed upward inside her so sharply that it made her draw in her breath.

"Or worse," he intoned. "You could have actually stayed pregnant. That would have been even worse."

Jess's head was starting to clear now. The nurse had come in and removed the IV; the effects of the medication seemed to be wearing off. Finally, he finished her exam and turned his back on her to wash his hands, raising his voice to talk to her over the sound of the rushing water.

"From now on, you two need to stay away from each other. It's genetic incompatibility that caused this. Cousins are not designed to make babies together. It's against the laws of nature!" And with that, he strode out the door, leaving Jess on the table staring at the yellowing tiles of the acoustic ceiling. She could hear the steps of the discharge nurse squeaking down the hall toward her.

———

The ride back to Wequetona was silent. Mamie said nothing—didn't even look her way. Jess, plastered up against the passenger-side door, stared resolutely out the window, watching the farms and fields go by, the funny broken-down castle walls at the old Loeb estate, and, finally, the gateway to Wequetona, the road past the neighboring cottages, and the broad back of Journey's End. Her mind was spinning. What was the doctor talking about? What did he mean by *cousin*? She cast an occasional sideways glance at her grandmother, but Mamie's eyes stayed firmly fixed on the road.

Cousins? It made no sense. Margaret never talked about the family, nor did Mamie, come to think of it. Jess realized she knew almost nothing—just that Mamie had been married only briefly, to someone named Cleves, and that Margaret had never known her father. But she had no cousins that she had ever heard of, and she had never heard the name Daniel Painter until this summer. She closed her eyes and tried to blot out all of it—the pain and bleeding, the doctor's words, and even the face of Daniel. It was too much to think about. She was exhausted and felt shattered inside.

Finally, once back at the cottage, Jess blurted out the question.

"Am I related to Daniel Painter?"

For a moment, the question hung in the air between them. Jess studied Mamie's face. She waited for her grandmother to look puzzled by such an off-the-wall question. Related to Daniel Painter—of course not. What an absurd idea!

But, in a split second, Jess knew the truth. She could see from the look on Mamie's face, all at once ashen and eager, that her grandmother was planning to tell her something. But instead of answering the question, Mamie put a firm hand on Jess's arm.

"Not now, dear. Not now," Mamie said. "Right now, you are in a delicate condition." Before Jess could think to protest, Mamie had guided her up the stairs, covered her with a cool sheet, and said a no-nonsense "Get some rest."

In spite of everything that had just happened, Jess fell into a deep sleep. When she opened her eyes, the slanted rays of late-afternoon sun were making a pattern of golden diamonds on the pine-board wall beside her bed. For a moment, she remembered nothing, but then it all came flooding back to her.

When Jess went downstairs, late that afternoon, Mamie had laid out the table for tea: two china teacups with saucers, the blue-and-white sugar bowl, and two carefully polished silver teaspoons. Mamie put a kettle on to boil and sat down at the table, and Jess sat down facing her, feeling her own weariness as she sank into the chair.

"I'll explain everything," Mamie said. "But I'll have to begin at the beginning."

CHAPTER FIFTEEN

JESS, AGE SEVENTEEN

"I am sure you know," Mamie began, "that I lost my dear sister in the flower of her youth. The year was 1922. My darling Lila left us, drowned in Pine Lake. As you can imagine, my entire family was devastated."

Jess had rarely heard her grandmother speak Lila's name aloud.

"I was several years older than Lila. But she was very beautiful, exceedingly beautiful, and so was the first to marry. Not that I was terribly plain myself, but I had come of age during the war, when all the young men were overseas. Still, I was not to be passed by in love either. The summer that Lila drowned was in all other ways a glorious summer, long, and at times hot. And that summer, it was my turn. I was in love, my dear, with a wonderful man, the most glorious man alive, and Jess, he was in love with me."

Jess looked at Mamie's face, her powdery skin lined with age but still soft, and scented faintly with the old-fashioned Sem-pray Jo-ve-nay lotion that she used. Mamie's eyes had a distant look in them, as though she were seeing past the cottage, past the kitchen, past Jess herself, into another long-distant time.

"Thomas Cleves was his name," Mamie said. "Captain Cleves. Oh, he was handsome, almost a foot taller than I was, and dark, with black hair and snapping brown eyes. We had known each other for several years, ever since his family bought a cottage on the other side of the woods. His father was the pastor at the little church in Ironton—they were not rich, but very respectable.

"When the soldiers came back from the war, they seemed so much older, inclined to stand back a little from the rest of us. I felt a funny kinship with them, because I was kind of an old soul too. When my daddy died, my mother almost went out of her mind with grief; she used to 'go to the country,' as she put it. She took to her bed, leaving me to manage our household. We lived quite nicely on Sycamore Street. The house was three times bigger than this one, so managing the household was quite a task. I proved quite adept at it, and I thought that my excellent housekeeping skills were as strong an advertisement for my qualities as running around to a lot of movie shows and cotillions, as Lila used to do. For the right sort of man, that is—the serious kind of man that I was looking for.

"And Lila . . . Well, my dear sister was a handful—so lovely, but the oddest ideas sometimes. Certainly, she had no shortage of beaux. She could have married any of a half dozen young men. But Chapin Flagg came along and just grabbed her. She was still a schoolgirl, not even out of her boarding school in Connecticut yet. I begged Mama to think twice before consenting to it."

"And . . . ?" Jess said, standing up to turn on the kettle, not wanting Mamie to see that she was still feeling woozy and had to steady herself on the edge of the table.

"Well, Mother wouldn't hear about it. A marriage to the Flagg family, a Wequetona family? She couldn't see any reason to worry. I supposed she was right, but I had my reservations."

"Why?" Jess asked. "What was wrong with him?" She could not see where Mamie was going with this story, but she understood that she was going to have to let her grandmother tell it her own way.

"The Flagg family had a great deal of money. But Chapin, he was . . ." Mamie paused, unsure of how to go on. "He was . . ." She stopped again. "I wasn't convinced that he cared about Lila," she finally said.

"I remember once he took her to a party at the Loeb estate, and then he just left her there. She did not even know where he had gone. She had to get Dickie Loeb to get one of the servants to drive her back. I used to tell my mother that there were stories about Chapin . . . He drank . . . Some say he gambled . . . He was . . ." Mamie stopped speaking again. Something about him, she was having a hard time putting into words.

"He had the swankiest car at the Club. I just thought he wanted the prettiest girl to go with it . . . Like a Rolex watch or something . . . Like something to wear. But then again, Lila had no sense. She just did not think straight sometimes. People at the Club were starting to say . . ."

Jess closed her eyes for a few seconds, trying to concentrate on Mamie's words, to follow them. She opened her eyes, then laid her head down on her arm.

"Jess, now is not the time. You need to rest. I can see that you're exhausted."

"No," Jess said, sitting up again. "You have to tell me now. I can't wait another minute."

Mamie hesitated, opened her mouth as if to protest but then thought better of it. She picked up two sugar cubes and dropped them into her teacup, making a thin pinging sound as she stirred with her silver teaspoon.

"People were jealous of her, so pretty and being courted by the heir to the Flagg fortune. Still, I was worried that people might believe . . ."

Mamie looked straight at Jess, studying her face. She seemed to be wondering whether her granddaughter was able to understand her, as though speaking about the past was like conversing in a foreign language—a language that Jess might not understand.

Jess turned her head and looked out the window; light was playing in the gently moving leaves of the old maple behind the kitchen. She could see that the tips of the leaves were already tinged with yellow and orange. Fall came so early up there in the North.

"Might believe . . . ?" Jess had no idea what Mamie was trying to get at, or why they were talking about this old forgotten story now. She kept thinking about Daniel. Was there something about him she should have noticed but didn't?

"Well, of course it wasn't true," Mamie continued, almost as though she were talking to herself. "I never believed it. Not for one minute. To think that a Tretheway . . ." It did almost seem as if Mamie were speaking a foreign language. Jess was unused to having to decode messages. Her own mother, Margaret, was always perfectly blunt.

"Anyway, Chapin married her. Right under the rose arbor in front of their cottage, Aldergate. He had a gown flown in from Paris, beaded all over, cut up above the knees in front, with a long train hanging down the back. Scandalized everyone in the Club, getting married outside, with her kneecaps showing and a beaded veil over her bobbed hair. Then, she went off with him, to Europe for a Grand Tour. It was that very summer, the summer that Lila married, that I met Thomas Cleves—and right from the start, we were in love.

Mamie sipped her tea, looking intently at Jess as though trying to see if somehow, across time, her granddaughter was getting it. Jess too was looking at Mamie, trying to see through her stern demeanor, stiff gray hair carefully coiffed into pin curls once a week.

"I thought that Thomas might propose to me almost right away, that very first summer, the summer Lila married. But Thomas was called away suddenly when his father took ill. So, hard as it was, we parted with our plans as yet unsettled, not to see each other again for almost a whole year."

Unexpectedly, Jess felt her throat tighten and the need to fight back tears. She looked away from Mamie and around the familiar kitchen, taking in the hinged beadboard cupboards, the faded green-and-white linoleum floor. She knew her plane ticket to Texas lay on the glass-topped vanity upstairs, the departure date less than a week away.

"You know, Jess, no sooner had I boarded the steamer to head back to Chicago than the porter brought me a telegram, and then another, and then another. Thomas Cleves sent me telegrams and letters every day, sometimes several times a day, and so I never felt apart from my beloved, nor did I ever feel lonely, though my own dear sister was away in Europe with Chapin, and I was home alone in our house on Sycamore Street, going about my solitary ways.

"We were to meet at Pine Lake, near the end of May. We arrived at the Club a few days before the Cleveses did. I still remember those last few days of waiting, pacing up and down the front walk, as though I could will the hours away, as though the lake wouldn't turn blue nor the trees green until I could look at them knowing that he was by my side."

Jess's own thoughts flew to Daniel.

"And then, finally, there he was. Oh, Jess, it seemed he was taller than ever, and handsomer still than I remembered him. The very first time I saw him, he dropped to his knees before me and offered me a ring." Jess could see that Mamie was fingering the emerald-cut diamond that she had always worn on her ring finger.

"And so, we agreed to be married, and the wedding was set for Christmastime. We were supposed to be married in the Ironton Congregational Church, with the reception at home."

"And you were?" Jess asked.

"No," Mamie said, suddenly sounding businesslike, more like her usual self. "Tragically, my younger sister drowned in the lake, and because of the need for a year of mourning, it meant that we would have to postpone the wedding. Lila drowned in May, and after a terrible year of waiting, suddenly we were facing another year."

A year, Jess thought, looking out again at the multihued leaves outside the kitchen, framed by the weathered, unpainted casement now pushed open to let in the soft August air. What would a whole year of waiting feel like? What about a whole lifetime?

"I'll never forget the day of the funeral. Lila lay in an open casket. You know, Jess, she was fair, like you are, but in death, she was almost a ghost, her skin whiter than whiteness can be, eyes closed, yes, but to me, they were staring up at me like they did when we pulled her out of the water, as dead and cold as a stone. Thomas took it very hard. He was there when she drowned, you know, right out there in the rowboat, rowing alongside; after all the killing he had seen in the war, it was as though it was just one death too many. He stood there at the funeral like a block of granite, gray as a tombstone, but he was crying—tears just slipping silently down his face. Miss Ada was out of her mind with grief, just wailing and wailing until someone finally had to lead her away. But you know how I felt, Jess? I felt angry. Angry at my sister for going off and getting herself drowned. It was supposed to be my turn, but that was Lila. She could always steal your thunder."

Mamie was quiet for a moment, and Jess looked at her, surprised at her candor. Mamie's eyes were still far away, looking through Jess to another time.

"So that night, after the funeral, we left," she continued. "Just took off, the two of us, down toward Indiana. I don't remember which one of us thought of it. But we just realized that we couldn't wait. Hitched a ride down to Traverse on Billy Webster's old Model T and then got the steamer from there. Oh, we were so much in love, and, Jess, it felt like the right thing to do. We took off and got ourselves married, no fancy wedding on Sycamore Street, no honeymoon Grand Tour, just two foolish young people in love."

And what had happened to all that passion, Jess wondered. He seemed to have left no trace behind but his name.

"And that's it," Mamie said, folding her hands primly in front of her. "The rest of the story you know."

Jess looked at Mamie with bewilderment. The rest of the story she knew? What on earth did she mean? She had just stopped the story at the part that Jess already knew. Mamie ran off with Thomas Cleves. And then what?

"Miss Mamie," Jess said, "I don't understand." An icy sensation gripped the back of her throat. Could she have misunderstood what the doctor had said? She did not want to understand.

"I take it that Daniel told you nothing about his mother?"

"His mother? Mrs. Painter?"

"Thomas Cleves left me," she said curtly. "Married again, had a family . . . had a daughter . . . named Elizabeth Cleves."

"But what does that have to do with Daniel?"

"Did he never mention his mother's name to you?"

"Yes, I think he said his mother's named—Elizabeth." Jess felt realization bloom as she spoke the name aloud.

"Elizabeth Cleves," Mamie said. Jess could hear the cruel edge in her voice. "Aunt Elizabeth. Your mother's half sister."

"That makes me and Daniel . . . ?"

"First cousins," Mamie whispered. "And I suggest you stop doing what the Lord never intended. It's just not right. Not proper. It's *sinful* . . ." Mamie's face crumpled, and as she covered her face in her hands, her shoulders started shaking. After a moment, she looked up, and Jess saw that her face was full of tears. "I'm sorry, Jess. I should have stopped you. I never imagined it would come to this."

Jess was stunned into silence, looking at her hands, the chipped Formica tabletop, out the window over Mamie's shoulder, anywhere but at Mamie herself. Jess did not have any cousins, did not have a family, just a line of solitary females, Mamie, Margaret, Jess . . . An aunt? A cousin? And that cousin was Daniel?

"Does my mother know?" Jess asked.

"I told her that her father remarried when she asked me."

"Does she know his family owns a cottage just on the other side of the woods?"

"Your mother can barely remember that *I* own a cottage. Has *she* ever been here? Why would she care a whit about that?" Now, the bitterness in Mamie's voice was not hidden, nor was the ugly twist at the corner of her mouth.

The words of the doctor were ringing in Jess's ears—*genetic incompatibility.* She heard what her grandmother and the doctor were trying to tell her, a kind of final and incontrovertible no, an incestuous no, a scientific and moral no. Just last night, she had not been able to think of anything that would make her give Daniel up.

But, of course, she had never thought of *this.*

When Mamie started to speak again, her voice was soft and trembling a bit. "It was raining really hard the night that Thomas and I left, ran away. We were running so fast, I never even got damp. We ran right through that rain, hand in hand, jumped in the back of an old Model T, no hesitation, never looking back. How I wish I'd had someone close by to tell me to stand still and let myself get wet. If I could have stood still and taken it then, a lot might

have been different, a whole lot. Now, Jess, I feel like it's my respon-
sibility to tell you. You are going to be a doctor, Jess; imagine that,
a young lady doctor. You've got a bright future ahead of you. Just
stand still and let the rain pour down on you. No matter how bad
you feel right now, it's nothing compared to what you would feel if
you gave up all of that bright future."

Mamie stood and neatly pushed in her chair, then clasped her
hands in front of her. It was clear that the conversation was done.

"Now, it's time for me to get to my correspondence if I don't
want to miss the post. And I suggest that you start packing. That
trip to Austin, my dear, is just a few days away."

———

Time to pack up—hard to believe. Jess stood next to the bed, folding
her white T-shirts and stacking them in perfectly symmetrical piles,
pressing her jeans on the ironing board into sharp creases. White
underwear, bleached and smelling like the dryer, folded, piled, and
tucked into a corner. Jess loved packing, had always loved packing
time, when all the complexities of her life, wherever she and her
mother happened to be, got reduced down to this: neat categories,
clean and fresh smelling, each item in its place. Life was never so
untidy, Jess always thought, that it couldn't be stowed neatly in a
suitcase, taken to the train station or airport, and carried away. She
was leaving the next morning, and she felt ready to pack up her
things and carry them away to this new place, her baggage clean,
well ordered, and spare, and her mind a blank slate.

She had not seen or spoken to Daniel. Mamie had taken to
answering the phone first, and when she saw his white pickup out
behind the cottage, she let Mamie open the door and send him
away.

Jess's mother was an untidy packer, jamming things into suitcases at the last minute, clean clothes tangled up with dirty, notes

and papers for deadline articles stowed in wrinkled piles. Jess remembered one time in particular, in the train station in Milan. They had flown out of the apartment that they had lived in for two years, rushing haphazard, no time even to make a final round to see if anything had been left behind. Her mother, as usual, had jammed any number of crumpled things into her suitcase at wrong angles, then sat on it, bouncing up and down to try to get it to close. When they got to the station, the train was late, as Italian trains often were, and her mother had dragged her off to a phone booth. Her mother's battered black Samsonite was precariously closed, and to Jess's extreme mortification, there was a bit of nylon stocking, the foot part with its homely darkened toe, hanging out of the suitcase, flapping along like an intimate flag as they walked. Jess sat outside the booth while Margaret made two frantic calls, one to her editor promising that her article would be along very soon, another to Giovanni, an ardent but hasty leave-taking conducted in broken, tearful Texan-Italian. That was Margaret.

That was not Jess, who was always packed two days ahead of time, neat and tidy, with no loose ends.

It did not seem right to her to leave it like that. Not speaking to Daniel was like leaving a loose end. *See him, don't see him, see him, don't see him.* It was a chant that went on and on in her mind, a litany coursing along underneath everything, underneath her folding and ironing and washing, her list making and floor sweeping. Clean. She thought, *just leave,* with the sterile finality of Dr. Coggins's *against the laws of nature,* the antiseptic, biological, unlived quality of those words. Or *see him,* the tears, the good-byes, the swimming in it. *Just stand still and let yourself get wet,* as Mamie had said. She had to leave without seeing him. She knew that she could not bear to see him again.

———

"*Daniel.*" Jess knew from the sound of her own voice, which startled her with its breathless urgency.

"Jess." She knew again from the sound of his voice, like a waterfall, a waterfall of sorrow pouring down.

"Pick me up at seven." And then it was done. He had said okay. He had hung up. She stood there staring at the phone in her hands, amazed at the way she had rushed headlong down the stairs, picked up the phone, and dialed the second she heard the screen door screech and knew that Mamie had gone out. No forethought, no plan, just pure action.

———

The Docksider was a townie joint. Nobody from Wequetona used to ever go there, and then some of the kids found out that they never carded anyone, and that the townies didn't chase them away. You could smoke there, eat burgers, and drink beer. They had those little jukeboxes that hang above the table, "Hotel California," "Cherokee Woman," "Midnight at the Oasis." Jess had not found a way to talk to Daniel yet. They had ridden out past the moonlit cornfields in silence. Daniel, hands on the wheel, eyes on the road, nothing different from usual. Jess, fiddling with the radio dial, switching it around, first country then gospel, lots of static, nothing decent, lots of Bible shows.

"I'm leaving tomorrow," Jess said. The only thing she managed to say during the ten-minute ride into town.

"I know when you're leaving," Daniel said. Then silence. Jess kept fiddling with the radio dial.

It was a chilly night. Fall came early up in the north part of Michigan, and there was a damp chill in the air that spoke more of autumn than summer. Most of the summer people had already left town; the sidewalks were mostly empty, and a cold, damp mist swirled around the lampposts that lined Main Street. Daniel was wearing faded blue jeans and a navy-blue sweatshirt whose sleeves were a little too short, as though it had been washed in hot water too many times, and his strong, bony wrists protruded from the sleeves. On one wrist was the woven sailor's bracelet, slightly grayish, that he always wore, couldn't take off. His ankles were bare too, as his feet were barefoot in an old worn-out pair of Bass Weejuns. He walked briskly, a step or two ahead of her. As he pushed open the door of the Docksider, an acrid odor of smoke-filled air spilled out into the street.

Jess and Daniel made their way toward the back and sat down in a booth with a scarred-up old wooden table. From where she sat, Jess could see out to the bar, where a few fat, bearded guys wearing lumberjack shirts were smoking and drinking beer. And beyond that to the door, where the neon OPEN sign was flickering, appearing backward, the top half of the *E* not lit up. Jess pulled out a cigarette and lit it.

"It's over," Jess said finally, simply, letting smoke out of her mouth as she spoke.

"I know," Daniel said, flat, miserable. For once not looking up at her, looking at the table. She had thought that maybe he'd be relieved, but she could see the regret that shadowed his face, making him look somehow older.

"You all right now?" he said.

How to answer? She felt light-headed, and there was this horrible roaring sound in her ears. She inhaled hard on the cigarette, blowing smoke rings up at the ceiling. She could catch a look at the side of her face in the smoky mirror—the pallor of her face took her by surprise.

For a few minutes, they just sat there, taking in the scene around them. Jess finished her cigarette and stubbed it out. Daniel ordered a pitcher of beer, and they sat, fingering their glasses, flipping through the racks on the jukebox, like it was any other night.

Jess was cold. She was hunched down low in the booth, with her nylon parka's collar still pulled up around her cheeks. Her head was edgy from the nicotine. She was feeling her way around what she was going to say.

"Daniel," Jess said finally. "I have a question. It's about your grandfather."

"My grandfather?"

"Your grandfather, Thomas Cleves."

He looked at her, quizzical. Clearly, this was not what he had expected her to say.

"Did you know him?" She could feel that she was still hoping, *even now*, that there was some kind of mistake.

But the moment he opened his mouth to answer, Jess felt the rest of the air suck out of her with a whoosh.

"Who, my mom's dad? No, I don't know anything about him, except I heard he was a war hero, or something. He ran off on my grandma when my mom was still a baby. I think he was kind of the black sheep of the family. Why do you ask?"

"Because he was my grandfather too."

She saw the look on his face, like the words she had just said were completely separate from their meaning.

"Your mother and my mother are half sisters," she said.

"My mom has a half sister?"

"We're first cousins."

They sat like that for a moment. The stunned silence that hung in the air between them was thicker than the haze of smoke.

Finally, she said, in a voice barely above a whisper, "That's why I . . ."

Jess felt the courage leaking out of her, air out of a pricked balloon. Like the self inside her had become slightly, almost imperceptibly smaller. Like her soul didn't quite fill her body and there was a little space that echoed in between.

Daniel leaned forward, reached across the table, reached out to her, like he wanted to steady her, to hold her there. He put a hand over her hand; she felt the warmth of it. Hers were like ice.

"What is it?"

"Why I . . ."

She opened her mouth to speak, but the words were stuck down in her throat somewhere. She inhaled on her cigarette again, slouched a little lower. Tried again to force herself to speak.

"Lost it . . ." she said.

Daniel had tears in his eyes. She could see them shining in his eyes, could see him willing them not to spill over.

When she opened her mouth to speak again, her voice was louder, more insistent, almost shrill.

"It's because we shouldn't have been together at all! Because we're genetically incompatible. We get together and make little freaky genetic accidents. That's why! Because cousins don't screw!" As she spoke, her voice was getting louder, and as she finished uttering "screw," she was closer to yelling, and a couple of townies from the bar turned around and looked at her.

Daniel's face had flushed a deep crimson and he was looking down at the table; his wrist, with the sailor's bracelet, was curved where his hand was gripping the ridged plastic beer glass. Jess stared at him, feeling a volatile mix of emotions, a deep, hot flashing anger combined with the visual images, his wrist, his hair, the curve of his chin that left her light-headed with desire. They sat there like that, frozen together in silence, until Daniel spoke.

"Are you sure about this?"

"Dead sure." She felt the word *dead* buzz on the end of her tongue a little.

Daniel's face turned from crimson to ashen.

"It can't be," he said. "It makes no sense . . ."

She thought of Phelps Whitmire, of Doc Coggins, of the little pink cross, of the red tint of the sinking sand. He was right—it made no sense. But something didn't have to make sense to turn out to be true.

They sat there for a while, still unable to keep their eyes off each other, separate miserable bubbles on either side of the scarred-up table.

"So I'm off to Texas then," Jess finally said.

"I'll be driving back to Ann Arbor in a few more days."

"Right."

They sat looking at each other for a few more minutes, Daniel wearing that same look that Jess couldn't read.

"So I guess this is it . . ."

"Jess, I'm going to wait for you," he said simply.

She responded with the barest shake of her head.

"I can wait for birds to alight in trees and for a cloud to pass behind that tree when the sun is at a certain spot. I can wait until the sky is a certain color and the wing is at a certain angle and the light is coming from a particular direction. I'm a guy who knows how to wait, Jess. Maybe you think I can't, or I won't, but I intend to. And I know that I can."

Daniel was looking straight at her now, brown eyes wide, mouth relaxed into the gentlest, the softest of smiles. Jess could almost feel herself reaching across the table and grasping his face in her hands, pulling it closer to her, but then she stopped as if jolted. What was she thinking?

"Are you out of your mind?" Jess said sharply, again a little too loud. "We had the bright idea to think of the one thing that can't *ever* work." And as she spoke, she saw the bloody sand dripping through her fingers, saw a flash of Doc Coggins's face.

Daniel was looking at her, hard at her, looking deep into her eyes like he was trying to see something inside that she wasn't saying, trying to read on her face a story that the words didn't tell. After a moment, he stood up and turned his back to her, and walked, almost ran, out the bar door, and stood just outside the window in the lamplight where she could still see him. It was raining now, and he was getting wet.

Daniel was not the type to leave her stranded, and he didn't. He just stood there in the rain waiting, water dripping down his forehead, looking out at the mostly empty street.

Realizing she had no alternative, eventually she followed him outside and got into the truck with him, and he drove her home. But Jess could see something different in his profile, something obdurate and hidden that she had never seen there before. And she was left feeling that indeed her heart was made of stone, because she felt better now, like she had closed that suitcase neat and tidy, no loose ends, no stockings hanging out the sides, and now she was ready to move on.

CHAPTER SIXTEEN

JESS, AGE THIRTY-THREE

Russ and Paul had gone to Traverse to look at granite counter-tops. Jess had the day to herself, so she decided to go into town. It would get her mind off the cottage to take a walk around. It was another glorious summer day. The sidewalks were crowded with tourists, standing in line at the fudge store or drifting in and out of the T-shirt shops, licking chocolate ice-cream cones that were melting and running down over their fingers as they strolled. She meandered past the marina, the post office, and out to the south, where the street became more residential, lined with trim ginger-bread cottages, window boxes overflowing with red geraniums, porch railings shining with fresh paint. The town straddled the area between Pine Lake and Lake Michigan. The smaller lake was connected to the larger one by a small circular harbor and the Pine

River Channel, which had been built, originally, to get the pine logs out to the lumber barges on the Great Lakes that would take them south to Chicago or Gary, Indiana.

As she was walking, Jess tried not to pay attention to the fact that there was a book stuck in her pocket, even though it was a little too bulky and so scraped against her butt as she walked. She turned the corner and descended a few steps onto the walkway that ran alongside the Pine River Channel. There were pleasure boats: big cabin cruisers and yachts with their sails down and motors purring, chugging calmly up the channel, bright flags fluttering in the wind. Pretty soon, she could see Lake Michigan, which appeared to stretch on forever, much grayer than the blue of Pine Lake.

Down on Michigan Beach, the wind was blowing straight off the lake. She liked the way it roared in her ears, the sound seeming to silence her own thoughts. She found a park bench and sat down, looking across the expanse of sand toward the water. Here and there were small groups of mothers and children, their bright-hued towels making vivid splashes across the sand; a solitary couple was walking barefoot on the hard-packed sand at the water's edge.

Jess looked out at the vast expanse of water. Shifting her weight slightly, she pulled the little book out of her pocket, turning it to gaze at the picture of the author on the back cover. He looked older, yes, face a little more bony than before, hair still longish. Now, there were laugh lines around his eyes. This was the first time that Jess had really allowed herself to look at his face. In spite of herself, she felt herself grinning back at him.

How many times had she thought about him over the years? Picked up the phone to dial 411 for his number, and then thought better of it and hung up? She used to imagine that she would call him just to ask him one question: *Did you stay in the North?* She had clung to the hope that he had, that he was out there somewhere looking at birds and walking light-footed through the woods.

But she hadn't ever tried to reach him, fearing two things in equal measure: That he would still be there, going on, without her. Worse even, that he *wouldn't* be there, that he would be gone, off into some cubicle, in an office somewhere, wearing a suit and tie.

No, he *had* to be in the woods still. It was essential to her system of belief. So always over the years, she had put the phone back in its cradle without calling. All in all, it was better not to know.

Even across the span of years, Jess still had the same familiar feeling: that this was a face that she knew, in some deep way, some way that predated her own self, like she had known him before she had ever seen him, that she knew him as she knew her own self. What had felt like love to her at seventeen, she had realized belatedly, was what kinship feels like. She, who had never had a cousin, or an aunt or uncle, no sister or brother, or a child. She who bore only the faintest passing resemblance to her own mother, but this face—it was not love, apparently, after all—it was the affinity of blood for blood.

What if they had been allowed to know each other as family? If he had known her mother as . . . Aunt Margaret? Jess stared at the picture, trying to formulate some feeling that represented what that kind of love must feel like. And as she stared at the photo of this cousin-man-stranger, her cheeks flushed and her heart pounded uncomfortably in her chest. What she felt when she stared at that familiar-yet-unfamiliar face was nothing like that.

Jess stood up and shoved the book back into her pocket without ever opening it. That she should find herself feeling like this, all hot and bothered, after all these years, was ludicrous even to her. Staring at his photo like some lovesick preteen staring at a pop star. Honestly. She turned onto the path heading back into town. Paul was returning to New York, and she and Russ would have dinner alone tonight together—Jess started making a mental shopping list: pasta and garlic, fresh coffee, red wine.

Thinking about Russ made Jess feel comfortable. Dwelling on the past was violating her own rules. *It was the place,* she thought. Journey's End *was* haunted in a way. Not by Great-Aunt Lila but by the ghost of her own past self that she thought she had left behind. Jess Carpenter picked up the pace as she walked back into the throng of summer tourists walking down Main Street. She had seen a good specialty grocery store around the corner, where she thought she could find some tortellini and decent olive oil. Looking forward to cooking a good dinner, Jess bustled about her errands, and then, arms full of packages, a copy of the *Times* tucked under her arm, she got in the car and drove to back to Wequetona.

"Dinner," Jess said, as she came in, plunking the grocery bags on the counter. "Those the plans?"

"Yeah, these are the basic plans. We'll just take down that wall, put in a new set of cabinets and the new appliances. Oughta look great. Most of the rest we can do with coats of white and yellow paint."

"What about Holcombe Gaines and the beauty of natural pine?" Jess said.

"Nah, never sell. Everybody wants white and yellow these days. Natural wood is dark."

Jess started to unload the grocery bags, putting a bottle of Chardonnay into the 1940s metal fridge.

"Hey, Jess, that Barnes lady called," Russ said. "Bringing some prospective buyers. She made it sound like pretty much a done deal. Somebody you know, I guess."

"Oh, who is it?"

"I can't remember the name. Something Republican-sounding?"

"Russ. Honestly? *Republican-sounding?*"

"Like Bush or something? You got any Bushes up here?"

"Bushes? Russ. Enough with the Kennebunkport thing."

"Well, I don't really remember, but the operative words were "boatloads of money" and "remodel sounds great."

"When are they coming?"

"I think she said sixish."

"Great, we'll eat after," Jess said.

At around six, Jess was sitting at Mamie's writing desk, looking out the window at the lake and the front walk. She saw Toni Barnes come striding down the path, this time dressed in red and white: white linen pants, red strappy sandals, and a red-and-white-striped sailor shirt. Following a short distance behind were two people that Jess didn't recognize. There was a thin, sandy-haired man with a slightly receding hairline, dressed in a Patagonia pullover, jeans and boat shoes. A very tall and thin woman stood beside him, her light-brown pageboy pulled back in a tortoiseshell barrette. Wequetona people, obviously, but if Jess had ever known them, she did not recognize them anymore. Jess watched Russ get up and go out to shake Toni's hand and make the introductions. She hesitated a bit, wanting to delay the inevitable greetings, the pretending to remember each other, the perfunctory condolences for Mamie. Jess stood up and walked out to the porch.

"Why, Jess, how nice to see you again. It's been too long, much too long. This is my wife, Martha. Martha's from the Belvedere Club. Martha . . . Jess . . . ? I guess it's not Carpenter anymore?"

"Jess Carpenter," Jess said, sticking out her hand, mentally ticking down the line of cottages. Who was this nondescript man? Was he an Addison? A Coffey? A Slade?

"What a delight to meet you," Martha said, holding out a cool hand with long, slender fingers. "I understand you're a researcher. How *in*-teresting."

"A librarian," Jess muttered.

"We were so terribly sorry to hear about Miss Mamie's passing. She was an institution around here," the man said.

"It's lovely to see you again"—Jess pretended that she remembered him—"and a pleasure to meet you, Martha. Please go ahead and look around. Take your time."

Jess was looking at the affable couple, so pleasant, though she still couldn't place the fellow; any one of twenty Wequetona boys would have grown up to look just like him. His wife, Martha, was an example of well-bred Midwestern good looks: even features, thin long legs, flat chest, and straight hair. She was stooping slightly, as tall women sometimes do; her husband, equally thin and angular, was about her height.

"You know, we used to sail out from the Belvedere, and always noticed your cottage, so *attractive*, sitting up here on the bluff," Martha said.

"Most of us Wequetona people think of Journey's End as almost a symbol for the Club as a whole," her husband said. "I'm sure you feel as we do, that Journey's End should 'stay in the family' so to speak . . ."

"Please," Jess said, wanting to cut the conversation short. "Go ahead and look around."

With Toni Barnes leading the way and Russ hovering, ready to be the obsequious guide, Jess left the little party to tour the cottage and went back to her work, reading through a bibliography of new works about Molière.

She could hear their chattering voices: Martha's little squeals of delight as Russ talked about the magazine piece, the wall coming down, and the stainless-steel Viking range. Toni and the husband talked about winter insulation, air-conditioning, and more closet space. Martha and Russ talked about working for the magazine, about New York, about Maine and the South of France.

It's all to the good, Jess thought. They could have their golf and their sailing and their summer cottage in the Club, on the lake. These were exactly the kind of people that Mamie adored, *such attractive people,* as she would say. Their children would grow up here, skipping down the front walk with white ribbons in their hair, just as she had. With any luck, their grandchildren would do the same.

By the time they were coming back down the stairs, Russ was already negotiating. There were only twenty or so cottages in the Wequetona Club, and most of them rarely changed hands. Journey's End was the largest and the most architecturally striking. Jess had heard more than once the litany of who these people were, people she saw walking around in bathing suits or golf shorts, the president of this, the chairman of that, one of the blah-blahs from blah-blah . . . Russ was betting that money was no object for these people. Jess actually heard him use the words "once-in-a-lifetime chance." Again, Jess felt as she had several times before during this trip. Let him handle it. Let him take care of this transaction, as though she wasn't even involved, as though the business had nothing to do with her. Wouldn't Mamie be proud of me, she thought, for finding this nice, boring, rich couple to sell to . . . so Wequetona . . . more like the Tretheways than the Tretheways themselves.

"That's our offer," Russ was exulting to Jess as soon as they had said their good-byes and walked back down the front path. "They're going to get back to us tonight. I'm sure the place is sold."

"Well, that's a relief," Jess said. "That's what we came here for, isn't it?"

She walked down the familiar mothball-smelling hallway to the as-yet-unchanged cottage kitchen and started assembling the ingredients for her dinner. Now, she was wishing they had just gone and picked up a pizza. She did not feel like cooking. The cottage kitchen was old-fashioned and awkward. There was no counter space. She searched through the cupboards until she found a cutting board and got started chopping up onions. *When can we leave*? she thought. She did not care at all about the stupid magazine article. She just wanted these people to sign on the dotted line so she could get the hell out and go back home. Even the humid, dirty hubbub of New York in July was preferable to this. The onion odor was sharp and Jess felt her eyes starting to tear up.

Chop. *I want to get out of here.* Chop. *I hate vacation.* Chop. *I'm sick of the lake.* Chop. Chop. Chop.

The mindless chore of cooking soothed her mind, and by the time Jess sat down with Russ out on the front porch, plates of tortellini balanced on their knees, she was starting to feel something close to happy.

"Just think of all that money," Jess said.

"Inheriting it," Russ said. "I've always said that was the best way to go."

"Who was that anyway?" Jess asked. "I didn't recognize him at all."

"I keep forgetting his name. It's like Wasp-mire or something like that."

"Not *Whitmire*?" Jess said, racking her brain again for some familiar feature in the bland, middle-aged face.

"Yeah, that's it. Phelps Whitmire. You know, as in *Phelps Gate*? At *Yale*?"

Jess's eyes widened in surprise.

Russ, not noticing, continued. "These are real substantial folks. Monument types. Come to think of it, isn't there a Whitmire Hall somewhere? Princeton?"

"That wasn't Phelps Whitmire," Jess said.

"Yeah, Phelps and Martha Whitmire. Can you believe it? Now those are the kind of people I like to take money from!" Russ whooped.

"*That* was Phelps Whitmire?"

"So you *do* know him?"

"You can't take their money," Jess said, her voice suddenly steely with fury.

"Oh, honey," Russ said, leaning closer to her so that his plate tipped precariously and a few drops of spaghetti sauce dripped onto the floor, "I didn't mean . . . I mean . . . I know it's your money . . . It's just that you and me . . . I thought . . ." Russ paused and looked searchingly at Jess's face, which now looked guarded and cool.

"I'm messing this up, aren't I?" Russ said. "I'm putting my goddamn foot in it. Jess, I . . ." He set his plate aside and fell down on his knees in front of her, in a mock-dramatic gesture of pleading.

"The deal's off."

"Wait a minute," Russ said from the porch floor. "I haven't even said what the deal is yet . . ."

"Phelps Whitmire is not going to buy this cottage. Over my dead body. That's final."

"Oh," Russ said. Looking baffled. Standing up. "You mean, it's about *him*?"

"That prick," Jess said, standing up, downing the dregs in her wineglass, and picking up her plate. And with that, she pulled open the porch door and went inside, leaving Russ on the porch, mystified, brushing the dust off the knees of his pants. She could see him considering following her in, but he must have seen the look on her face, so he retreated into the kitchen. Jess returned to the porch alone. She spent the remainder of the evening staring out at the lake, until she saw the bedroom light go on and then turn off again.

———

"I need paper!" Russ was hollering from the bedroom. Jess could hear the thunk of drawers being pulled open and shut a little too roughly. "Every drawer in this goddamn house is full. Isn't there any paper around here?

Jess was standing in front of the grainy mirror combing her hair. *Thunk.* A tight door was slammed shut. Jess felt herself wince, just slightly. This was Margaret's routine, the anger at little things accompanied by thunks. It was the thing about Russ that she liked the least. *Thunk.* Jess winced again.

"I need printer paper!" Russ called out in the general direction of the bathroom. "I'm going to run into town."

Jess stood gazing at her reflection. When Jess had gone inside to bed the night before, she was thinking that Russ would ask her what was going on, but he was already asleep. She was so frustrated—just when she thought she was going to get enough money to set aside a little nest egg for her mother's retirement, it turned out that the man holding the checkbook was the one person to whom she would never agree to sell. Phelps Whitmire? Maybe he could politely forget that he had mauled her at the beach picnic, but she couldn't. No indeed, that memory was still fresh in her mind.

Jess pulled the string attached to the single-bulb light fixture in the outmoded bathroom, and walked through the dressing area back into Mamie's room, where she noticed that Russ had left every drawer in Mamie's writing desk ajar. She bent over to close them, hating the unfinished business that half-closed drawers implied. With his rooting around, Russ had left a jumble of stationery boxes tilting at odd angles, and Jess could not get them to fit back in the drawer without taking everything out to square them again. She opened the boxes of stationery. A small jewelry-sized box contained stamps of various denominations nesting on a bed of smooth cotton. Next under that was a box of note cards, with an engraved sketch of the cottage on them. The third box contained simple Crane's stationery, engraved *MTC*, pearl gray, with matching envelopes, which Jess recognized from countless letters from Mamie to her over the years. She used to cherish those letters during her childhood. Always the same paper and envelope, the same neat and even hand, the same news of Mamie, shopping at Neiman's, Red Cross luncheon, dinner at the country club. Just plain news, ordinary things. Margaret, in contrast, always dashed off notes—lunch with Mobutu, attended an execution, momentous happenings, great world events—that did not touch Jess like the notes from Mamie: lunch with two sorority sisters, a foursome of golf, played bridge.

Jess took out a couple of sheets of the fine paper stock. There were only a few sheets left in the box, and underneath, she saw what appeared to be a small bundle of letters in envelopes. The one on top was a squat blue envelope that looked fairly new. Clearly, the pile contained letters that were quite old; some of the envelopes at the bottom of the pile were brittle and yellow. Jess could feel that her heart was beating faster as she regarded this hidden pile of carefully hoarded letters. She felt sure that they must be love letters; they *must* be letters from Thomas Cleves. She studied the flowery engraved monogram on the back flap of the blue envelope, having trouble discerning the letters. She pulled a brittle envelope from the bottom of the pile and, with some difficulty, extracted a yellowed onionskin paper. The ink was faded and difficult to read, but she could see the date was 1920-something; the exact year was smudged, and the signature, very ornate, read *Chapin Flagg*. Jess took the packet of envelopes and laid it on the top of the desk, closing up the now-empty stationery box and nesting it just so with the other boxes so that the small drawer closed smoothly. A part of her realized that this was a useless gesture. The cottage and its contents were going to be sold soon. She might just as well have taken the boxes and pitched them into the trash.

Her disappointment over the author of the letters was palpable. So palpable that she realized now that this was what she had been looking for all along, what she had secretly been looking for as she had gone through all of Mamie's receipts and bookkeeping and other papers. Something, anything, about her missing grandfather.

Jess picked up the little packet of letters again, glancing at the first letter that she had opened. She vaguely dreaded Russ's return— she was relieved that he had gone out for a while. She flashed on the image of Russ down on his knees on the floor in front of her the night before, with two small, perfectly round blotches of spaghetti sauce on his blue shirt, just over his heart. *I'm not ready for this*, Jess thought. Holding the letters, she flopped onto the bed, propping her head on a small chintz pillow, and began to try to read the first letter, the oldest letter in fact. Curious, she noted that it had been mailed from Berlin.

My dearest Mamie,

 I did indeed receive your letter. Germany is in fact accessible by post, and though in fact "terribly far away" from where you are, those of us who are here do not feel far away at all, but rather feel that this is quite a nice close-by place.

 Indeed, Mamie, if you are looking for a keeper of secrets, you have come to the right person. I fear that I keep secrets better than I thought I did, for I never realized that people did not actually see the truths that were staring them directly in the face.

 I am greatly grieved about your sister, Lila, and hold a terrible heaviness in my heart about whatever may have been my part.

 Money is no problem, and I dispatch what seems an ample sum forthwith, but please let me know if more would better do the trick.

 I offer my congratulations on your becoming a mother. My own role, shall we call it avuncular, I consider to be quite an honor. Let us hope that we will both be equal to the task.

Your humble servant,
Chapin Flagg

CHAPTER SEVENTEEN

MAMIE

Thomas said that he could see Lila all along, that he watched her even as we kissed, as she made her steady progress in toward shore. I have racked my brain a thousand times to ask myself if I was thinking about Lila then. Thomas's embrace was the warmth of the sun, and I felt as though the cold blue lake were a thousand hours behind.

But it was Thomas who was facing the lake, who broke from the embrace and stepped toward her, running through the shallow water even with his shoes and trousers on. I never saw Lila and so could only imagine how he saw her stand up for a moment, there a few feet out from shore, and then topple, face-first, into the water, as though pushed by an unseen divine hand. It couldn't have been more than a split second that it took me to spin around, could it have? But I saw her first as she floated there, head on the surface, feet bobbing down, then Thomas grabbed her by the shoulder and heaved her up over his back, wading out of the water. That sight I will never forget. My sister slung over Thomas's white-shirted shoulder like a fatted calf, her wet hair hanging down in green strands almost to Thomas's knees.

What I remember is how she lay there, body clumsy and awkward as though it had been thrown there, mindless of the sharp rocks that studded the narrow beach. Thomas gave me terse instructions in a voice I had never heard before, and I followed them. Each task, in its concreteness, reminding me that I was in fact awake and not dreaming. I got the thick wool blankets from the boat and laid them across her. He bent over her, his cheeks close to her nose. No breath, he said. He took his wide fingers and placed them on the V-shaped groove of her neck. A heartbeat, he said, just barely, it beats.

I remember I was thinking that he was going to save her. He seemed to know how to go in and find the shadow of life there in the valley of death. I saw him marking the beats of her slow pulse with his fingers. I saw him placing his lips upon hers and blowing. Thomas, I thought, had enough vitality in him to share. I expected that at any moment she would flutter her eyes open and bloom with color again, like Sleeping Beauty in an illustrated color plate.

There was no mistaking though that something was terribly wrong with Lila. That seems silly, doesn't it? There she lay motionless on the beach, not breathing, no sign of life. But her color, even now I cannot think of it without shuddering. She was not the color of a person at all. Her skin was whiter than a bleached, clean-picked bone. Her lips were the blue that lurks in the deepest recesses of the lake. I stood by, motionless, frozen, numb, and watched Thomas caring for her so tenderly, like a lover. Still, at that moment, trusting entirely that he would fix her, breathe life into her, just as surely as the Holy Spirit had breathed life into the Virgin Mary's womb.

When he stood up though, nothing had changed. Thomas's lips were a soft warm pink, the beach was a sun-warmed ribbon of rocks and sand, and across it lay Lila's blue body, at rag-doll angles, motionless, lifeless, and cold.

"I don't understand," Thomas said. "She was standing . . . right there in the shallow water . . . Did you see her? Did you see her, Mamie?"

"Is she . . . is she drowned then?" Shocked that I could ask the question, shocked that this horror could stand right alongside an ordinary day.

"No, it's impossible. She couldn't have drowned . . . I saw her standing right there, in the shallow water. I thought . . . I thought she had just tripped on a rock and stumbled . . . It makes no sense."

"So she's alive," I said joyously, falling on my knees beside her, daring to touch her for the first time. I pressed my lips across her forehead. Never will I forget what that felt like. It was just like bending over to kiss a block of granite, a stone.

"No, Mamie, she's dead," he said, so gentle, like he was saying any old thing, like he was passing the time of day.

Only then did I hear a strange sound on the beach: someone was screaming, yes, that was it . . . someone was screaming. I was shivering so hard I could barely stand up. I could feel my knees knocking underneath me, about to give way. Thomas picked up one of the thick wool blankets, picked it up right off Lila's lifeless body, wrapping it tightly around me. He pushed on my shoulder firmly, almost rough.

"Sit down," he said. "And stop screaming. Please, oh please, Mamie, try to stay calm. We've got to get her back into the boat."

I looked up at Thomas, standing there. His clothes were wet, his shirt on one shoulder stained a pale pink.

"Sit, Mamie, and try to warm yourself. I'm going to carry her into the boat."

He bent over to pick her up, not cradling her in his arms but lifting her up under her armpits, as though he was preparing to drag her.

"Thomas, don't!" I cried out, but still he lifted her, upright in front of him, her head slumping downward, her legs flopping, and he started to back toward the boat, her bare feet just clearing the ground.

It was then that I saw it, something, hanging out from under her bathing dress, so strange-looking that it caught my eye—and then I saw it all at once, first the thick white jelly of the rope with a chewed-off-looking end, then the trickle of pink streaming down her leg—

All of a sudden, something hideous slithered down her bare, lifeless leg and fell onto the sandy beach. I know that I then shrieked again. I thought I saw a jellyfish, all silvery across the top and angry dark brown underneath; for a fleeting second, I thought I understood—she had been stung by a horrible poison fish and . . .

"Oh dear God no!" Thomas had stopped and caught sight of the thing. "Mamie!" he said. "Do as I say. Look away, Mamie, look away."

———

There have been two times in my life that I have been a party to formulating a tale that was not true. Both of those times were during the same few days in May, so many years ago. How many times have I prayed to God to tell me if it was right to keep my secret, and down on my knees I have only heard the Lord's voice come back as silence. I have always taken that silence as an affirmation, and if I did not hear that silence right, then only God in his infinite wisdom will know.

Thomas speared the vile thing with a stick and tossed it up into the woods. Then, he dragged my poor sister's lifeless body and put it into the boat. I still remember how it looked, when he reached over and grabbed her two legs, lifting them over the gunwale; they fell into the boat's bottom with a thud.

His strokes were rapid; it took only a few minutes for us to traverse the short distance back to the Wequetona dock. Then he was gone, sprinting up the stairs carrying her body, shouting:

"God help us, Doc. Lewis, get the doctor, for the love of God."

After that, it was only the sound of the clubhouse bells that filled my head—clanging, clanging the emergency call.

CHAPTER EIGHTEEN

JESS, AGE THIRTY-THREE

"So are we going to talk?" Russ asked. He was hovering in front of her face, sticking his head between her and the phone receiver as she was leaning over to put it back in the cradle. She had just hung up with Toni Barnes.

"Talk?"

"You want to tell me what is going on here? I take it something is bothering you about selling the cottage to this guy. You want to tell me what is?"

Jess stepped back, just half a pace, and looked at Russ's face. She could see concern and curiosity; the hint of aggravation was pretty well veiled. How odd that the sale of the cottage seemed to be turning into a joint venture. Wasn't it just a few days ago that she was not going to even bother to tell Russ where she was going?

Now, all of a sudden, they were doing this together, like it was something that concerned both of them. Did this mean that the trip was bringing them closer? But when she looked at his inquisitive face, she felt, same as ever, that she just wanted to back away.

"Jess?"

"Oh, I was just thinking . . . Listen . . . we'll sell it . . . just not to him." There it was, her own voice, saying *we . . . we'll*, just the way that she always heard other people do it, couple people.

"Well, I really think you ought to rethink that . . . I mean . . . I take it you must have some kind of a reason, but this is just a business transaction. What is it? What is it about those people, Jess?"

Jess recognized the look on Russ's face. She saw that face a lot. That was how he looked when he wasn't going to take no for an answer. The one that pushed their way into crowded galleries, that got them a better table at restaurants, the one that, Jess swore, would make the Pakistani taxi driver pass others and stop for him. As a rule, Jess didn't argue with him. There really wasn't any point. She didn't face down that face, just stood shoulder to shoulder with him while he used it to mow other people down.

"There is nothing to rethink. I do not choose to sell this cottage to a person whom I particularly dislike."

"Now if that isn't the stupidest . . . Jess, that's crazy. They made a great offer . . . no contingencies . . . What does like or dislike have to do with anything?"

"You know, I inherited this cottage from my grandmother. It's been in the family for years." She glanced around them for just a second, her eyes falling on the shadowy recesses up under the eaves, and the blurry blue of the lake shining through the glass. "It does matter who it goes to."

"Jess, you live in a one-room walk-up in Fort Washington. How many times have you told me you don't feel comfortable walking around your neighborhood late at night? And you're always sending money to your mother—you could use the money. You have a right to it—why not take it?"

Jess stood looking at him without answering. Russ was standing in front of the windows. The light coming in from outside formed a halo across the top of his head, his light-brown hair shining like oat straw in the sun. She hadn't answered him yet, and she did not have the slightest idea what she was going to say next. As if, instead of waiting to speak, she were waiting to hear what someone else in the room had to say.

Russ was right. What did it matter? If you don't care about a place, you don't care about it. She would take the money and move on, putting the cottage back where it belonged, in the past.

But she *did* care. She couldn't forgive Phelps Whitmire for what he had done to her, and didn't want to surrender Journey's End to the wrong sort of people. There it was, Toni Barnes's expression: *The wrong sort of people*. Well, it was clear that no one wanted any part of *them*—it just wasn't clear who *they* were.

"Jess?"

Jess couldn't read his face. Unexpectedly, Russ turned to look out the window, clasping her hand as he did, his palm soft, dry, slightly cool to the touch.

"Do you want to tell me what it is?" Russ said.

He looked up sidelong, his silky hair falling over one eye, his long nose sharp at that angle. "You know what I want, Jess?" Russ said. "I want to get you out of here. You've had a death mask on ever since we got here. Some people do better away from family. It seems like even dead family gets you down."

Jess had to laugh a little at that.

What she hadn't told him, yet, was that she was starting to want to keep it. Because this cottage was the closest an only child, daughter, and granddaughter—all in a lonely single-file line— could come to feeling a part of a family.

What if you kept coming back to the same place, as your mother did and her mother before her? What if four generations of women kept coming back and living their lives and depositing their stuff: old letters, telegraph receipts, photos, or dramatic stories of loving and drowning that got told and told again. Then, couldn't it be that the house itself became the family story? Narratives bending, circling, and turning around the same set of rooms. She envisioned the rooms of Journey's End as they encircled the central living room, layers of a family, intertwining and overlapping over time. Maybe, she thought, she was sunk in a lot deeper than she'd realized.

As it happened, when Jess opened her mouth to say all this to Russ, when she tilted her chin up, preparing to make a speech that she had never expected to hear herself make, Russ read that upward tilt as an amorous invitation, and so planted a full, wet kiss on the lips that were preparing to speak.

Afterward, Russ's voice was husky.

"I love you, Jess," he said, then waited for her to reply in kind, but the words, as always, stuck in her throat.

In that moment, Jess realized that the time to cling to the past was over—she needed to sell the cottage, and Phelps Whitmire had money.

"All right," she said. "We'll sell."

Russ grabbed her and kissed her again. "You're making the right decision," he said.

———

Toni had accepted a glass of chilled white wine and was leaning against the counter in the kitchen, the papers for the sale ready to be signed. She was wearing white-linen pedal pushers, a lime-green T-shirt, and matching thong sandals. Her frosted hair was short; fat pearl earrings were hugging her minuscule lobes.

"Phelps and Martha are just beside themselves. You know, it's been so hard for them being up at Aldergate with the four boys. You know how Muffin is, so difficult. They still dress for dinner every single night. Martha has to drag the boys up from the beach or sailing or whatever and dress them for dinner." Toni looked so pleased, sipping her white wine.

"Muffin, now, that would be the cat?" Russ said.

Jess giggled.

"No, that's Phelps's mother." No trace of irony from Toni. "*She's* the Phelps."

"Muffin," Russ said, snorting through his nose. "Are there really grown women who go by Muffin in this world? God, you have to love this place."

"Mrs. Wendell Randolph Whitmire, née Phelps. Her great-grandfather founded half the newspapers in the Midwest." Toni recited the pedigree with assurance.

Russ topped off Toni's glass. Jess could tell he was starting to enjoy himself. He loved hearing Toni talk about the Wequetona Club. Jess could see why Toni had done well in real estate. She had a knack for dropping names and making things sound even better than they were.

They all stood in the kitchen basking in that particular kind of warmth, an illusion at least of affection shared all the way around, an ample amount of California Chardonnay. Jess had been scrimping and saving her money for years—this would give her a little bit of comfort room. Her eyes felt blurry, she was sure, from the rightness of it, and she leaned into Russ's arm as Toni regaled them with stories: about Muffin, about the Founder's Day Regatta, about all the people who weren't around anymore: Pete was a gay Episcopal priest. Sal had been in and out of drug rehab. Megan, God forbid, married a schoolteacher—"they're poor as church mice"—couldn't afford the Club membership, sold out to her cousin, the one who had done so well in real estate. Jess drank and laughed, allowing herself to think a little bit about the money. Maybe she could move somewhere a bit nicer and still afford the rent.

"And, of course, I haven't even mentioned the obvious one you know. The riverboat captain-cum-poet—he's a local boy."

Jess got quiet, waiting to hear what Toni was going to say next.

"You remember Daniel Painter—didn't you date him one summer for a while? He has one of those adventure outback kinds of enterprises, leads canoe trips up north of the Sault. You really ought to stop in and see him sometime. His office is right in town, behind the chamber of commerce. Course, this time of year, he's probably out with an expedition."

"Daniel . . ." Jess said, her voice trailing off in confusion.

"Oh, maybe you don't remember him. Their cottage wasn't part of the Club—he was always kind of an oddball anyway."

Jess got a flash of Toni's face that seventeenth summer, when her hair had been down to her waist and streaked through by the sun. She remembered the first time she saw Daniel at the beach picnic, for a second could almost remember the way he smelled, like fresh ironing and pine needles and the damp loamy earth.

She shrugged off Russ's arm from where it was resting, draped around her shoulder, and walked out to the porch to get some cool air.

CHAPTER NINETEEN

MAMIE

With the clanging of the clubhouse bells, it did not take long for the whole citizenry of the Club, still sparse at that time of year, to gather outside the Lewis cottage, The Rafters, everyone abuzz with the words "Lila Flagg has drowned." Thomas was inside the cottage, where he had carried Lila's body, emerging a few moments later out back to get into Alvin Whitmire's Studebaker.

"He's gone to Ironton to get the reverend," people were whispering among themselves.

I saw my mother, Miss Ada, come keening down the walk, a lady at each arm. She didn't look at me at all, but blubbered past calling, "I'm coming, Lila, don't worry, Mommy's here." As far as I know, she did not ever look for me or ask where I was. When she walked past me, she seemed not to see me at all.

I sat at the base of the big Dutch maple, still wet, clad only in my bathing suit and the thick wool sweater, watching The Rafters, the people swirling about with an air of frantic urgency. I observed all the activity with detached confusion. As I sat, I saw that, as always on Thursday afternoon, two Indian girls had come to sell flowers; black haired and barefoot, they were carrying their baskets full of white gladiolas and yellow daffodils. They were wending among the small crowd that had gathered there, the Iveses, the Whitmires, the Millers. To my confusion, everyone was ignoring them. I was thinking, *Buy the flowers from the Indian girls—you will need them for Lila's grave.*

I do not remember leaving there, only that I was gone. I remember too that the sun was gone and that the lake had turned to a brooding, wind-lashed silver. The sky was darkening with clouds, giving a late-afternoon cast.

I walked down the empty sidewalk along the bluff toward Journey's End, but when I reached the front steps, I could not go in.

The two dark-haired Indian girls, young girls, perhaps nine or ten, were now standing upon the Journey's End porch in front of the doorway, the daffodils in their baskets bright splashes of yellow in the now-darkened day. Miss Ada always bought flowers from the girls—as did most of the other cottagers—and the girls stood patiently, shifting from one foot to the other, expecting someone to open the door.

I did not speak to them but kept walking instead, straight off the cement walk onto the little path that led into the woods.

What drew me into the woods that day? Was it simply the effort it would have taken to speak to the flower girls? Sorry, no flowers today because my sister is dead?

I was never much one to venture into the woods, preferring the pleasures of manicured lawns. It was Lila who loved the woods.

Lila why lila why lila why—it was a song with a coda, repeating over and over again in my head. The simplest explanation was that the path led me there. At the end of the sidewalk at Wequetona, the woods are all that is left.

The canopy of leaves spread over my head. With the clouds gathering, there was very little light, and that peculiar hush that seems present in the woods, where the silence is full and even quiet footsteps seem to echo in your ears.

I do not believe that I went there looking for something, but perhaps I did. I was dazed with grief, but something made me stumble down the same path that Lila had. Something made me know where she would have been, to look for the thing that she had left behind, in the place where she had left it.

I reached the place where the trees were so tall that they seemed to soar up out of the woods, appearing to cross overhead as if you were staring up into a church's nave. *Christian soldiers* is what we used to call them, tall and straight, like soldiers marching, pointing the way to heaven. Lila and I used to go there to play as young girls. Journey's End was completely hidden behind the wall of thick trees, but we were close enough that we could hear our mother's call. I did not like it much, too many bugs, and soon forgot it. It was Lila's place, and on that terrible day, I saw it as a place to hide.

Crying, the sound of crying.

I was crying and I did not know it. Could not hear the loud sound of my own rib-cracking sobs. So I could not have heard more crying, could I have? No, I do not think so. I think that I heard nothing but the sound of the woods, the wind whipping through the trees, urging them to speak.

And next I saw color—dark, heated, angry crimson, stark and vivid against the pure white of a white hand-stitched petticoat made of fine Savannah cotton. A petticoat just like mine.

Coiling out from under that petticoat was a hideous bluish and yellowy jellied cord, kinked and cold-looking, with a shredded gnawed-off end.

I would never have dared to move that petticoat; I was bone frightened, and ready to bolt, but at the horrible sight I started retching so violently that I could not move, and it was then that I saw something else peeking out from under the petticoat.

It was a tiny single hand opening and closing, its tiny perfect domed fingernails shining like pearls.

So I did what life must do when it sees life. I picked up that horrible, blood-stained, leaf-strewn bundle, and I held it close to me, right up against my skin under the thick sweater, and I held it there until I heard shrill crying again, and this time, I was sure that the cries were not mine.

CHAPTER TWENTY

JESS, AGE THIRTY-THREE

Later that night, they were celebrating. Russ had even cracked open champagne. Jess was wearing a sleeveless cotton T-shirt that glowed faintly in the moonlight. The air was cool enough to raise gooseflesh on her bare arms, but not cool enough to make her put on a sweater. They were sitting out on the Adirondack chairs at the top edge of the bluff. She still felt stunned that she had really gone and done it, sold the Tretheway cottage, Journey's End.

Jess knew that the people who had first built the Wequetona Club were not wealthy people; they were ministers and Bible professors from a little college down in Illinois. The Wequetona Club had started out as a kind of spiritual retreat, a place to be devout and quiet in a spot less humid and bug-ridden than the cornfields of southern Illinois. Jess supposed that the college people had taken this place as a wilderness, approachable, as it was, more easily by water at that time. She didn't suppose that they thought much about the Woodland Indians, who had settled at the edges of these lakes for millennia, before the good gentlefolk of the Presbyterian Bible Seminary reimagined it as a wilderness retreat. Jess did remember the Indians selling beaded trinkets on the street corners in Ironton—how she had begged Mamie to buy them for her on Sunday mornings when they were leaving the white-clap-board church in Ironton. Mamie always herded Jess quickly to the other side of the street, a firm hand on her shoulder, making little clicking sounds under her breath.

Jess sat sideways on the Adirondack chair, her knees pulled up under her sleeveless shirt now, bare feet tucked up, and arms clasped around her legs, trying to warm herself. She could see "down the line," the cottages lining up along the bluff like maiden ladies, so decorous, each waiting her turn. The wooden footbridge over to the north side was invisible even on a bright night like this one, but she knew that down the north side it was the same: some cottages with screened porches, some with wide verandas, most of the front walks littered with plastic tricycles, discarded roller skates. Here and there, a forgotten beach towel draped over a porch railing or trailed up the cottage steps. Some of these cottages had been loved to death, passed along from generation to generation, parceled into ever-smaller and smaller shares, every two weeks a new batch of cousins and new babies and gay uncles and elderly widowed aunts. Jess supposed that must have been Mamie's vision for Journey's End when she bequeathed the cottage to Jess—as it must have seemed that it would be back in 1922, when they had hung their sorority banners in the balcony, before Lila had drowned and Mamie had borne an illegitimate child.

Well, she might get married yet, Jess thought. But what Mamie did not understand, could not ever understand, was that Jess was going to marry someone like Russ, someone who would never want to come here.

"Do you really think I'm doing the right thing?" Jess finally spoke.

"Selling to someone you don't like very much is of perfectly no consequence as long as he has the cash in hand."

"I don't mean selling to Phelps and Martha. I mean selling at all."

"Jess honey, when would we ever get up here? It's nice and all, but it's a little dull."

"It's like getting your dead mother's diamond ring and then hocking it."

"What any sane person would do, in my opinion," Russ said. "But you know, Jess," he said, his voice curiously thick, reaching out and grasping her thin bare hand, smoothing the backs of her fingers, where she wore no kind of ornamentation at all. "I feel like coming here was like coming to meet the family, and even though I still haven't met your mother, the fabulous Margaret Carpenter, I still kind of think that . . ."

Jess sat suspended in a frantic kind of silence, aware only of a high-pitched buzzing between her ears.

"I never would have shopped for a ring or anything outside of the city, and I guess I came here more in mind of a photo shoot than a . . . Well, I didn't know things would happen so fast, emotionally speaking . . ."

Emotionally speaking. Jess realized that she was mourning the cottage like she was mourning a death, much more than the loss of Mamie, but the loss of a whole family of forebears who had gone away before she had ever had a chance to know them, leaving only yellowing photographs, malleable stories, and the faded stately grandeur of the house itself.

Russ paused again and Jess became aware, uncomfortably aware, that she had been unable to come up with a single word to fill the vibrant silence that Russ's words had created. He looked at her deeply, cocking his head a little, like a golden retriever that thinks he's about to be tossed a tennis ball. He took her hand, awkwardly attempting to embrace her but only managing to get ahold of the hand, which he drew up and pressed against his mouth.

Jess sat perfectly still like that for a pained moment, her hand resting passively against his lips. Mercifully, the ripping sound of a motorboat cut through the silence. Jess turned toward the lake, seeing the foamy boat-wake shining whitely in the black water. Peals of teenage laughter rang out each time the boat cut a sharp turn.

"Of course it's blood money," Russ said, his voice calm again. "Funding all the internecine strife in Sierra Leone. I don't know how you feel about that. I'm sure you know more about that than I do—your mother, you know."

Jess had to rack her brains to figure out what he was talking about, had trouble remembering that Sierra Leone was in Africa, couldn't see what her mother had to do with it. It took her a lot of thought to realize he was talking about diamonds. She was feeling that same brain-glazed feeling that she always got when Margaret started discussing African politics. Russ was talking about buying her a diamond engagement ring. She was at a total loss for words.

"I have to go to the bathroom," she finally said, like a kid in the middle of a scolding who can't think of any other way to get away.

"Of course, most other gemstones have problematic political issues attached, and I suppose you could make a moral argument that if the diamond was mined in the Rhodesian era . . ."

Russ just kept talking as Jess turned and walked back toward the yellow light on the cottage porch; he was, in fact, a little like a radio, left on so that a soothing, unintelligible rhythm could be heard from another room.

———

The next morning, Toni Barnes phoned and said that Phelps had been called back to Saint Louis on urgent business, so the closing would be delayed for another twenty-four hours. Jess and Russ would have to postpone their departure for one more day. Russ would be coming back in August for the actual shoot. Jess did not plan to accompany him. Phelps and Martha had so wanted the cottage as it was, with the Indian collection, that they had matched the appraiser's generous lump-sum estimate. Jess could scarcely believe the numbers involved—enough to put a generous down payment on a house in New Jersey, where she could have a little yard of her own.

She had chosen a tiny number of things to take with her: the file with Margaret's birth certificate, the packet of Chapin Flagg's letters, and the ghostly picture of her aunt who had drowned. The few papers looked small and insubstantial laid out on the pink-and-white bedspread.

As she removed the picture of Lila from its tarnished silver-plate frame, a small newspaper clipping, dark orange with age, slipped out from between the picture and the velveteen backing and fluttered to the floor. Jess picked up the clipping, dated at the top June 5, 1922. The headline read: "Drowning at Wequetona Club."

Last Thursday, May 30, Lila Tretheway Flagg, wife of Chapin Flagg of Wequetona Club and Winnetka, Illinois, daughter of the late Harris Tretheway of Brenton, Texas, drowned in Pine Lake. Despite efforts by Capt. Thomas Cleves, a visitor to Wequetona, and club member Dr. George Lewis, Mrs. Flagg could not be revived. The memorial service will be held tomorrow at the Ironton Congregational Church. She is survived by her mother Mrs. Ada Louise Tretheway and her sister Margaret Adele Tretheway, both of Wequetona Club.

Jess stared at the clipping, unsure what to do with it. It seemed hard to throw these documents away, and yet the cottage was going to another family. After all, what difference did it make? After a moment's hesitation, she let it drop into the wastepaper bin, watching it fluttering until it came to rest on top of used Kleenexes and tangles of hair.

As for the photo albums, she left them where they were, on the shelf, next to the moldering books on botany and trout fishing and golf. She figured that in a generation or two, the Whitmires would forget that these were not their own ancestors, Phelps and Martha's grandchildren looking with wonder at the strange wide-eyed faces in the sepia prints that looked mutely out at them, unable to tell their stories.

Time to get on with it. Jess looked once more at the little pile of things that were left, gazing for a moment at the picture of Lila, puzzling momentarily over the packet of letters from Chapin, with one that looked more recent than the rest. Then, the urge to pack took over. Moving briskly, she bound the documents carefully in brown kraft paper, sealing the edges at perfect right angles with clear packing tape. She labeled the package with black marker in neat block script with her name and address in New York. As an afterthought, she added: *Documents: Journey's End.* She liked the tidy, finished way that the package looked. It could fit neatly in a suitcase.

That task finished, Jess now felt that time hung heavy upon her. She was ready to leave, all packed up. The extra twenty-four hours seemed needlessly painful, a kind of purgatory. She had been skirting Russ all morning, unable to look at him except crosswise. She had feigned sleep when he woke up, drunk her coffee in the kitchen while he waited on the porch. She wasn't sure that he noticed she was avoiding him.

Jess reached down and plucked the yellowed obituary from its resting place among the crumpled tissues in the wastepaper basket. She smoothed the wrinkled paper with the side of her hand against the cool glass tabletop of her grandmother's desk, and reread the few words written there.

CHAPTER TWENTY-ONE

Mamie

It was raining so hard the night we left, a deluge, a downpour as cold and dense as a rain could possibly be. It seemed to me that the world had turned upside down, that the lake was up and the sky was down and the cold contents of the lake were dropping on us, drowning us in their fury. Thomas and I stumbled down the back road, unable to see more than a few paces in front of us. He carried the two little bags and I had my bundle gripped tightly in my arms, so tightly that I thought for sure that I was harming it, but I was afraid to grip any looser. It was only Thomas's firm hold on my arm that kept me going. The pressure of his broad hand on my upper arm was like eyes to see with, like one warm spot in a body that felt so cold that I would have sworn there was no more blood coursing through my veins. Thomas Cleves had big feet—I remember the sight of his size-twelve boots stomping through puddles and I kept looking at those puddles feeling afraid, afraid that beneath a puddle there was an infinite depth of water and that he would sink down and disappear in front of me, and leave me alone on that back road, blinded by rain and too cold for my heart to keep on beating in my rib cage.

But stomp, stomp, his boots stayed the course, good and solid, and I followed him, away from the cottages, past the stone gates, and up the hill to the road, just a wet, dark ribbon in the night. And there we stood, waiting for headlights, believing that by the grace of God we would see headlights. I held my little damp bundle to my cold bosom and hoped that there was somehow enough warmth in me to maintain a tiny spark of life.

If I have ever put myself in the hands of the good Lord, it was that night. And if I have ever felt a cold, hollow, empty place inside that worried that the good Lord wasn't listening, it was that night too. I felt the muddy hem of my dress knocking against my legs, and I felt my curls pulling loose from their pins and clinging to my forehead as I looked up that wet, empty road, hugging my bundle with fear and calling to the Lord in the loudest unspoken voice that I had, willing that curtain of water obscuring the road to part.

I often wonder, looking back, how long we would have stood there. I remember, and Lord forgive me this, that the longer we stood there shivering, the more the bundle in my arms felt heavy, the more I wondered if I had enough strength to carry out my plan, and I started eyeing the clumps of bushes on the side of the road. But the waters did part that night, the rain sliced apart by headlights, a tinny Model T truck rattling through, and we climbed in and got carried down that wet road to our destiny, and the bulrushes I had been contemplating, there by the side of the road, were left behind us, spooling away farther and farther as that good farmer took us south in his truck toward Indiana, not saying a word about our sorry bedraggledness, nor even taking notice of the damp bundle of rags on my lap that from time to time took to mewling like a pitiful half-drowned cat.

Nowadays, everybody drives up in Michigan, but in those days the roads were so poor that even to make it down to Alpena was a full night's journey. The good farmer took us all the way down there without asking any questions, and I didn't know which way to look, nor what to do, when the little bundle set up a steady and persistent howl, but after a while it gave up and then silence again, and I do believe I must have even fallen asleep. I just remember my head banging against the stays of the cover that the driver had put up because of the rain. At the train station, we got out and thanked him, then I sat on a park bench by the lake while Thomas went and rounded up some evaporated milk and a clean, dry length of flannel. We looked at that little baby with the smoke-blue eyes with a kind of nervous wonder. Sure enough if it wasn't still bawling and breathing. If ever there was a miracle, it seemed to be that.

The home for foundlings and orphans in LaSalle, Indiana. That was our destination. That was the place Thomas had told me about, the name floating up to me through the fog of my intense confusion. The little church in Ironton, our summer church, sent a collection box there every year. I didn't have any idea where LaSalle was, but I knew that Indiana couldn't be that far away.

It is a testament to our love that I went to Thomas first. Without thought or plan, I cut right through those woods to the Cleves cottage, holding that strange bundle wrapped in my own damp sweater. I presented myself before my beloved with my awkward burden, rapping on the window under cover of darkness, heedless that almost any member of his family could have heard my solic-itation. He came out into that night with me, cloud cover already thick, though the rain had not yet started to fall, and walked into the dark forest with me.

"Thomas," I said, looking up at that face, trying to see into his brown eyes in the shadows. "Lila left the baby . . . in the woods . . . I found it . . . Thomas . . . can you . . . ?"

"Mamie," he said, and I couldn't see his face because the night was too dark.

"I need . . . I need to take it away," I whispered.

"Mamie," Thomas said, his voice gentle. "If you run away, you will be disgraced."

The bundle I held in my arms, wriggling, wrapped in my sweater, seemed unreal and insignificant; the bulk of Thomas's warm presence seemed real and great. I looked at his silhouette against the bits of indigo sky and the black trunks of trees. I searched his face for answers, but it was too dark out for me to see. My nostrils were full of him though, of the smell of his body.

"If I stay, then the disgrace is upon my sister, a disgrace she will never be able to rectify from the grave." That was the first time that I had linked those two ideas, my sister and the grave. I could feel my body shivering, colder than ice. I did not cry, as I truly believe that my tears were too frozen to flow.

"Mamie," Thomas said, peering dubiously in the shadow toward the shapeless white bundle in my arms, "are you sure the baby is still alive?"

At that very moment, the little bundle started howling, first feeble, then more convinced. I could feel the stirring in my arms like the very force of life. And like I was born knowing how, I nestled that bundle against my bosom and set up a rocking motion with my hips that came from somewhere inside I didn't know about.

If I were a woman with a better imagination, would things have come out differently? Standing there in that dark wood, holding that poor, accursed orphan babe, I couldn't think of any path that led back through the woods to Journey's End. I did not see how to walk up to my mother in her wild-eyed craziness and hand her that tiny kernel of life that had turned up on my path in the woods. I could only see going forward.

"Couldn't you come with me?" I said, speaking up a little louder since the baby was wailing. "We could run away."

Thomas did not answer.

"There's a home in Indiana. We send a church box there. We could take the baby there, and leave it."

For a long moment, Thomas was silent, though I could feel him looking at me, and smell him, and feel the heat coming off his body. Then, his big strong hand circled the base of my head like a cradle, and he pulled my face closer to his, pressing the warm sweet heat of his lips against mine, drawing my small self close to his big body so that the bundle I was holding was caught in the warmth in between.

"Baby must need milk or something, right?" he said finally. "I don't know what else to do but leave you here in the woods. I'm going to gather a few things and meet you back here. You won't be afraid now, will you?" When I did not answer, he loped back out of the woods toward the house.

I stayed there for what seemed like an eternity, rocking that baby whose cries were so loud they set my teeth on edge, lusty and sharp edged with what must have been a fierce hunger. Finally, he came back with a jar of warm milk that I dropped into the baby's mouth with a teaspoon while Thomas held up a lit candle to see by. It was just after that that it started to rain.

———

LaSalle, Indiana, was a gray town. On the river, it was lined with textile mills, a small downtown with three churches and a courthouse. Beyond that central square, the houses were jerry-built, their paint peeling. The rain had finally stopped, but it was a wan sun that shone down, and the skies were less blue than a smoky yellow. Thomas and I had spent the night in a little hotel off the Main Street, and we had spent it as man and wife. I guess there is not much convincing to do if a couple shows up with a baby in tow, and they gave us a narrow room upstairs. I believed that the Lord saw us as wedded right from that first night in the woods, and I did not think He would insist that there be a signed piece of paper from the courthouse as long as He knew it would be along in a day or two.

Even to this day, I can tell you that I loved Thomas Cleves with all my heart and I believe that he loved me too. Two days I spent with my beloved, and I drank at the font of his soul and discovered all that can be beautiful between a man and a woman. Is two days enough to last a whole lifetime? I can only say that I believe you can only ask so much of a man, even a good man. I had myself a good man, but I made my choice.

On the day that I go to my grave, I will be able to describe every detail of the corner of Main and Bunting in LaSalle, Indiana. My beloved took me for breakfast in a coffee shop that morning. We ate thick slices of bacon and drank steaming coffee from white-porcelain mugs. Thomas had gone to the dry-goods store and found some little pink clothing for the baby. She may have been a foundling, but I wanted her to look pretty so that she would be loved. She wasn't a pretty baby. She looked yellow and shriveled and scrunched up, but that morning she looked more like a human being than she ever had before. Does that make any sense? Up until then, it was only her eyes that convinced me that she was human at all; I thought of her more as moss from the woods, or a mushroom, or a rotting wooden stump. Until that morning, when my eyes took her in for what she really was: a jaundiced starveling baby who was mewling in the world, smart enough to know she was hungry but not smart enough to know that her mother was dead.

Thomas and I ate that breakfast with appetite; it tasted like the best food in the world, and we were catching the corners of each other's eyes, having that private knowledge of heat and soreness that we shared, far outside the sunny world of that breakfast shop.

We had talked a little about our story and decided what we would tell people when we got back home: in the confusion of grief after Lila's death, we had eloped. Thomas and I made a plan to stop at the little courthouse in LaSalle and make it official. It was not the wedding or the circumstances we had dreamed of, but, in spite of the terrible events that had brought us to this point, it is true: we had carved out a measure of true and delirious joy. We would leave the poor baby at the home, and we would pray for her, that she would go on to have a life better than the one promised by the way it had started.

Thomas had his arm linked through mine as we walked down Main Street past the plate-glass windows and the imposing granite edifice of the bank. He held me firmly as we stood at the corner of Main and Bunting, looking across the street at the white-frame building, whitewashed and jerry-built, with a painted sign that read: LaSalle Home for Foundlings and Orphaned Children. At that moment, the baby who was to be Margaret set off with a screaming racket. Without thinking, I shifted her just so, and I felt her little body go soft, grateful because I was learning her ways.

It was at that moment, about half past nine in the morning on a half-warm early-summer day, that my body just stopped doing my bidding. Thomas held me and was guiding me to cross the street, but my foot just wouldn't step off that curb. It was like I was frozen there, and I believe that God stepped down and put a hand on my shoulder, because I could not move, not a step. Thomas tightened his grip on my arm, not noticing when he felt my resistance. He stopped and looked at me.

"What is it, Mamie?" he said, turning to me. Even then, at that fateful moment, his voice was thrilling to me.

I looked down at that little baby I was holding in my arms, and like a movie theater picture in front of my eyes, I saw that awful blue of the lake, Lila's face staring at me like a block of ice. And in this vision I couldn't hear her speaking, but I could see her mouthing words. And what she was saying was "Mamie, don't."

I thought about that moment a lot, later on, later when Margaret was living with me on Sycamore Street, an ill-tempered, ungrateful, dark-skinned child. And I thought about it when she up and left me, off to Miss Porter's School in Connecticut, and never came back again, just blew in for a few days at holidays. I thought about it when her name used to show up in unexpected places: on a newspaper wrapped around shoes that I picked up from the shoe repair, or left behind on a park bench, or half wrinkled and shoved in a wastepaper bin. I thought about it, and I wondered if I couldn't have given that little pink-dressed baby to someone else to raise, someone who didn't see a ghost every time she looked at her, someone for whom the joy of having her wasn't always shadowed by the pain of loss.

What I know is that I couldn't do it that day; there was something in me that held on to that baby in spite of every single thing that says I should have given her up. I don't know if it took me a long time to answer, but I know that I looked up at my beloved's face and tried to memorize that gaze of kindness, took it in and studied every angle of it. Before I opened up my mouth and said, "Thomas, I can't."

He did try to talk me out of it; we spent half a day upstairs in that little hotel room, crying and then kissing, then crying again. Only stopping now and again to get some milk ready for Margaret to drink.

He was such a big man that when he sat on the edge of that hotel bed, he made the springs sag halfway down to the floor. There was only one window in that room, set up high. From where we sat on the edge of the bed, we stared at the rusting washbasin, and at the faded gray posies on the wallpaper, which was brown-singed and peeling up near the ceiling.

"Mamie," he said. "I don't talk about the war much, but I learned something there."

I looked at his big face, eyes looking at that gray wallpaper. He was pausing between each word, like he was really struggling to speak.

"It happens sometimes in wartime that a buddy gets shot. And the fellow standing next to him, could be you yourself, is still standing there, looking around, not even sure at first what made such a loud thunk. And then you look down and there's your buddy bleeding, and he's looking at you. And then you hear orders shouted and you realize that you are supposed to run. There's the guy on the ground, there's you, there's your superior shouting, and so you leave him there, and you run for cover. At the end of the day, you're still alive."

I guess I was just looking at him, wondering what the war story had to do with us, when he said, "Bad things happen and we can't always fix 'em. I can't build my own life based on the fact that somebody dumped their little baby in the woods and then went away and drowned herself. That's too much pain for me, Mamie."

So there it was. I reached out with my two fingers, and I rested them there, in that heart-shaped groove where his collarbone was. I could feel his pulse beating under my fingers. I saw a pain haunting him behind the eyes, and I could feel it too. Like we both knew that he was already gone.

Before Thomas Cleves walked out of that room and left me there, he left thirty dollars on the rickety wooden dresser, and he wrote down how I could wire him if I found out I needed more. I begged him not to say anything to my mother, let her think I had run away, so that she could mourn her two daughters at the same time.

He turned to look at me before he left, his large frame filling the doorway. Looked like he wanted to say something, then didn't, then did again.

"I think you're going to come with me," he said, his voice quiet, weak sounding. "Aren't you, Mamie?"

I picked up Margaret, who was fussing a little, and I shook my head.

"She'll need a name," I said.

"If it's a name she's wanting, give her mine," he said. "That's asking me for something that is easy to give."

Looking back, I try to go back to that moment at the corner of Main and Bunting, before everything changed, and keep my eyes on those big brown eyes of his as they were, kind and gentle and sweet.

In the end, I went to Chapin Flagg for money; what else could I do? I couldn't bear to see his name or think upon him, so great was my rage against him. I never asked him how he could have sent my sister home in that condition. I asked him only to support me and his daughter and to keep my whereabouts a secret. He did as bidden; sent money and asked no awkward questions. Mercifully, it was not much longer after that Miss Ada died, and from then on, I took charge of myself and managed my dear daddy's fortune. I have always taken a great deal of pride in my ability to do so.

CHAPTER TWENTY-TWO

JESS, AGE THIRTY-THREE

Jess walked down the front walk, past the Wequetona cottages. Most had painted signs hanging over the front porches, some with Indian names, "An-wa-bo-ka," "Kin-ka-ya-ming." There were a few people, dressed in pastels, sitting out on the porches, enjoying the gentle afternoon breeze. As was the custom, she nodded to each group of cottagers as she passed.

The Rafters was the last cottage on the south side, just at the spot where the stairs led down to the bathing beach. It was a gracious cottage, with large gabled windows across the front that had always been painted a creamy yellow with white trim. Across the side of the cottage was a large solarium. The front porch was screened, making it hard to see whether anyone was inside. For as long as Jess could remember, this cottage had always been empty except for Mrs. May Lewis. Mrs. Lewis was already a widow when Jess was growing up, and she had no children. May Lewis had been Mamie's closest friend. They played cards together, and had a weekly ritual of shopping every Thursday in Petoskey.

Back in the days when everyone had dined in the clubhouse, Jess used to think it terribly sad to see Mrs. Lewis all alone at her linen-covered table, sitting ramrod straight in her wooden chair. The Lewis table was in the corner of the dining room.

"Why does Mrs. Lewis have to eat alone?" Jess asked Mamie.

"She sits at the Lewis table," Mamie had replied. "At Wequetona, that is the way it is done."

At the Tretheway table, in the far south corner, there was only Jess and Mamie. Jess used to sit chewing her food and banging one Mary Jane absently against the table leg, looking out across the dining room and seeing the tables of other families that would swell almost to bursting, surrounded by cousins—big families that were noisy and boisterous, with boys who would jump up before the meal was finished and run outside, letting the heavy doors bang behind them. It did not occur to Jess at the time, as far as she remembered, that Mamie must have sat alone whenever Jess was not there.

Jess approached The Rafters with hesitation. What exactly did she want from Mrs. May Lewis? What made her think that Mrs. Lewis would be able to tell her anything she did not already know, and what good would it do her anyway? Jess stopped halfway up the walk and peered at the blank front of the cottage, the dark screens shrouding her view of the porch. Perhaps she shouldn't even bother.

"Why, Jess Carpenter, welcome to The Rafters—just let yourself in if you wouldn't mind. My rheumatism is bothering me a touch this morning."

Jess heard Mrs. Lewis's voice, and now could just make out the outline of her head. She walked up the steps and pushed the screen door open.

"Well now, Jess," Mrs. Lewis said. "I had a feeling you might be coming to visit me. Please sit down."

"Oh, I'm so sorry," Jess said, feeling embarrassed, looking at tiny Mrs. Lewis, sitting in a wicker rocker, her knees covered in an afghan, an open book and reading glasses lying in her lap.

"I should have come sooner. It's nice to see you looking so well. I've been busy, you know . . . with the cottage . . ." She was thinking about her grandmother, who had been a few years older than Mrs. Lewis. She felt tears pricking her eyes at the thought of Mamie—was this how she looked, near the end?

Mrs. Lewis's face was deeply lined, but her blue eyes were still as sharp and alert as ever, and though her voice was frail, her diction was clear.

"Sit down, Jess dear," she said, gesturing to a wicker armchair.

Jess stared at her hands like an awkward child, and then she found herself blurting, "Mrs. Lewis, I was wondering . . ." She stopped and looked searchingly at the old woman, wondering what it was exactly that she wanted to know.

Mrs. Lewis gazed at her patiently, waiting for her to finish.

"I'm wondering if you know what happened when my great-aunt Lila died? I found a newspaper clipping, about her death, and it mentioned that Dr. Lewis was there when the accident happened . . . I guess I'm just curious what happened to her exactly. Mamie didn't like to talk about it, but I know she drowned."

Mrs. Lewis nodded. "It was a long time ago, but I'll be happy to share what I know. My husband kept a log of all his cases. Back in those days, he made the occasional house call during the summer, and he left the summer logbooks up here. I'm sure your aunt Lila's case is recorded there. There's a built-in bookcase right under the stairs, on the top shelf, left-hand side, you'll find a series of brown leather-bound ledgers. Find the one labeled 1922–23. Could you just bring that to me?"

Jess stepped into the small living room. The Rafters was bright and sunny inside, filled with white-wicker furniture with light cotton upholstery, the walls painted pale yellow with bright white trim. There were fresh daisies in a silver vase on the piano. The air smelled fresh, not at all musty, and there was light streaming in through the large glass windows of the solarium. Jess found the large bookcase built into the corner of the wall beneath the stairs. On the top shelf, which was at just about eye level, Jess saw the set of leather-bound books. They were embossed with gold numbers on the binding—starting with 1922 and ending with 1935. Jess carefully picked out the first volume. The brown cover left an orangish stain on her fingertips. Carefully, she carried it out to the porch.

"Is this what you're looking for?"

"Now, let me see, dear," Mrs. Lewis said, tipping her head back and putting on her glasses.

"Yes, that's it." She reached out to take the small musty volume from Jess. She did not open it, however, but placed it gently in her lap, and smoothing the blanket over her knees, she began talking, her voice rather soft so that Jess had to strain to hear.

"The year was 1922. I was just married then, a newlywed. My husband, George Lewis, was a good bit older than I. He was a physician and had been in the war. Of course, I had been coming to Wequetona since I was a baby, but it was George's first summer. I found it very strange to be here that summer. I had lost both my parents to pneumonia during the previous winter, and so it was just the two of us. You wouldn't know this, Jess dear, but my only brother, Arbruster, was lost at Ardennes. So it was just George and I, newlyweds, sharing The Rafters for the very first time. He had insisted that we come up early that season. It was oddly warm that year, and there wasn't much water in the lake; there had been

an early thaw. By the beginning of May, it was already swelter-
ing in Saint Louis. George, always a dear, was worried about my
nerves—the loss of my parents so suddenly, of course, had been a
terrible shock. He thought that the cool air of the north would do
me good, and indeed, as soon as we stepped off the steamship and
breathed that fresh Michigan air, I did feel infinitely much better.

"There were not many people in the Club when we arrived.
Most of the cottages were still empty and shuttered, the height of
the season not starting until later into June. The Tretheways were
here though, just Mamie and Lila and the poor widow Tretheway,
who everybody thought was out of her mind with grief—she was
never quite right after her husband, Harris, passed away."

Jess leaned forward, listening carefully.

"It seemed that many in the Club had been touched by tragedy.
I was a young woman in love, and my grief at the loss of my parents
and brother was tempered by the joy of being newly married. Mrs.
Tretheway was in middle age when she lost her husband. She never
seemed to get over it."

Jess suppressed the urge to hurry Mrs. Lewis through her
story. She settled into her chair, looking out at the sunlight playing
over the lake, waiting for Mrs. Lewis to compose her thoughts.

"I was not the only newlywed at the Club that summer. Lila
Tretheway Flagg was here, though she had come home and left
her husband off in Europe somewhere—Berlin, I believe it was.
I found that to be quite odd. I was so besotted with my own dear
George that I could not bear the thought of being parted from him
for even a day, and tried to imagine what had made Lila agree to
leave her handsome young husband so far away. I assumed that she
had come to help care for Miss Ada, even though, I'll admit, Lila
made an unlikely nursemaid. She was not a practical sort."

"What were Chapin and Lila like?" Jess asked. "I've seen pictures. They were very good-looking?"

"Oh, they were terribly glamorous. Lila Tretheway was far and away the most beautiful girl in the Club. Her parents had sent her away to a boarding school for girls in Connecticut, and she had clothes from New York that were up-to-the-minute. Her hair was bobbed too—something which the others of us were dying to do but didn't quite dare. The Flaggs were very flashy with their money, and Chapin was no exception. He had this car that everybody admired, a Stutz Bearcat. He used to drive Lila around in it, and we all thought they looked just like movie stars. People said that they used to go into Charlevoix to gamble at Koch's casino—a terrible scandal. People here were Presbyterians and didn't go in for that kind of thing."

Jess smiled in agreement.

"But when Lila came back from Europe, she had changed. It was like someone had pricked a balloon and let all the air out. Even her prettiness was almost gone. At the time, I thought it was a cruel thing, that Lila had been turned into a nursemaid for her cranky old mother. I thought that Mamie could have just as easily done the job. I'll never forget how Lila looked when I saw her. She had the oddest way of walking, almost a shuffle, and I never saw her when she wasn't covered up by some thick and bulky wrap—as though she was cold. Lila Flagg was a girl. She was younger than I, not much more than seventeen, but that summer, seeing her from a distance, you might have taken her for a middle-aged lady with indifferent health."

"And what about Miss Mamie?"

"I remember Mamie so clearly that summer. Never more beautiful, and so happy all the time. She was in love with the handsome Captain Thomas Cleves. Happy—but not for long. It was early in the summer when her sister died."

Jess folded her hands in her lap and stared out at the lake. Today it was a bright clear blue, and still as a sheet. "Do you remember the day that she died?"

"Oh yes, my dear. As if it were yesterday. I saw both Mamie and Lila at breakfast that morning. It was unseasonably warm, and everyone in the room was wearing fresh light linen or cotton, except for Lila, who was all bundled up in a heavy woolen cloak. George was looking across at their table, and he said to me, 'What is it about the younger Tretheway girl? Is she not quite right in the head?' I told him about how gay and pretty Lila had been and how she was now nursing her cranky and difficult mother. I remember he said, 'Why don't those people hire a nursemaid? It's far too much stress on the poor girl's nerves.' As I recall, that was all we spoke about it, moving as happy young people do, quickly on to lighter matters."

"Was she not quite right in the head?" Jess asked, studying Mrs. Lewis's wrinkled face.

"Well, to be honest, I never thought too highly of Lila Tretheway. She was all flash and no substance, if you know what I mean. But was she crazy? Hear me out for the rest of the story, and then you can decide for yourself."

Jess cast her eyes quickly down to Mrs. Lewis's lap, where the little brown 1922 ledger still lay untouched, and then back up to her face as she started to speak again.

"I was sitting right here on the porch that afternoon. I had some mending to do, and I was in this very chair with my darning basket in my lap. George was puttering around inside. It was hot in the cottage and I was hoping it would be cooler on the porch, but that afternoon the air was heavy and still. The first thing I saw was someone in a dory, rowing round Loeb Point. Because it was early in the season, there weren't that many boats out and about, and the little red-and-white dory caught my eye. A few minutes later, I saw Mamie hurrying along the front walk, a picnic basket in her hand. She was bare legged and wearing a big fisherman's sweater that fell almost to her knees."

"Why was she wearing a sweater on a hot day?"

"Oh, we all did that in those days. We all wore wool-flannel bathing suits that took forever to dry. Sometimes, if the wind came up, you could start to catch a chill. The big men's sweaters were all the rage then. All the girls wore them to cover up. The thick wool would repel the water, and it would keep you warm if a breeze came up before your bathing suit was dry. When I saw her dressed like that, I figured that she was going for a swim. We liked to swim long distances, always with a rowboat rowing alongside, in case we got tired. A few minutes later, Lila came by, dressed just as Mamie had been in a big fisherman's sweater. She was walking the same way she had been walking all summer, uncomfortable, as though she hurt a little bit somewhere. I thought about calling out to her, but I didn't. She gave no sign that she saw me as she passed.

"I'm not sure how long I sat there on the porch. Not too long after, I saw the rowboat pull out with Mamie and Lila swimming alongside. Thomas must have been in the boat. They were heading out toward Hemingway Point—you know that's not far, can't be more than a quarter mile. Anyway, that's all. I watched their progress across, but I wasn't actively watching. Then, I lost sight of them. You can't see the point from here, as you know."

Jess followed Mrs. Lewis's gaze. The lake was such a warm and friendly blue today, not the slightest bit menacing.

"And that's when she drowned?" Jess asked. "On her way out to Hemingway Point?" The old woman nodded, but she seemed far away, lost in a time long past.

"I don't understand. If Thomas was in the rowboat, didn't he see her struggling?"

"Hold your horses, Jess dear. I've got to tell the story in my own way. It's an old story and I'm afraid if I mix it up, I may lose my grasp of it entirely."

Jess blushed. Mrs. Lewis looked so tiny sitting there wrapped in the afghan. She was embarrassed to be pushing on her like that. She turned away from Mrs. Lewis and gazed out over the lake. The view was different from The Rafters—you could see a part of the cove, but the point lay hidden just out of view.

"Well, as I said. I sat there a while longer, doing my darning, and just enjoying the peace of the day. Then, it seemed like just a few minutes later, I heard someone hollering 'Doc Lewis!' And I saw Thomas Cleves charging toward our house, carrying Lila's body in his arms. George came running out the front door and gestured for him to bring the poor girl inside."

"Where was Mamie?"

"I didn't look to see where Mamie was. I ran straight over the footbridge to the north side, to the Clubhouse. There was a big old farm bell that we rang in case of a fire, or any other emergency. I just ran right in and started pulling that rope as hard as I could, ringing that bell until I could feel rope burns on the palm of my hand. Then, I hurried back home again, and sure enough, the few people that were on the grounds then had soon assembled outside our cottage, standing around not sure how to help, and I stood there by the door, calling out to them, "It's Lila Flagg! No news yet!"

"What was going on in there?" Jess asked.

"No one knew, but we feared the worst. Alvin Whitmire had a car, so we sent him over to Ironton to fetch the minister. I remember that Thomas's whole body was shaking with these deep, horrible sobs—the sound filled the cottage. A big man like that, you just don't expect to hear him cry. I wanted to shoo all the people away from the cottage. I remember I was afraid that someone would hear him crying, and I thought that later he'd be embarrassed. The oddest thing I remember was that the Indian girls were out front."

"The Indian girls?"

"Oh, you're too young to remember. There used to be a camp, about half a mile up the road. On Sunday afternoons, the squaws came, selling sweetgrass baskets woven through with porcupine quills. And on Tuesdays and Thursdays, the young girls came, selling cut flowers, gladiolas and such. Everybody used to buy them then. The flowers looked pretty, and then, of course, you felt sorry for the girls having to live out there in the camp."

"So then the minister came and they buried her?"

"Well, dear, there's a little more to the story than that." Mrs. Lewis was peering at Jess, her blue eyes sharp and alert. "I need to be sure that you really want to know."

"That's what I came here for," said Jess. She paused for a minute, then forced herself to continue. "Coming here has made me realize that there are a lot of things about my life that I've never really understood. I should have asked Mamie . . ." She looked up at Mrs. Lewis, and when she saw that the old woman's face was kind and encouraging, she continued. "I guess I've always had the feeling that I never really got the straight story . . ."

Mrs. Lewis smoothed her afghan again and then put her hands down on the little leather-bound volume in her lap, about to open it.

"Do you think you could be a dear and bring me a tumbler of water, Jess. I'm afraid my mouth is a little too dry to read."

Jess found a glass in the kitchen cupboard and filled it with cool water from the tap. She hesitated, looking out the window.

Jess wasn't exactly sure what she was looking for. Was there something important in that little brown book? Something she should have known? Would it have mattered if she had known sooner? Jess picked up the glass of water and walked back out to the porch.

She was ready to find out.

"When George examined Lila, he found neither pulse nor breath of life. She was as cold as a stone. Thomas was in the greatest state of shock. He kept repeating over and over again, 'But she didn't drown—she made it across. I saw her standing in shallow water. She was standing there, and then she just keeled over.' George poured him a stiff shot of bourbon, wrapped him in a Pendleton blanket, and said sternly, 'Captain Cleves, get yourself dried out and pulled together.' The man had been through the war and everything, but somehow he just couldn't handle the loss of that young girl." She shook her head, remembering.

"George shut the door to the back bedroom, there where the poor dead girl lay, telling me that he needed to do a more thorough examination. A few minutes later, he came out and went into the washroom to wash up. Before long, Alvin Whitmire came in with the minister and George explained that the poor girl had drowned."

The slim leather volume still lay unopened on Mrs. Lewis's lap, but now she started stroking the binding with her index finger, still deep in thought. Jess thought the old woman had nothing else to say, but then she continued.

"Three nights later, George woke me in the middle of the night. He had not come to bed that night—he was still wearing his rumpled clothes, and in the dark bedroom, his face looked haggard. It was not unusual for him to be called out in the middle of the night, you see. He often went out to the Indian camp and was always called out in the case of a difficult labor. 'May,' he whispered to me, 'I'm not sure if I have done right.'

"I sat up, now fully awake, saying to him, 'What, what can it be, my love?' He said he had not told me whole truth because he didn't see the point. The girl was dead, her mother was crazy, and her husband was abroad. Nobody knew the whole truth except for George and Lila's sister, Mamie—and me, now that he had told me."

Mrs. Lewis paused and stared intently at Jess. "It was a terrible burden. I've kept that secret through all of these long years."

Jess nodded but said nothing.

"I remember that night so clearly. Moonlight shone in our bedroom window, casting a diamond of light on our white bedspread. The terrible rainstorm of early evening had passed, and in the pale light, I could see my husband's face—the handsome, craggy contours, the wide brow of intelligence and the soft eyes of compassion. He held my hands tight as he spoke to me in his soft voice: 'Lila did not drown. She had recently delivered a child. Such a slim chance, so slim, that the baby was born alive . . .'"

When Mrs. Lewis finished this recital, she had such a distant look that Jess had the impression that she could see her late husband's face before her. She sat in silence, until Jess prodded her to continue.

"A child . . . ?" Jess said.

"The truth is that your great-aunt Lila didn't drown. She died of a massive hemorrhage."

"But she was out swimming. I'm sorry. But it doesn't make any sense."

"Well, I'm not a medical person like my dear George, but I'll explain as best I can." As though she had forgotten all about it, she caught sight of the ledger in her lap. She picked up the crumbling volume slowly and opened it to a yellowed page covered with handwritten script. She coughed a little and then picked up her glass and took a sip of water.

"Perhaps if I read this to you, it will all be more clear. These are Dr. Lewis's medical records." Taking another sip of water, she began to read.

"*Thursday, May 30th, 1922 . . .*"

Mrs. Lewis paused, then cleared her throat.

"My voice is getting tired, Jess. Perhaps it would be better if you read it to yourself." She handed the volume to Jess.

Summoned at emergency behest to examine Mrs. Lila Tretheway Flagg, female, seventeen years of age. Two o'clock in the afternoon, Mrs. Flagg is carried to me by Capt. Thomas Cleves, who states that Mrs. Flagg had lost consciousness and fallen into shallow water after swimming approximately fifteen minutes. Mrs. Flagg presented with the following physical findings: Color: pale. Temperature:

*cool. Pulse: none. Respiration: none. Pupils: fixed, dilated,
and nonresponsive to light. Serous fluid in vaginal vault and
on mediolateral aspects of thighs. First-degree lacerations of
perineum, boggy atonic uterus, fundus three fingerbreadths
superior to umbilicus. Retained placental fragment adher-
ent to posterior uterine wall. Probable cause of death: puer-
peral hemorrhage. Fetal condition: unknown.*

Jess held the small dusty volume in her hand. The pages were
so yellowed, the handwriting so florid, and the ink so stained that
it was difficult for her to make out the words. Though she understood most of them individually, she was having trouble under-
standing what all of it meant. She read over the entry three times,
and then looked up at Mrs. Lewis, who was peering at her with the
greatest attention.

"I'm sorry, it's very medical. I'm not sure I understand it completely . . ." Jess said.

"As close as Dr. Lewis could figure, from what he explained
to me, she had to have delivered a baby earlier that day. She must
have abandoned it somewhere. Dr. Lewis believed that she bled to
death, out there in the lake, and then she passed out, just as she
reached shore."

"Is that possible?"

"There are times when a hemorrhage is delayed, when a
woman can bleed to death hours, even days, after she has delivered
a child."

"But are you . . . It makes no sense . . . How can you be sure?"

"Dr. Lewis trained at Boston Lying-In. Obstetrics was his
specialty. I was a maternity nurse. We met there, in Boston, just
after the war. This was an unusual case, but sadly, not unheard-of.
Sometimes, a woman delivers a baby alone, and abandons it. Rare,
of course, and so sad. It can be very dangerous as well."

"But nobody knew? She told no one?"

"She hid it from everyone—perhaps even from herself. I know I saw her many times that summer, and though I knew she had a problem, I did not suspect that one."

"Did anyone ever find out what happened to the baby?"

"The baby was never found. You know, it wouldn't have lived more than an hour or two if it wasn't born dead in the first place . . ."

"Do you think she . . . killed it?"

"I think that's something we will never know. In a case like this, you wish the mother had lived long enough that you could have asked her why—but then, of course, think how awful for her, for the family, if she *had* lived and then had to forever deal with the truth of what she had done. Lila was whiter than the driven snow when she lay in her casket. I've never seen a corpse so pale."

"Strange. That's the one thing about Lila that Mamie told me. She used to tell me about her funeral. She said that she lay in an open casket, and looked as white and cold as a stone. The only other thing I remember her telling me is that Lila's funeral was the only time she ever saw Thomas Cleves cry."

May looked oddly at Jess.

"Your grandmother wasn't at the funeral, Jess dear. Thomas Cleves wasn't there either. They ran away that very same night Lila died. Left in the middle of a rainstorm, and never came back . . . not for a few years anyway."

Jess sat without speaking, looking out the window at the placid blue lake, the still waters that held so much of her family's history. She gently rubbed the outside of the brown-leather book, seeing the orangey dust coming off onto her fingers. There were a few sailboats out on the lake, not many as there was little wind. From The Rafters's porch, Jess could see a bit of the bathing beach: a cluster of mothers in beach chairs and swarms of children dabbling in the water.

"Mrs. Lewis," Jess said. "Did you know that May thirtieth is the day that my mother was born?"

Mrs. Lewis paused before speaking.

"I think that I did, child. Yes, I think that I did."

CHAPTER TWENTY-THREE

Mamie

The night that Jess went off to the picnic at Hemingway Point with the Whitmire boy, I spent a long time sitting out on the porch swing. I had my mending basket and was enjoying the solitude. It was a pleasant night, though a bit cool, and I was wearing my little black cashmere sweater; it was just cool enough for that.

I had noticed the way that Jess arranged herself, taking extra time in front of the mirror, touching at her hair with nervous, fluttery fingers. The girls in those days all seemed to dress like boys anyway, jeans and T-shirts all the time. Still, there was something fussy about the way she tied her blue sweatshirt around her waist, and pulled a few loose hairs out of her ponytail to frame her face. Indeed, she was lovely—she had the high pink flush of a girl just come of age. Jess was seventeen. The very same age at which my dear sister, Lila, departed. She looked so much like Lila too. That summer I always had the urge to keep her close to me, even as I knew that she needed to live her life.

"Take care, Jess dear," I said to her, trying as I might to let her go on thinking that, as an old lady, I was bat-blind when it came to matters of love. Looking through the cottage windows from the porch, I watched her white T-shirt fade into the shadows inside and then disappear. Then: *bang* as the kitchen screen door slammed shut behind her.

Earlier that day, I had seen the big, good-looking Whitmire boy looking at her. She was playing Ping-Pong on the clubhouse porch, and he was hanging around with his clubs, hitting golf balls down the bluff, swinging around with each arc of his stroke to catch sight of her.

I was already feeling the brittleness in my bones, the ache with the early-morning cottage chill. I knew that I would not always be there to keep my summer vigil over the lake. How lovely it would be if Jess grew attached to a Wequetona boy.

I remember how I felt that evening, looking at the shining path of light that the moon traced along the water, hearing the gentle clanging of a sailboat moored to its buoy, the buzz of the cicadas, louder on the wooded side of the cottage. It was hard to believe that at one time, so long ago, I had left in despair, assuming I'd never come back. My eyes took in the familiar look of a Pine Lake evening, and I felt that night that I had been rewarded for my patience. I had lived through hard times, but the truth is, the hard times had passed. I had lived long enough to see Margaret grow up and then Jess grow up after her. Now I was an old woman, on my Wequetona porch; it was only the house itself and I that could bear witness to where we had been. The chain supporting the porch swing made a soft, rhythmic creaking sound as I sat there, a woman, a house, a place, all one.

With a start I awoke later; I had fallen asleep there on the porch swing, my mending still clutched in my lap. Mortified, I wiped away the thin stream of spittle from my chin, even though it was dim on the porch and there was no one around to see. I was just patting my hair straight and gathering up my things when I saw a figure come around the side of the house.

Before I could even see him clearly, I felt the strangest sensation, a tug, like the pull of gravity had just gotten stronger. There was something about the way the figure walked, an economy of movement, a kind of catlike grace. Deep from a part of my heart that I thought had shriveled up and died forever, I felt it thump hard. For a moment, I was sure I was seeing Thomas. But of course, that was impossible. A second later, the figure emerged from the shadows and I saw that he was just a boy, dark haired and slight of build. He was ever so like *him*. And yet not. Like him, but not him, a shadow, a visitation. Not unlike the way I would come upon Jess and see a glimmer of Lila, but then again, not Lila, not even slightly like her at all.

"Miss Mamie?" The boy said, his tone deferential.

"What is it?" I was surprised by the sound of my own voice, an old lady's voice, reedy and dry.

"Miss Mamie, forgive me for intruding like this, I'm terribly sorry, it's just that . . ."

"Do I know you, son?" I said, leaning forward, peering at him. His face, which at first blush had seemed familiar, now seemed to be a stranger's face, one of those unkempt teenagers who wore his hair hanging down around his shirt collar.

"Oh, sorry," he said, now seeming awkward. "I'm Daniel Painter . . . I need to talk to you . . . It's about Jess . . ." I must not have registered his name, because I was immediately panicked that something had happened to Jess.

"Jess?" I said, sitting up straighter, now wide-awake. "What is it, young man? Is something wrong?" I could feel my heart banging against the inside of my rib cage. "Has there been an accident?"

I still remember the grace of that boy as he knelt down beside me, an old lady and a perfect stranger to him. I remember the poise with which he spoke to me.

I saw a yellow patch of light illuminate the dark grass in front of the cottage, which let me know that Jess was in her room. The boy's voice was grave as he spoke, telling me about Jess, that Jess was okay, just a little upset.

That Whitmire boy had gotten fresh with her. Too fresh. Well, the boys drank Wild Turkey in my day too, and that kind of thing is to be expected. Expected, but not tolerated. So I left the boy standing there and marched straight down the walk to speak to Erskine Whitmire, and the good judge did the honorable thing and sent his son packing for a while. The boy turned out just fine too, went to law school and married a girl from the Belvedere.

I went to bed that night perfectly peaceful, feeling I had taken care of the matter, and sure that the Whitmire boy wouldn't bother Jess, poor lamb, again that summer.

But the next morning, I awoke heavy with dread. When my eyes opened, I lay rigid, staring at the grooves in the pine ceiling. Never before or since have I felt more like a stray thread was about to be pulled; that I would see my whole life unraveled before me.

The young man whom I had seen the night before—it was Thomas Cleves's grandson.

Of course, I knew that Treetops was still in his family. From time to time, I'd hear it referred to as the Painter cottage. That cottage was not formally part of the Wequetona Club. In the early days, the Cleveses used to come over for Vespers. They were friends of the Addisons. But as time went on, those early ties were lost. The elder Cleveses had both passed on not long after the summer of

1922. People said that Thomas had sold his share of the cottage to his brother. Quite frankly, I did not want to know about it.

You can never imagine how I weighed my words the next morning when Jess came down for breakfast. I was churning up inside like a young girl in love, but it's funny being old—most of the time that dried-up husk of a self you carry around with you is all anyone sees.

I took a good, hard look at Jess. She looked the same as usual, wearing blue jeans and a T-shirt, her clean hair pulled back in a ponytail. She did not speak but went straight to the toaster to fix herself some toast. My mind was flitting anxiously over what I should say to her. How do you begin with a fresh-faced girl to talk about anything that matters . . . and *where* to begin?

I had in mind that I would convey some sympathy to her, stepped forward, but I felt her body stiffen at my slightest touch. How do you tell a young girl: I was once young too, and I know what it is to be female? Jess, as usual, was cool as a cucumber, and I felt inadequate, a foolish old lady faced with an accomplished modern girl, a girl who could do things I could never have imagined, like go to the university and study for medical school.

I did not burden her with my pats and sympathy. I resolved not to say anything. But my secret, after all these years lying dormant, was eating at me, and try as I might, I could not keep my mouth shut. Would it not have been wiser to say nothing? But I was more nervous than wise. Since those fateful days so many years ago, our family had never had any contact with the family of Thomas Cleves. I could not take the risk that Jess would establish a connection with them. I told her to stay away from the Painter boy. Did I in fact drive her toward him? I'll never know.

———

May and I liked to play cribbage together, in the afternoon.

We were at the Lewis cottage, The Rafters, facing each other at the card table, in the lovely glassed-in solarium that stays so nice and warm in the afternoons. I was wearing gray wool slacks and that pink raw-silk blazer with the three-quarter-length sleeves, and May was in her turquoise silk that I have always liked, the one that brings out the blue in her eyes. May winters in Palm Beach, and is quite frankly not careful enough about the sun, being, I think, more wrinkled than is necessary for a woman of her age, but she is still lovely, and ever so careful about herself. I appreciate that. Nothing is more repellent than an older lady who lets herself go.

"I never knew that Jess was so fond of canoeing," May said. She was peering at me, the way she does, tipping her head back, since her eyelids are a little droopy. I caught right away the sharp look in her eyes.

"Canoeing," I said, careful. "Oh yes, lovely way to spend time."

"And isn't it lovely that she's getting on so well with the Painter boy." Just like May, she took a moment to peer out the window, so that I could gather myself before she turned back to look at me. I had never told my dear friend the whole story, but she knew, as a friend does, that Thomas had broken my heart.

"Such a bright girl, and she's going to medical school," I said to May, and we were done with it.

It was a second shock when I saw that they were in love. You know what it was like to see them together? Like heat and white lightning, that's what. They gave off so much heat I thought they'd light the house on fire. A force of nature—you'd think you'd finally get old and forget about it, but you don't. I remember with Thomas I used to think about spontaneous combustion a lot, and it was just like that with them. Daniel Painter had a fire inside him. They did not know that an old white-haired lady could see that flame, but there was nothing wrong with my eyesight, and see it I could.

So I settled down to wait. I waited and waited for Jess to come upon me. It was only a matter of time before they discovered the family connection. I looked deep inside myself to try to open that fathomless spot that was locked up tight. The spot that had got locked up so many years ago that I thought it was permanently sealed, grown over like a scar with a keloid on it. I was almost eighty years old, and I had not revisited that spot in so long that I liked to pretend it wasn't there anymore.

I promised myself that I would unlock the secrets of my heart. I would tell her when she asked. But the problem was, there was only one person alive who knew the whole story, and it wasn't me.

So I decided to write him a letter. I sat down at my writing desk, and looked out toward Hemingway Point, out toward the same view that I had looked at every day of every summer since *that summer*, and which still looked the same as ever, a narrow strip of beach, a few scrubby pines. I sat there at my desk, and I penned that letter. When I look back, and the good Lord knows it's true, that was one of the hardest things I've ever done. I wrote the letter, and after all those years, I asked for an explanation. But I asked that the letter be addressed to Jess—not to me—because there are some things in life that we may be better off not having to know.

The letter came back, in due time, and it sat there on my desk, the square blue envelope, staring at me, reproaching me. I steeled myself for the moment I would hand it to her. I waited for her to come to me. It wouldn't take long for the two young people to put two and two together, and then she would come to me and ask me to explain.

There was only one problem. Something an old lady didn't count on. Jess never asked. Those two were not thinking one blessed thing about the past. I felt like the past was right before them, all around them, the time between then and now no more than a few blinks of an eye, the events of long ago still crowding up into the present—but they couldn't see it at all. I guess I started to think that maybe no harm would come of their association. Maybe the events of the past no longer mattered at all.

It was a shock like being doused with cold water when I realized that Jess might have gotten herself in trouble. Naively, I had assumed that Margaret would have taught her how to take precautions, but it seemed she had not. Nowadays, they have these little kits you can buy in the pharmacy and you test yourself right at home. I had seen advertisements for such things in the ladies' magazines, and Jess, not like her to be careless, left the printed instructions splayed out across the back of the bathroom sink for all to see. I was upstairs in the pink bathroom putting in some fresh rolls of toilet paper, and in spite of myself I saw it. I did not know what result she had gotten, but I knew that she needed to see a doctor right away. I was, more than anything else, furious at Margaret. I was an old lady. Far too old to have to think about this kind of thing. What with the time change, there was no way to call Jess's mother right then. I resolved to phone Margaret the next morning.

Call me superstitious, but there is something not right in Northern Michigan when it is unseasonably hot. It had started to warm up that very evening, the evening I spoke to Jess and tried to tactfully suggest that she needed to see a doctor. By the following morning, it was stifling. I awoke early when I heard the screen door bang. I knew that Jess had gone out. I tried for a while to go back to sleep, but it was impossible. So I got up, put on my lace dressing gown and slippers, picked up a *Reader's Digest*, and tried to read.

I'm not sure how much time passed. I was sitting at my little table looking out over the lake. Since the day was very hot, the lake was the color of cement, and the sky above was a flat pale yellow. I picked up the phone several times to try to call Margaret, but all I got was a message telling me that all the lines were occupied in the country I was trying to reach. So I worked my way through the

Reader's Digest, steadily and without much interest, feeling old and tired, unready to face a hot and difficult day with my granddaughter, who was suddenly causing so much trouble.

I had just placed the receiver in its cradle for the third time, still unable to reach Margaret, and was staring out the window, momentarily idle, when I saw a sight that frightened me so much that I became completely disoriented.

There, out of that hot, lifeless landscape, burst two figures in a pose that was already indelibly burned into my brain, and for a second it seemed as if the worst day of my entire life was being played out again. For the second time in my life, I saw the same horrifying scene—a young man, dark haired and painfully handsome, carrying slumped in his arms a blond girl, limp and wan, her legs stained crimson with blood.

I tried to calm myself, not to panic, to take a moment to compose myself and get dressed and ready to take her into town. Unlike Lila, Jess was alert, and talking, and she didn't seem to be in imminent danger, but I was terrified that at any moment she would stop breathing, right in front of my eyes. Neither one of them knew that I lost hold of myself completely in the hospital, blathering to the doctor, crying and wailing—*she's lost her baby, she's bleeding to death and her baby is lost.* Neither one of them knows that I was forced to sit there with a blood-pressure cuff on while a stout, bossy nurse asked me, *Do you know your name, do you know what day it is, do you know where you live?* They gave me some sugar water to drink, and then a tranquilizer, and then finally let me back into the waiting room. When Doc Coggins came out to tell me that she had a miscarriage, he asked me if it was true that they were first cousins—he thought Daniel's mother was the daughter of Thomas Cleves, Pastor Cleves's son. I hesitated, thinking of Jess, of Daniel, of the love that burned between them, like the love that had once burned between me and my beloved.

But if Margaret was my daughter, then they were first cousins—to deny it was to deny the story upon which I had built my
entire life. Because in the end, we didn't have much besides my
story; it was the shaky foundation upon which we had built our
family. Margaret Lila Tretheway Cleves was my daughter, and
Jess was my granddaughter. That made Jess and Daniel cousins,
and their love had nowhere else to go except down into sacrificial
flames.

"I'm afraid so," I said.

Doc Coggins shook his head. "Those two need to stay away
from each other. Mother Nature never intended for cousins to
mate. It causes genetic issues."

Once again, I couldn't find a path out, couldn't see the road
back. My story stayed locked up inside me. And Jess left me, ran
away. She had no choice, I know, because her love for Daniel was
so hot it was ready to burn. One week later, she flew off to Texas.
I paid her bills, but she never came back to see me, and I never
pressed her on it. She didn't know I had betrayed her, but I did.

————

It isn't until now, as I lie in the clean and sterile confines of Coventry
Manor, where finally the last of my things have been stripped away,
alone in a bed with a call button and a motor in it, rustling on stiff
sheets that worry my skin—now that I see that Journey's End must
go to her. I doubt it is possible for her to go back, as it seems impossible for all of us. That's what I've learned, in this long life of mine,
above anything. That what's past is past. But still, the cottage sits
up on the bluff proudly, full of Tretheway things, the final keeper of
secrets, and now I pass it on to Jess to unravel. The message is there
for her if she wants to read it. If it's too late, then so be it.

CHAPTER TWENTY-FOUR

JESS, AGE THIRTY-THREE

There had been a path here. Once, Jess had known it as well as she had known the sound of her own beating heart. But now it was gone, no trace of it, and she was stumbling as she walked, tripping on branches and ducking under thorny overhangs. She wanted to see the place—even though, properly speaking, it wasn't there anymore. Even the pathway to get there was gone. The underbrush was so dense here that the lake was scarcely visible, just winking at her now and then, intense electric blue glowing through the green.

It hadn't been so hard after all. She had just taken the bound packet out of her suitcase and slit the tape open with a knife.

Documents: Journey's End. She couldn't believe she had sealed the package up so tight, just that very morning. Sealed it up without looking more carefully at the packet of letters from Chapin

Flagg she had found in her grandmother's desk. She had that quality, selective blindness, when she just didn't look straight at things she didn't want to see. Kind of like that book of poetry that was *still* unopened, the cover itself already more than she could bear. The letter that Jess now held in her hand was so unassuming-looking: it was a square blue envelope, with a San Francisco return address. The letters *CEF* were engraved on the back flap in a flowery script.

It had never been opened.

Of course, she thought now, brushing a pine branch out of the way, looking for footing down the steep slope, she should have turned the letter *over*, to look at the *front* of the envelope, where the name of the sender and addressee were written. She should have *looked* at it before she had packed it away without reading it. At some level, she had known that, but Jess was slowly coming to comprehend that about herself, that sometimes she could just slide things out of the way, sealed up tight with packing tape, unread and therefore unknown.

She was getting close to the water's edge now. She scanned the unassuming surface, looking for a landmark to orient her. Then, she saw it—the flat rock, now looking ordinary, mostly submerged under the murky greenish water near the shore. There was no beach here, not anymore. What used to be beach was completely submerged, the water up just past the tree line; already here, she could feel the thick, peaty ground squelching under her shoes.

She backed up a few paces, to where the ground was dry again, and found a place to perch, on a mossy fallen log. It felt damp under her bottom and craggy with broken-off twigs. A couple of gnats buzzed around her face. She batted at them with the letter (still not looking at it), scanning the surface of the water, measuring with her eyes the distance from where the flat rock was. She was *certain* she could see something. *Certain* there had to be something, bubbles on the surface, like little breaths of life, hinting at the cold troubled waters below.

Spirit waters.

But there was nothing. The waterline was at least fifteen feet above where the sinking sand had been, and the surface of the water lay smooth and untroubled, reflecting back the color of the surrounding woods.

Here was the one place in Wequetona that had completely changed, that had become unrecognizable. Jess shifted her bottom on the uncomfortable log. She glanced once more at the placid surface of the lake.

Slowly, she turned the letter over and saw what she knew she had seen already—that the letter was addressed in an elegant, old-fashioned cursive, that it bore a sixteen-year-old postmark from San Francisco, and that the letter was addressed *to her.* If Margaret wasn't Mamie's baby, if she was really Lila's, then there was one person who might have known the truth: Lila's husband, Chapin Flagg. Now, it turns out that he had tried to get in touch with her. Why hadn't Mamie given her the letter? Why had she kept it all these years? She must have known that there was a chance that, one day, Jess would find it.

There was a strong wind blowing across the lake. She tipped her chin up, letting the wind blow across her face; with her eyes closed like that, it gave her goose bumps and made the hair stand up on the back of her neck. Even now, it bit into her—that roaring sound that filled her ears. It was and would ever be the sound of helplessness.

She could still feel the facts of that long-ago day imprinted on her body—the way the thin paper covering kept slipping off her bare knees, the cold metal stirrups biting into the tender arches of her feet, her breasts so swollen that she kept her arms crossed tight across them, as though she could make herself invisible, unseen.

You are genetically incompatible with the baby's father. That's what the doctor had said.

Jess was lying there, legs up, bottom exposed, head turned to the side, like she wasn't even there. They were doing things to her, squirting her belly with gel, wheeling in something that looked liked a TV screen; she could see it, kind of, out of the corner of her eye. She craned her neck trying to see, but the nurse told her to hold still, please. She injected a cloudy liquid into the IV bag; moments later, Jess felt her head go cottony, and it seemed she was floating above the bed.

It was harder to follow what the doctor and nurse were saying, now that her head felt like it was wrapped in cotton. But still she tried as if it were a matter of life or death. She heard them saying words, but she couldn't piece them together properly. She tried to speak, but they ignored her.

A heartbeat.

Maybe there were two sacs.

Seven-week size.

This one looks okay.

See that little flicker.

A heartbeat. A heartbeat. A heartbeat.

Then, there was Doc Coggins's face bending over her, breathing on her; his breath was hot and smelled antiseptic.

Hearing for the first time the words that would tear her apart.

Your cousin.

Your cousin.

You were pregnant with twins. You lost one of them.

Better to take care of the other one now. You can't have a baby with your cousin. It would be . . .

It would be a freak.

The room seemed to be spinning around her. The face of the doctor and nurse zoomed in and out of her vision. She saw all kinds of images mixed up, swirling around her then.

Cousin. Cousin. Cousin. Cousin. Twisted, distorted monsters with yellow eyes and two heads.

There was Doc Coggins, bending toward her again. Saying, "I'm going to take care of it for you."

Jess tried to ask: *There is a heartbeat? A heartbeat? A heartbeat?*

"Don't worry. It won't hurt. It will all be over in a minute," the doctor said.

"It's for the best," the nurse said.

Jess imagined herself getting up and running away, but she was so dizzy, and she was strapped down by the IV. She just lay there, cotton-heady, nakedly dressed in paper. Staring up at the ceiling. She was afraid, and she did not know what else to do, so she nodded her head, just once, to say "Okay."

Just once, she turned her head toward him. She looked up at Doc Coggins, his height, and the blinding white of his lab coat. Then, she turned to face the wall again.

After that, a horrible sucking sound. A roaring in her ears, and then, the machine switched off, and nothing more than a deadly deafening silence.

Jess was halfway through her second year of the premedical curriculum at the University of Texas, an excellent student, near the top of her class, when she went into the stacks and checked out *Williams Obstetrics*. She looked up twin gestations, early miscarriage, and the procedure called suction and curettage. The next day, she went to her advisor and dropped out of the premedical program, changing her major to French. Since that day, she had never looked back.

Jess still did not know, truly, if she had done the right thing that day in the hospital emergency room. She knew that she was too drugged, confused, and surprised to be able to make a decision at the time. She wished someone had been with her, someone to hold her hand and help her understand the consequences of her decision. But the one thing that bothered her more than anything was that she had never told Daniel the truth. They had parted seventeen years ago with a confession on the tip of her tongue. And not confessing, she had also never forgiven herself.

Now, she had to confront the possibility that she and Daniel were never cousins in the first place. If Margaret was Lila's daughter . . .

Jess could not imagine what horror lurked in the mind of a person who had chewed her own umbilical cord, abandoned her newborn, and then set off in the lake to swim. The horror was unfathomable, and this lake, calm, blue, beautiful, mutely held on to her secrets.

Spirit waters. Maybe they had released her from whatever place she dwelled.

The envelope flew open, the old seal brittle with age—she slipped out the contents; there were two sets of pages. With a start, she saw that clipped to a sheaf of handwritten papers was a small sheet of her grandmother's familiar pearl-gray writing paper, inscribed with Mamie's tidy blue script.

> *Dear Chapin,*
>
> *It is time for my granddaughter to know whatever part of the story that you know.*
>
> *But I fear after all these years it is too late for me. The story that I choose to live with must be my own. I know that Margaret is Lila's daughter, but there must be a piece of the puzzle that only you can tell.*
>
> *Please address the letter to my lovely granddaughter, Jess Carpenter. Write what you like. I will not open it myself.*
>
> *May God bless you and keep you in good health.*
>
> *Mamie*

Under it, on plain white writing paper, were several pages written out longhand. Jess started when she noticed the date in the upper left-hand corner: *Tuesday, July 30th, 1980—San Francisco, California.*

Sixteen summers ago. Jess's last summer at Wequetona. The summer of farewell.

CHAPTER TWENTY-FIVE

CHAPIN

Dear Jess,

A few days ago, I received by post an odd request from your grandmother Mamie. It brought me back to a place and time that I thought I had forgotten entirely. But then, one doesn't actually forget, does one?

She has asked me to tell you what I know about her sister, Lila, to whom I was once briefly married, so long ago that it now seems part of another life, and I have decided that I shall endeavor to do so, and hope I shall acquit myself reasonably of the task.

I should start by saying that I admire your grandmother greatly, and believe her to be a woman of character. She said that I should write what I like, and I trust your grandmother knows that there's no way to tell this story unless I leave in the parts that wouldn't normally be discussed in what used to be called "polite company." I do hope you'll not be shocked, but then I doubt you will. You're Mamie's granddaughter, after all. Without doubt, a young woman of character, and of course, you have the benefit of being born into a more enlightened time.

The story starts in summer, of course. When else would a Michigan story start? My family, the Flagg family, was fortunate. My father had made his money in shoe leather—you remember this was just after the Great War—and we had become impossibly rich helping to boot up every young foot soldier who marched off to be slaughtered in the war. If I recall correctly, my father had bought his cottage, Aldergate, from the penurious sister of an officer who was killed at Verdun, no doubt killed with Flagg soles nailed to his shoes. We were new money—bright as a minted penny, and quite unknown by the Wequetona set; had they known me better, I trust they would have pinned fewer of their hopes upon me and recognized me sooner for what I was. Of course, this is not my story, this is Lila's story, but our tales ended up getting entwined somehow. That was the trouble with how we used to do things in those days—Lila and I did not ever belong together. Trouble was, to those around us, we looked as though we did.

Lila was a great deal younger than I, which suited me quite well. She was a skinny girl with a face that would have been unremarkable except for her eyes, which tended to violet and were set wide apart. Her hair was flaxen colored and hung perfectly straight. She was the first of the group to bob her hair. You could say she was an ordinary-looking girl, but as people sometimes do, she had a look that suited the spirit of the time. She did not talk much. In all honesty,

*I did not think her very bright. But that summer, there was
something luminous about her. Like a firefly, Lila Tretheway
lit up the dark.*

*It was the summer of 1921, Lila was, well, I guess she
must have been about sixteen, and I was just up from Yale.
There were always groups of us going into town. The young
girls prized driving with me because they fancied my car,
a Stutz Bearcat, yellow, the only one in town. I'm sure you
don't imagine it like that—the way Charlevoix was in those
days, but Jess, there was a moment, back between the wars,
when those thirty-room "cottages" were being built, when
people used to arrive at the Pere Marquette station in private railway cars to be picked up by chauffeured limousines.*

*Not a big enough town for me though. I was fidgety
there, lived with a weariness that was bone deep. I used to
go into town, into Koch's almost every evening to play roulette. The Wequetona girls were, for the most part, whole-
some sorts, but Lila was always willing to sneak out on a
pretense and bump with me over the bone-rattling roads
between Wequetona and town. Her clothes were fabulous.
(Not that I found her attractive, in that way, Jess. I trust
you have understood, by this time, that my proclivities did
not lie in that direction.) Your Aunt Lila was at boarding
school at Farmington then, and she must've been up in New
York at the dressmakers almost every weekend. You could
just see the older Wequetona ladies, the matronly sisters of
Bible professors, frowning at that girl when she tripped into
the dining room looking every inch the flapper. But stout
Mrs. Tretheway had apprised herself of the interested looks
of the young men toward Lila Tretheway's legs, and she just
let her gad about like that. When Mrs. Tretheway wasn't in
bed, that is; the grieving widow, who had lost her husband*

three years previous, suffered from a nervous condition, and on physician's orders, spent much of her time in bed.

Lila did not demand much from me. She was just looking for a good time. Koch's was a Georgian building, right in town, that made little pretense of hiding that it was a first-class gambling joint. I remember walking in the front door with Lila Tretheway. She always reeked of smoke, pulling out her Chesterfields the moment she and I left the Wequetona grounds. There were a lot of chauffeurs around town then, bringing in the families from the Chicago Club and the Belvedere, but I drove us right up to the front door in my Stutz, and you could just see the way people paused a little, and said, "Who are those two?" Inside the front hallway with its polished wooden floors, we would shrug off our coats, mine white cashmere and Lila in a little ermine wrap. At the end of the hallway, there was an arched window and a buffed mahogany table with a silver vase kept full of dozens of red roses. Mr. Koch had them sent up from Chicago every day.

That moment, when we were standing there in front of the vase of roses, with eyes looking up from the dining room and the card room, was the moment that I cherished. We were just it, Lila and I. I knew how people saw us: young, fair haired, and lanky legged.

I think that's what she married me for. Somehow, standing next to each other, we were the thing that everyone wanted to be, the stars that had aligned just so in the sky. I'm sure she truly believed that she would always get precisely what she wanted. I myself was less convinced. Both of us should have known that looking fabulous in a hallway in front of a vase of roses is not the surest route to happiness.

Lila was a born gambler. She would keep playing in the Ladies' Room as long as I would leave her there, shooting craps with ten-penny bets. I could see the gleam in her eye when I came back to get her, the relish with which she scooped up her pile of silver and copper and let it fall tinkling into her beaded bag.

I did not care if I won or I lost; I just loved sitting there in the game room, surrounded by stout middle-aged men who had made fortunes in things—rubber, sugar, guns, shoes—watching the roulette table, spin clatter clatter clatter spin, inhaling that intoxicating odor of Havana cigars mingled with the sweat of powerful men.

One afternoon, a warm sunny day in mid-July, we were bored, looking for some amusement. We decided to go down to the Pine River Channel and watch the lumbermen bringing in the logs. The Pine River Channel was a man-made throughway that connected Pine Lake to Lake Michigan. The lumbermen used to ride the logs down through the channel; big chested and bare backed, they would wrestle the huge logs through the narrow channel to where they would be loaded up onto the waiting freighters.

Lila and I stood on the banks of the channel. I remember that Lila looked especially lovely that day in a cream-colored linen sheath with a dropped waist. She was one of the few girls actually thin enough to wear a dress cut like that. It hung loose past her hips in graceful straight lines.

Down the channel, straddling a huge log, came a big, strapping fellow, tanned a deep brown, with a powerful muscled chest that immediately caught my eye.

I noticed that Lila was looking at him too, and she started pointing to him, shouting out, in that silly, girlish way of hers, "Oh look, Chapin, do look . . . It's Billy, Billy McKawber . . . the Indian . . . from the Club. It's Billy." Just like, that she was hopping up and down like a girl half her age and yelling, "Yoo-hoo, Billy . . . It's me . . . it's Lila."

I felt a fool with her hollering out like that, but at the same time, I was hoping the fellow would take notice, and then he did. He smiled and waved at us. Even at a distance, I saw the white flash of his teeth, the smooth arc of his muscled arm.

"Chapin," Lila prattled on excitedly. She had a nasal tone of voice, curiously flat. "You remember Billy. Billy the caretaker's son. He used to live right next to Wequetona. His father did work for the club all the time. You remember him. The Indian. We used to play together all the time, when we were kids. We were best friends. Mamie couldn't stand him. She said all Indians smell."

Lila always talked like that. Like a small child. Her chatter was just background noise to me; I couldn't get past the thought of the fellow with his legs wrapped around the enormous virgin pine log.

"He still lives out at the club, then?" I asked. "In the caretaker's cottage?"

"Oh, Chapin, don't you know anything? Old Joe McKawber got fired. They said he was a drunk, and people worried he might steal. That's when they built the caretaker's house. Don't you remember? When John and Mabel came. A lot of folks just thought they'd rather have a white couple living there year-round. What with the Indian camp being so nearby."

"Well, if you want to say hello, let's go find him," I said.

So we found him. He was standing on the rough dock down where the freighters loaded up, still bare chested, leaning against the iron railing, swigging root beer out of an amber-glass bottle.

"Well, aren't you the swell," he said to Lila, and he gave a slow, easy smile that poured down me like hot molten steel.

I bit down on the inside of my lip until I could taste the iron bitterness of blood.

"Need a lift?" I said, hating the thin quaver in my voice as I tried to hide how badly I wanted him to agree. "If you're all done working, we could take you somewhere."

He might not have bothered with us at all if it hadn't been for the car. He and everyone else in the world wanted to ride in a Stutz Bearcat. It was a two-seater and he climbed in between us, the stick shift nestled up snug against his crotch. He had the stink of hard work on him, and I felt so faint with desire that I wasn't sure I could drive. I reached over to grab the stick shift, letting my forearm press hard against his well-muscled thigh.

Some men are like that, so easy in their body that they'll let you touch them and they don't draw away, they just accept it, like it's their due. I felt a shiver of hope building inside me. I was blind though, because I didn't notice what was going on over on the other side of the car. He was in the middle, and Lila and I rode along each side of him, both of us, always alone when together, just breathing him in.

When we got to the county road just about a quarter mile from the Club, he leaned over and breathed in my ear, the tickle shooting jarringly down my spine. "We can walk from here," he said, and I pulled over, light all the way down to my ankles, my heart beating wildly, thump thumpty thump. It was a perfect summer day—you could just catch a glimpse of the blue water through the trees, and I got this momentary feeling of infinite possibility, like all was right with the world. But before that feeling could even sink in enough for me to name it, Lila grabbed his hand and they were out of the car, in a flash, just like that. Into the woods, hand in hand, under an umbrella of green leaves. And I was left alone in the car, hand on the polished cherrywood of the stick shift.

Believe me, Jess, I can still call to mind the precise shade of the water that day. I call that summer blue, the color of water in July—all of promise wrapped up in it, and every disappointment too.

That was what I married her for, Jess. Because I wanted what she seemed to get with so little effort. That day, she had just stretched out her hand and taken what she wanted, so easy on a sunny summer day. That's why everyone wanted to be near her—because they hoped that some of that quality would rub off on them. But that Lila, the one I saw, the one everyone else thought they saw, was flimsy, and inflammable. Light a match to her, and she just flashed up into smoke and was gone.

After our wedding, during our trip abroad, it should have been clear to me that Lila was feeling poorly, but by then I was scarcely aware of Lila. We had two large, separate chamber rooms. I shared mine with a redheaded valet named Paul. Though the crossing was smooth, I rarely saw her above deck, and when I did see her, she was sallow and pitiful-looking, sometimes shocking me with her wrinkled frocks and uncombed hair. She was my wife, after all, and I wanted her to be a credit to me. I wanted her to glitter and shine and to deflect the glare away from me.

Once, early in the trip, she had come to my chamber in the evening, dressed in a silk peignoir. I opened the door and saw her standing there, small and pale, her blue eyes large and moist.

"I'm lonely, Chapin," she said, and I saw the note of puzzlement in her eyes as she looked around the small anteroom and took in Paul reading the newspaper in his silk dressing gown.

At that moment, when I saw her there, I realized that she had not understood; what I had seen as a tacit agreement was only Lila's girlish inattentiveness. I would like to say of myself that I felt sorry for the pitiful green-faced, lonely girl who came hoping for something that she was never going to find. Looking back, of course, I feel sadness, sadness for both of us, but at the time I was filled with nothing—nothing but indifference and a cold, deep dagger of disdain. I had given her trunks full of gowns and first-class accommodations. I had given her an allowance and a Grand Tour. It had never once occurred to me that the girl who had so easily stolen into the woods with Billy McKawber would someday come looking for affection.

After that, Lila and I kept our distance. Though we were traveling together, we rarely spoke. I could see that she was rapidly losing her prettiness. She went from being wan and green on the ship to taking on a fishwife pudginess—not surprising, as she rarely went out and dined on rich food. Finally, she started begging to go home again, and I thought to myself, Let the girl go. I supposed that she was going mad on me, like her mother. I thought it was just something that ran in their family.

I had been in Berlin for several weeks when I got the wire that Lila had drowned. Several weeks that had been the best that I had ever lived in my young life, a taste of what life was supposed to be like for others, for people who weren't like me. I was sitting at a café on the Nollendorfplatz with Paul, drinking bitters, the warm sun slanting down on my face, when the concierge brought me the wire.

Lila drowned. Stop. Pine Lake. Stop. Funeral tomorrow.

I must not have shown much emotion at all, because Paul did not even ask the contents of the wire. I just kept looking at him—coarse red hair, translucent skin, and a gap between his teeth—and smiled just seeing him sitting there. I did not leave then—there hardly seemed to be a point. By the time I got there, the funeral would be two months past. I would never return to Wequetona. Thankfully, I would never return to the ghost-man-shadow that being there had forced me to be.

And what of Billy McKawber? He didn't last long. The winter that followed our joyride together, he went out fishing on the frozen lake, fell through the ice, and drowned.

I never tried marriage again. Deciding not ever to go home, for me, was a much better solution. What I regret, looking back, is that I did not find a way to help Lila. I thought we had the same problem—that each of us had a love problem. I thought both of us loved across boundaries—I loved red-haired valets, and she loved Billy. I used to imagine ways I could have made it work for her, another servant along to carry our trunks, a villa in Italy somewhere, a flat in Paris. Those were the 1920s, and on the Continent, it could have been done. But whenever I mentioned Billy, Lila's eyes went flat with utter hopelessness, an expression that I don't think she even realized she was making. I guess her imagination wasn't big enough to imagine a future that included the two of them.

Your grandmother did not tell me why you needed to hear this story now, Jess, but I'm willing to guess, this being July, that yours may be a love story too. I spent but a few brief days of my youth up north in Michigan, and I have seen many lovely places since. But to this day, I can close my eyes and see the exact shade of the water that day, and I'll feel a stab of regret that I'll never see it again. I've seen blues in my life: Italy, Aruba, Carmel, but never once quite that same shade, tinged through with want, and desire, and regret.

But I'm not sorry that I didn't sacrifice all to stay there, like Lila, and like Billy. I walked away long ago, and I hazard a guess that someday you will too. (Everyone swears they won't, but in the end, most people do.) But it's still there for me, in my mind's eye, blue water, and youth, and love frustrated, and I daresay, when you leave, it will still be there for you too.

I shall take the liberty to sign myself as,

Your great-uncle,
Chapin Emelius Flagg.

CHAPTER TWENTY-SIX

JESS, AGE THIRTY-THREE

Jess walked around the cottage slowly now, hesitant, the way you walk around a place that you know you are leaving, that is no longer yours.

With Russ gone, the life seemed drained out of the cottage—his newness, his oddness, his very *wrongness* had at least made the cottage seem a living place. Now, Jess saw the cottage for what it was, a summertime lair for Miss Havisham—old, faded, worn out, already dead.

Typical Russ, he hadn't really seemed to quite get it when she had said, "Leave."

He was looking over his shoulder, saying, "What about the photo shoot?" as she was practically shoving him out the door. She had called a cab for him, said, "I need to be alone for a while."

She stopped answering the phone. Found two of Toni Barnes's RE/
MAX cards stuck in the back screen door. The papers for the closing lay, unsigned, on her grandmother's writing table.

It had turned to August now, you could feel it right away, the
lack of sincerity of summer, the hint that it was already planning
to leave. There was a fierce north wind blowing across Five Mile
Point, bringing cold air down from Canada. She could see the
Slades's American flag flapping on the flagpole. Up from the lake
came the clanging sound of sailboats at their moorings. The sky
was a sharp, cloudless blue. Out the window, she could see the
branches whipping back and forth—a smattering of green leaves
were falling. It gave the impression of sunlit snow.

———

A week ago it had all seemed so easy. She would fly up for a week
and sell the cottage; she would then pack her bags and return to
her life in New York.

That long-ago afternoon when she and Mamie had sat on
the upstairs bed folding pillowcases—what was it that her grandmother had said? Mamie's face flashed in front of her, the way it
had been that summer: pale-blue eyes, white skin soft but already
lined with age. *Hold on to what matters.* She hadn't understood,
then, what her grandmother had been talking about. Now, after all
these years, it was possible that she did.

———

Jess looked down at the desktop. There were two photographs, side
by side, held down by the beveled glass tabletop of the mahogany
desk. One was of herself, another of Margaret. The one of Margaret
bore a caption: *Winner of the Pulitzer Prize.* Neither picture was
recent. Her mother was truly striking—thick, confident black

eyebrows, wide dark-brown eyes, and a full, determined mouth. Of course, Margaret was much older now. You couldn't get her to admit it, but she had pretty much retired. She could still turn heads in a restaurant though, even at her age. Margaret was a person who always looked like she mattered.

Jess had called her mother, of course, about the inheritance. Before she had left on the trip. Right after she got the official call from Mamie's lawyer about the will.

"What cottage?" her mother said.

"Mother," Jess said, "don't play games with me. I know you *know* what cottage. What do you think I should do?"

"What do you want to do?"

"Sell it," Jess said into the phone.

"Then sell it! For Christ's sake. She gave it to you. If the money makes you feel guilty, give it to Oxfam or something."

"But Mamie said . . ."

"You know, Jess, I think Mamie raised the both of us to know how to do what we want."

"I guess you're right."

"What's past is past," Margaret said, sounding just like Mamie, the way she seemed to more than ever these days.

Jess was still surprised by such a clear international connection. She hadn't gotten used to hearing her mother's voice without the familiar crackling of static overlaying it, the tinny faraway sound that Jess had eventually grown to associate with comfort.

"Mom," Jess said, not wanting to lose such a good connection, "when are you coming to New York?"

———

Jess edged back the glass top. She grasped the corner of the picture and slid it out from under the heavy glass. Underneath, Jess saw that there were several more pictures of Margaret, each one showing a younger face. Jess shuffled through the little pile of pictures: Margaret in a cap and gown, Margaret in a white dress holding flowers, Margaret holding a microphone.

With surprise, Jess came upon the last picture in the pile. It was not a picture of Margaret at all, but the image of a young man wearing a soldier's uniform—a tall man with broad shoulders, very young to be a soldier. He was wearing a peaked navy cap and tunic, and was holding an ornamental sword in his hand. For some reason, he looked a little familiar, though she was certain she had never seen the picture before. Jess turned the picture over.

On the back was written: "On the occasion of his enlistment in the Navy. Thomas Cardwell Cleves. 1917."

The big old cottage ticked and creaked around Jess, never perfectly silent, always with its own faint music. Jess recognized the melody now. It was made up of the songs of a family whose lives, like familiar refrains, still mattered.

All this time, she had felt guilty about the cottage, thinking that Mamie wanted her to hold on to it, imagining that was what Mamie had in mind. But she should have known Mamie better than that, should have known right away what Mamie wanted.

Hold on to what matters.

What matters . . .

Jess sat at Mamie's desk looking out toward Hemingway Point. She could see the spot, about halfway across, where the water was bluer, deeper, and where the surface was always flecked by the path of the wind. Through the doorway, she could see into the shadowy interior of the cottage, the interior that would always have the patina of so many summers past.

She glanced at her watch. It was not yet noon. The closing was scheduled for two, the flight for four. She hesitated, not long, just enough to hear her heart beat once or twice, then, leaving the unsigned papers lying on the desk, she walked slowly toward the back door, ever so slowly, like she wasn't going anywhere. As she crossed the sill, she broke into a run.

CHAPTER TWENTY-SEVEN

Jess, age thirty-three

She had known that it would be easy to find him, but that she would have to look. At first, every time she had rounded an aisle in Olsen's Market, or turned a corner when walking in town, she had that tiny anticipation that she would look up and there he would be. But in the end, she had known that it would not be a chance meeting. She would have to seek him out, if only she could find the courage to do so.

She rushed headlong out the back door, letting the screen door screech and then slam behind her. She moved so quickly up the back slope, up the stone steps in front of the garage, past the row of hollyhocks that stood brightly in a line in front of the stone wall. For a moment, she sat still, key in the ignition, inhaling the new-car smell of the blue-plush upholstery in the rental car, then she flipped the ignition and gunned it a little bit, spraying gravel as she went down the back road and out the stone gates toward M-66.

In town, the scene around her was tranquil—not too many tourists in the streets at this time of day. She saw an elderly couple, almost matching in blue and white clothing, walking slowly down the sidewalk just barely holding hands. From behind, a boy in a neon shirt raced up on a scooter, neatly arcing around the old couple and skimming on down the street.

Jess forced herself to think about the possibilities. He was out on an expedition. Hadn't Toni said he would be? He would surely be married (his wife would no doubt be a beautiful marine biologist). What if he was married and his wife was handling the front desk? What if he answered the door with a baby balanced on his hip?

She just wanted to see him; that was all. Trying to conjure a feeling that seemed platonic and mild, Jess stood up from the bench and walked down Pine Street toward the chamber of commerce building. Without hesitation, she followed the walk around the back of it, where a small office, more of a shack, really, was built close to the water's edge. She saw a sign that read: Soo Expeditions. D. Painter, Proprietor. Forcing herself—feeling outside herself—she walked in the half-open door.

Surprised to see no one behind the desk, Jess took a moment to look at the simple surroundings: some brochures in a metal rack, an electric clock on the wall, a gray-metal counter across the middle of the small room, a feed-store calendar with a grainy picture of a couple of grazing cows. It took her a moment to see the little paper tent resting on the countertop scrawled in pencil with the words *Out Back*. Jess pushed the door open and blinked for a second in the glaring light; she peered around the rear of the shack, but it appeared to be flush with the wharf. Around the other side, however, the cement path continued, where there was a cement parking lot backing up to the water. There were several white trailers, each of them stacked with green and red canoes resting on white-metal railings, two across, three up. One canoe, a worn-looking red one, was resting on cinderblocks. Next to it, a broad-shouldered man was squatting in shorts and Teva sandals, facing away from her, holding a small can of shiny black paint. She stood there watching the man's back, not sure. Cottages, she had found, don't change much over the years. She could recognize Journey's End in her sleep, in a trance, in her dreams; but a person . . . Broad shouldered, close-cropped hair with a few visible flecks of silver. The man put down the paint pot and stood up, turning so slowly that she realized he had known she was there all along.

"Toni told me you decided to sell it," he said. "Somehow, I kept thinking that in the end you wouldn't."

Jess held her hand up to her brow, thinking that if she could block the sun she would be able to see more clearly.

"Forgive me," he said. "Where are my manners?" Wiping his painty hands on the sides of his frayed khaki shorts, he stepped forward, holding out his hand.

"Welcome home to the North Country, Jess."

Later, looking back, it was the word *home* that struck her first and hardest; that left an immediate and indelible mark.

Daniel Painter had perfect white teeth that showed as his lips parted into an easy grin.

"There is something I need to tell you," she said.

EPILOGUE

SEVEN YEARS LATER

Jess leaned against the door frame in her sunny kitchen, cradling the phone in the crook of her neck, listening carefully and nodding, asking the occasional question while looking out the kitchen window at the sunlight playing on the surface of the lake. The window was open, and a white-cotton gauze curtain ruffled slightly in the mild summer breeze.

"What time did they start? Have you had any bleeding? When's the last time you felt the baby move?"

At the faint sound of a beeper buzzing on vibrate mode, Jess looked down at her waist where her beeper was clipped, pushing the buttons and scribbling a phone number on the paper in front of her, all the while murmuring listening sounds and nodding.

"It sounds like time for you to head in . . . I know, I know," Jess said, her voice soothing. "Yes, I'll come to the hospital as soon as you get there. Don't worry. You know I promised you that."

Jess scribbled a note that she left on the kitchen counter: *Gone to the hospital. First labor. Might be long. I'll try to be there by seven.*

———

Driving in, she was a few minutes late, her hair still damp from the rapid hospital shower. About an hour ago, she had delivered her patient's healthy six-pound baby boy. She caught sight of the Wequetona gates, the painted sign, the trim row of trees. Even after all these years, Jess still got a funny feeling when she drove past the Wequetona gates. She didn't drive through them anymore. Of course, the conservancy had opened a new roadway, which led around the back of Wequetona Club to a widened gravel parking lot. Down along the left side, there was a massive row of arborvitae towering up, over eight feet tall. The trustees had insisted on planting them when Journey's End was no longer part of the Club. Straight in front of her, the cottage looked exactly the same as ever though—except for the sign, which read: LITTLE TRAVERSE CONSERVANCY HEADQUARTERS. PINE LAKE.

Inside, of course, everything looked completely different. The walls to the downstairs bedrooms had been taken out, so that now the whole first floor, except for the kitchen, was one enormous meeting space. There were massive lines of track lighting everywhere. The lights blazed down on the banks of chairs. From the kitchen, the scent of percolating coffee wafted out, and there were tables set up with red-felt tablecloths, covered with pamphlets about conservation and petitions to sign. She caught sight of the framed *Town & Country* cover; it showed the front of the cottage looking better than it ever really had looked—red-white-and-blue bunting, bright geraniums, and borrowed brand-new wicker, with the caption *The Other Kennebunkport* emblazoned across the front. She smiled for a minute, thinking of Russ. Last she heard, he was still in New York and had gotten the coveted editor's job at *Architectural Home.*

Inside the main conference room, she was pleased to see that people were still milling around and not yet seated. She was shocked, though she shouldn't have been, to see how elaborately everyone else was dressed. Jess saw a number of Wequetona people, not surprising, she guessed. It was funny. Even though they lived just down the road year-round, they almost never ran into the summer people. There was Toni Barnes dressed in a butter-colored linen sheath, holding a plastic cup filled with white wine and a little green cocktail napkin, talking to . . . someone . . . Wasn't that Philip Cartwright? Over in the corner, Jess saw a tall, thin woman, slightly stooped, who might have been Martha Whitmire—hard to tell since so many of those women looked alike, and with her back to Jess, over near Martha, she saw a gaunt figure in a navy-blue blazer, a small bald spot glowing faintly on the back of his head, probably Phelps.

It took a moment for Jess to see Daniel. As always, it was like she felt his presence before she really saw him, felt that momentary clutch, even still, after all this time. He was standing in the corner wearing jeans and a sage-green hand-knitted sweater. She could see several people clutching his new book—*Soo Tales: A Canoer's Story*—standing in line, waiting for him to sign. Jess saw that he had seen her, saw the flash of white teeth, the little piece of a smile. Clutching his hand, sucking on her fingers, there was Maggie, hair in long black braids, dressed in a tie-dyed T-shirt and her best purple velveteen pants.

"Mommy!" she shouted out, skipping across the weathered floorboards of the old cottage. "You came back!"

DISCUSSION QUESTIONS

1. Early in the story, Jess is reluctant to return to Journey's End. She thinks: "This could not properly be called returning. There was no call to feel like this. She was imputing qualities—breath, flesh, blood—to a structure made of pine board, shingle, and stone." Why is Jess so reluctant to return to Journey's End? Why does she seem to think of the house as a living person?

2. How are Russ and Daniel different? Why is Jess trying so hard to convince herself that she is in love with Russ?

3. Early in the story, Mamie tells Margaret that she is planning to sell the cottage, but she decides to leave the cottage to Jess. What makes her change her mind?

4. Mamie and Margaret are completely different from each other. How does each of them affect Jess's own personality?

5. Mamie calls Journey's End "the final keeper of secrets." It's striking how much upheaval the family goes through, while

the house hardly changes at all. What role does the house play in the life of the family? Is it a good role or a bad role?

6. Mamie keeps a secret throughout Margaret's and Jess's lives, and she continues to keep the secret even when it means breaking up Daniel and Jess. Mamie calls her story "the shaky foundation upon which we had built our family." What do you think of Mamie's decision to keep her secret?

7. At the beginning of the story, Jess seems to feel that she never reached for her dreams. What changed to allow her to follow her passions?

8. Daniel and Jess were young when they met, and they fell in love quickly. Do you think this kind of young love can endure? If they had stayed together in the first place, do you think they would have been happy together despite the difficulties they would have faced?

9. Chapin writes, "I can still call to mind the precise shade of the water that day. I call that summer blue, the color of water in July—all of promise wrapped up in it, and every disappointment too." How does the title of the book tie into its central themes? Do summer things—vacation houses, summer romances—hold a special place in our lives? Why?

10. The character of Lila was something of a mystery, and even after the reader discovers what happened to her, it's still hard to understand. What do you think of Lila as a person? Do you think Mamie did the right thing? What would you do if faced with a similar situation?

11. In the end, Jess leaves the Club and donates the house to a nature conservancy. Why did she decide not to keep it? Why did she think that Mamie's words, "Hold on to what matters," provided the key to her future?

ABOUT THE AUTHOR

Nora Carroll is a pseudonym for #1 *New York Times* bestselling author Elizabeth Letts. A former obstetric nurse, Nora Carroll now writes full time. She lives with her husband, four children, and a madcap golden retriever in Southern California.